Carla

THE
END OF
REASON

Michael Gryboski

**Jan-Carol
Publishing, Inc**

"every story needs a book"

Carla: The End of Reason
Michael Gryboski

Published July 2020
Little Creek Books
Imprint of Jan-Carol Publishing, Inc.
All rights reserved
Copyright © 2020 Michael Gryboski

ISBN: 978-1-950895-46-5
Library of Congress Control Number: 2020942253

You may contact the publisher:
Jan-Carol Publishing, Inc.
PO Box 701
Johnson City, TN 37605
publisher@jancarolpublishing.com
jancarolpublishing.com

For God, Family, Country

ALSO BY MICHAEL GRYBOSKI:

CARLA

CARLA: THE ANTITHESES KILLER

Table of Contents

I

Some wanted reform. Some wanted revolution. There were those who sought anarchy, lumped in with the ones who sought moderation. Everyone desired a shifting of the paradigm, a moving of the present status. The degrees varied, the measures slanted by the biases of groups, factions, and individuals. They had not agreed on the specifics, though the general ideas were collectively endorsed. And the strategies, save for the violent minority, all tilted toward the peaceful, massive demonstration.

The land for which they congregated was in the old Spanish Empire. It's historical development mirroring that of its Latin neighbors. First were the pre-Colombian city-states of Pagans and human sacrifices. Societies that, while logical enough to calculate the stars and the calendars, still, maintained the savagery for ritual murder. Then came the Conquistadors, with their God, their steel, and their disease. Independence came during that so-called enlightened age, known both for the many intellectuals who spoke of man's basic rights and the thousands summarily executed by Madame Guillotine.

Their heritage was the world after the twentieth century. Supporters of the Allies during the Second World War, yet condemned to a decades-long sentence under a military dictatorship influenced by fascism. Radical elements tried to change things for generations. They were not without success. By the end of the 1980s, elections took place, literacy expanded, and life expectancies increased. A long constitution was passed, its foundational document a meteor with a bright tail of amendments.

Still the upheavals persisted, still the inseparable link between politics and violence, sophistication and barbarism. As the politicians continued their discourse, below them many dissenting voices found repression. It was far less cruel

1

than the days of the dictators, to be sure, when many an uppity student, actor, writer, teacher, and even the occasional priest were disappeared for stepping out of line. Still, the current regime was not tolerant of too many folks publicly repudiating the rising inflation, unemployment, dwindling grocery supplies, and a host of other social and economic ills.

Dissent came with regulation. The leaders for the protest slated to take place at the university had to meet with authorities. With grudging hearts, they compromised with their enemies. The course for the march was shortened, as was the time for the rally. Demonstrators conceded the presence of police checkpoints along the march, so that no weapons of any kind could be brought in to the rabble. More police were going to surround the campus, preventing any possible expansion of the demonstration beyond the prescribed limitations. Students had to have a professor's permission to skip class.

The campus was a nice location: well-paved walkways, modern buildings, grassy fields, a student union with large locker room facilities for men and women, up to date classrooms, and a sizable parking deck. The university was the largest industry for the small city, with nearly all things connected to it. Locals were employed at various levels at the university; numerous restaurants, cafés, convenience stores, grocers, farmers' markets, and book stores thrived on the students' money. The relationship went both ways, as many students were employed in part or in full at local businesses.

It was mid-morning when the crowds gathered. They were young; few were north of 30, even fewer beyond the 40 mark. Many wore bandanas around their faces, sunglasses as well, and demanded that camera-wielding journalists not capture their image. When going through the checkpoints, these folks briefly removed the disguises, though not without covert anger. Most were willing to have their countenances broadcasted online and offline. There was no repercussion they feared. The fight was for positive change, political reform, economic improvement. How could any take issue?

Thousands were already present. They formed globs of people, many beginning chants and holding signs with declarations in Español. Hundreds watched them gathered on a wide pedestrian-only street that hugged the south side of the campus. They were planning to go from there for about a mile off campus, to a large rally area before a government building. Most of the spectators were students, a few having cut class to behold the sight. The majority of the impressionable idealistic folk were sympathetic to the radical calls. However, some felt it a waste of time that made it harder to commute to class.

"No justicia!" shouted one of the organizers with a megaphone, standing in front of a large group of protesters.

"No paz!" they replied.

It was beginning. While their ranks were by no means in perfect order, the participants nevertheless coordinated into informal companies and regiments, led by organizers who coaxed them to give declarations. They moved forward, covering the pedestrian walkway like a stream of water coursing down a river bed. A few beat drums, adding a rhythm to the shouts for change. Many saluted with raised fists or two-fingered peace signs. Organizers walked backwards to face their audience as they continued the liturgical call and response.

"Reforma!" said an organizer.

"Ahora!" they responded.

"Reforma!"

"Ahora!"

"Reforma!"

"Ahora!"

"No justicia!" shouted a leader through the amplifying megaphone.

"No paz!" shouted back the chorus.

"No justicia!"

"No paz!"

One group of a couple hundred protesters and a duo of leaders chanted in unison, echoing the classic slogan of "Si se puede! Si se puede! Si se puede!"

As the checkpoint lines shortened, she came forward wearing a backpack. Officially, she was a foreign exchange student, hailing from los Estados Unidos. Like many of those in the country, she had black hair and dark eyes. Her skin was an Asiatic pale, reflecting the continent of her birth. Her face bore lines that came more from experience than aging. A barely visible indentation stretched from her forehead down to the level of her eyes. It was a reminder of a brutal struggle that had occurred months earlier. Yet all of these lines only added to her emotional expression and complemented her intrinsic beauty.

Her fit, medium frame had some muscle derived from an active life, though not so much that it made her look especially intimidating. Modestly dressed, despite a warm day, her legs were covered with blue jeans that extended below her ankles. Her torso was covered by a T-shirt with a high neckline. Her hair was in a pony tail that swept a few inches below the shoulders. One of those shoulders supported a black padded strap of a backpack. The pack in question was dark blue, and had multiple zippered pockets.

She stopped at the checkpoint, where a pair of officers in full body armor were standing guard. Obeying every command, she slowly swung the pack off her shoulder and onto the table. While showing her student identification card to one officer, the other unzipped the pockets to check for suspicious materials. He found the usual items: a couple of books and notebooks in the main pocket, several pens and pencils in another. Some loose-leaf paper was in another pocket, and a smartphone in another compartment. After less than a minute, she was given the okay. She smiled in gratitude and picked up her book bag, hanging it over both shoulders as she joined the marchers.

For a time, her purpose seemed obvious. Chanting, raising her fist to the heavens alongside fellow radicals. Moving along the wide and crowded walkway, joining the river of angered youths, she looked like anyone else. Yet through it all, she was gradually shifting. Not in ideology or sentiment, but literally moving from one side of the throng to the other. A few steps to the left, then chanting and saluting. A few more steps, then shouting with the other chanters. After a few minutes, she was on the other side, with spectators to her left. After another round of declarative statements, she unceremoniously shifted leftward and exited the rally, slipping between two students who stood on the grass by the occupied pavement.

The boisterous echoes of dissent got milder as she kept walking toward the student union. Droning noises from the sizable crowds still filled the background, though most of those around her were involved in other matters. Many were reading, mainly for study. Some socialized with friends and classmates. A few were catching brunch, heading to class, leaving class, going to a library to meet others for study. On a flat rectangular grassy field beside the student union, eight students engaged in a pickup game of fútbol. Backpacks served as goal posts.

She entered the student union without being noticed. It was normal inside, the typical mix of students casually sitting around on chairs and couches: talking, studying, doing homework, complaining about minor things, and enjoying coffee or other refreshments. She was another one, just another student in a campus with nearly ten thousand pupils. Few paid attention as she went to the locker room, and the few who did notice dismissed her presence just as quickly. Invisibility accomplished.

The locker room was mostly devoid of people. A wall of lockers stationed in the middle of the room obscured the view of the two students present, preventing them from seeing her. The janitor had already cleaned up for the day. Her locked compartment was in the upper row of two levels of blue-hued metal doors. Placing the backpack on the floor near her locker, she unzipped a pocket and removed her smartphone. Turning her head one way and then the other, she saw no one. She punched five buttons on the keyboard attached to her locker, listening for the sound that indicated that the metal door was unlocked. Knowing that the system locked again after five seconds if no action was taken, she opened it immediately. Inside the locker was a backpack identical to the one she had brought.

She switched the two, taking greater care when handling the one that she had placed in the locker a week earlier. Metal door closed and locked, she slowly put on the other book bag and walked away from the locker room entrance. A turn of the corner and there was the door for a back hallway used by janitors and other help. She knew it was never locked. No one was with her in the hallway. She knew the schedule for the cleaners and when the next truck was coming for supplies to the student union. Turning right, the woman opened a door that led outside, but not before taking hold of the chunk of wood used to prop the portal open. Unlike the other, it locked upon closing.

It was a quick walk to the parking deck. Cameras rolled at various corners. Before entering the large facility, she took out her smartphone and texted an American number a simple query:

"Abierto o Cerrado?"

There was a pause. Then a few gray blinking dots appeared on the bottom of the screen, confirming that the other person was tapping out a response. It came with a smiley face emoji:

"Abierto. ☺ "

After sending a brief text message confirming receipt of the answer, she put away the mobile device and walked into the parking deck. Cameras rolled, but on a loop. Security lacked any direct sight of the corridors of the structure, so she slipped in without notice. Parked cars vastly outnumbered people. Only a few folks walked by her, heading out of the deck for the campus. Few entered the deck at this hour. She turned to walk up the sloping divide between the first and second levels.

Her search for the correct vehicle was brief. She knew where he parked. He had an official reserved space that put him close to one of the administrative buildings. Looking around the level, she confirmed that she was alone. The woman went toward his parked car, which had another vehicle adjacent to it. The two metal structures aided her in hiding when she knelt down, unzipped the backpack's main pocket, and took out a handheld controller and a thin metal stick. Before zipping it back up, she briefly looked at the explosive device. She then pushed the pack so that it was under the car. She did not place the book bag all the way to the center, but rather slid it closer to the rear of the vehicle. Turning her face away, she gripped the short metal stick and jammed it into one of the car windows.

His phone alerted him. A buzzing noise that broke his concentration on the admissions information he was updating. Four students had dropped out of the university and he was looking over the report. He knew the noise well, and considered it more annoying than worrisome. Looking at his phone, he confirmed his theory: the car alarm had gone off again. It had done so a few times in the past month or so. He briefly considered turning off the noisemaker from his office, but decided that it was best to check out the situation in person. He saved his work, closed the files, and left his office.

"Yo volveré," he said to his secretary, who nodded without making eye contact.

A few minutes went by before he showed up. No one else had shown up on the second level since the alarm went off. Someone had come and parked on the first floor, looked with curiosity at the flashing car lights and buzzing noise, but then went about their own affairs. She kept vigil. Eventually, he appeared via an elevator. With his key fob, he turned off the alarm. Slightly perplexed as to why no security had arrived, the administrator nevertheless approached the car sans trepidation. As he zoomed in on the broken glass, a hidden Carla al-Hassan Sharp pushed the two necessary buttons on the controller and blew him away.

A rumbling went through the security office; the cameras remained on loop. Carla ran toward the fiery vehicle, threw the controller and the metal stick into the blaze, and then ran down the sloping ramp between the first and second levels. No sooner did she exit the parking deck than the cameras began to roll again, showing horrified campus police the thick smoke emanating from the second level. They assumed this was due to an accidental conflagration rather than an assassination, and called the fire department.

Meanwhile, Carla rushed toward the student union back hallway door, seeing to her relief that it was still ajar. She pushed it open, taking care to place the wooden block beside the portal where it had been before. Both the back hallway and the locker room were empty, in large part because the noise of the explosion led most people to go out the other end of the student union to stare in wonderment. She opened her locker and took out the backpack, settling a strap onto each shoulder. She walked at a peppier pace than before, leaving the locker room and then the main room of the student union, quickly blending into the growing crowd of onlookers. Carla looked with the others, who chatted about what it could be. As more kept joining the crowds, she slowly backed out and turned away.

Extinguishers defeated the fires to reveal a burned and broken corpse. Security soon concluded it was a car bomb and called in more authorities. They tried to seal off the campus, to prevent the killer from escaping, yet the protests hindered their efforts. Unknowingly, the demonstrators did their part to help Carla escape. The sight of more police trying to cross the pedestrian walkway led to heightened agitation. Soon, the more radical elements of the march were fomenting greater hostilities, picking fights with both campus and city officers, pushing and being pushed, punching and being punched. At best, the parking deck could be closed off. Others had to be directed to the growing riot.

Carla walked away from it all. The smoking parking deck, the emptying student union, and the newly instituted mob rule of the march were soon behind her. Following the straight beige sidewalks, she exited the campus on the other end, where the single patrol car that had been there earlier was ordered to go to the other side to handle the many arrests. Smiling at the thought of her ease of escape, she appeared to be just another student who was glad class was over ... until she checked her smartphone. Her eyes widened when she realized how much time had passed. Her brisk walk became a dashing run, made awkward by the many pounds of academic materials on her back.

Still, her two-block race got her in sight of the white compact awaiting her arrival. Its engine turned on as she got within twenty feet of it. In a panic, she slapped her hand on the passenger side of the frame in an effort to alert the driver. Without hesitation, she opened the unlocked backseat door and got in, tossing her backpack to the seat behind the driver. He was Latin American by heritage, with moderately tanned skin, a slim figure, and well-combed black hair. Without looking behind him, he knew the woman who had entered the compact.

"Estas tarde," stated Alfredo Hernandez flatly.

"Yo se, yo se," Carla replied in annoyance between breaths. Hernandez smiled, put the car in drive, and turned onto the street, leaving behind the chaos.

* * *

"Get in the front," ordered Hernandez. They were several blocks away, hidden between two apartment complexes. Carla obliged without speaking, leaving the harmless book bag in the back while getting out of the vehicle. The narrow alleyway gave just enough space for her to open the front passenger door. Hernandez continued as she fastened her seatbelt. "We want to be as unremarkable in our appearance as possible. Since this is not a cab, there is no valid reason for you not to be beside me."

"Understood."

"Being on time next time will make it easier to correct this mistake before it happens."

"Understood," she said with rolling eyes.

Engine ignited, the car rolled forward, turning right onto another street. Hernandez knew where he was going; he had been studying the city layout for weeks in preparation for the mission. The trip was sluggish, for the chaos behind them was affecting traffic all over the urban center. It took them three green lights to cross the next intersection. Their reward for this progress was to take another four lights to pass the intersection after that. For the following intersection, things moved a bit faster. By the second time the green became red, they were in the front of the line of automobiles awaiting permission to go.

"At least we know we're next," Hernandez remarked to his passenger. She looked at him fleetingly before turning to peer out the window once more. Both were listening to local news, the fast-talking Spanish fully understood by the driver and mostly understood by his company. They spoke of the upheavals and the fatality. Few details were revealed, though. Lots of talking transpired, nonetheless. It was necessary to listen, just in case something alerting the public to their culpability was transmitted on the airwaves.

Across the vacant square, the duo saw the cars starting to move. The cars ahead were already moving, promising a slightly faster commute once their light changed. Or at least, that was until emergency sounds were heard. Hernandez had a handgun in a holster at his side, while an additional firearm rested in the glove compartment in front of Carla. She contemplated reaching for it when the alarms sounded, prompting serious consideration that the authorities had figured out the culprits. Then the vehicles became visible, turning left from a side street to drive past the duo. Tension eased as a police cruiser led the way for three trucks carrying armed personnel.

"National guard units," observed Hernandez, who turned to Carla with a smile. "I guess we really did a number on them this time."

"It's green," said Carla as more government vehicles inhibited their ability to cross the intersection. Then it became yellow, and then back to red. Carla looked at her driver with annoyance as his prediction of their eased progress was debunked.

"Well, next time –"

"Don't ... say anything," she ordered. Hernandez nodded in response.

Several minutes later, they were finally out of the gridlock. The radio reporters had nothing on Carla. Witnesses offered numerous faces and bodies as suspicious; a chameleon must have done it. While they listened, Hernandez drove them out of the city. They ended up on a backroad, unpaved and leading to a small shantytown. They were more numerous last century. Passing the impoverished, the vehicle made its way up a collection of hills within sight of an imposing mountain chain.

That was where they stopped, a few hundred feet higher than their starting elevation. Alone on the hill, the sun high above the city, they could just make out the distant gray smoke rising from where the explosion had taken place. Hernandez turned off the automobile and the two got out. Alfredo took out a packet of cigarettes and chose one stick from their number. They both leaned against the passenger side of the vehicle, watching the cityscape. A lighter flame touched the front of the cigarette, Hernandez indulging in the chemicals as they watched in silence. He exhaled a plume of smoke before speaking.

"This time, I'll be leaving first," he began, getting Carla's attention. "I have a ticket for a flight that leaves in three hours. I should be back in the DC area before sundown. Tonight, you may text me for confirmation."

"I thought Mavis didn't want us texting."

9

"I'm changing her mind, with time," said Hernandez with a grin. He inhaled more nicotine and exhaled more smoke before continuing. "You will leave the country in five days. Your luggage and new identity papers are in the trunk. I'll be driving you to your hotel. Don't worry, it's already been paid for."

"Muchas gracias."

"De nada," replied Hernandez. "While there, stay inside your hotel room often, but try to occasionally walk around town. You stay in too much, you'll generate suspicion. But if you stay out too much, you might be detected."

"Even though they have no idea I was responsible?"

"Assume they have an idea," Hernandez countered.

"Yes, sir."

"It is very beautiful, the city," he observed. "Even the nasty parts have a certain urban allure about them."

"Yes."

"It is almost as beautiful as yourself," he said with a smile, which she reciprocated. The two got back into the vehicle and arrived at the hotel soon afterwards.

* * *

"Su carne asada, señorita?" asked the waitress as she approached a seated Carla. The inquiry prompted the agent to look up from her square table to behold the well-dressed restaurant worker.

"Sí, gracias," Carla responded as the plate was put before her, placed beside a water glass that was two-thirds full and a trio of utensils atop a napkin.

"Algo más?"

"No es necesario," replied Carla with a smile. "Gracias."

"Disfruta." She nodded and walked toward another table to inform the couple seated there that their meals were coming soon. The portion before the agent was smaller than what was typical in the United States, but still sufficient to satisfy hunger. Carla crossed herself before beginning the meal, likely turning some heads in the majority Catholic country for her Orthodox tendency to go up-down-right-left. A brief silent prayer of grace, a second crossing, and then she started eating her dinner.

It had been four days since the assassination. She was scheduled to leave the Latin American nation the following morning. For the past few days, the assignment had transformed into a vacation. She went about the city, enjoying the sights. There was the old market, with its produce and local products, including jewelry, domestically knitted clothing, and a few paintings by local artists. She had also toured a colonial-era cathedral that stood over the ruins of a Mesoamerican temple where human sacrifices were once performed. Earlier that day, she had hiked to the hill where she and Hernandez had parked.

Excursions notwithstanding, she had most of her meals at the hotel and spent little time outdoors after nightfall. This habit traced its existence to the days before she was either working for the government or working for a domestic terrorist organization. Her grandfather was a fairly permissive parental figure, but he was unequivocal about her never walking alone in the city past eventide. While her extralegal work often led her out in the moonlit hours in solitude, there was still that deeply ingrained hesitation.

Her room for the wait was decent, at least. It had running water, electricity, a full bath and queen-sized bed, wireless internet that worked more often than not, and a small television with hundreds of channels. It was on the second floor, with a window that gave a great view of the city. The panorama was potentially an effective tool in case she was discovered by the authorities, or even the cartel for whom she had just removed a key recruiter. While in her temporary domicile, she regularly watched the news, getting all the updates officials could give.

They knew a lot about her actions. They knew that an explosive device had been planted under the car of the decedent and they knew it was remote-controlled. They had discovered the charred remains of the backpack it was kept in, leading them to suspect either a student or someone masquerading as a student. Police were aware of the time of death and cause of death. During one press conference, they graphically described how hundreds of pieces of metal shrapnel from the car had torn into and through the body of the late cartel recruiter. Death was virtually instantaneous, as every major organ was shredded and burned.

To Carla's relief, they knew little beyond that. The lead theory, which garnered momentum due to social media and social commentators, was the protest. A radical did this, they reasoned; one of those opposed to polite society, the masked ones, those violent extremists who seek the end of law. Many government officials were happy to join in the narrative, viewing this as an ideal opportunity to ratchet up some dissent-crushing. However, the press was still free and many an editorial online and offline denounced the proposal. There was no consensus as to the origins of the perpetrator.

Ignorance was also seen in their speculation of what the murderer looked like. Everyone who appeared to walk away from the incident was a suspect. Some witnesses pointed to students, others to radicals. The suspect imagery included long hair, short hair, a mask, a hood, both, neither. Eyes were dark or blue, or obscured by sunglasses. Male, female, thin, fat, tall, and short. That was the best they had for a person of interest. At least one of the descriptions vaguely resembled Carla, but she paid it little mind. *After all*, she thought, *there are hundreds of female students with dark hair and pale skin.*

"Esta disfrutando su cena, señorita?" asked the quick waitress, who had just delivered the meals for the couple.

Carla waited to finish chewing before responding. "Sí, muy bien."

"Bien," she responded with a smile and then quickly walked away. Carla realized a moment later that she should have asked for the check. A small issue, of course.

And then the police arrived. They were in plain clothes, but Carla saw them show their badges to the maître d'. She acted normal, looking down and taking a few more bites of her dinner. Carla had requested and received a table facing the main entrance, just in case. She could hear them going around the other tables, asking for identification. Obliviousness was the part she played. Some nerves, but not too much. Enough to warn her to be careful. Surely, they had not figured out it was her.

"Perdóname, señorita?" asked the detective above her. "Señorita?"

Carla slowly looked up. "Hola."

"Hola," began the detective, a middle-aged fellow in a jacket and tie. To his right was a younger man, dressed in similar work clothes. "Yo soy con la policía y me gustaría a pedirla algunas preguntas."

"Lo siento," she began, "pero yo se sola poco Español."

The older detective looked to his partner, who nodded and spoke up. "Well, miss, I speak English with fluency."

"Okay."

"Are you American?"

"Sí."

"What is the purpose of your visiting our country?"

"Vacation."

"How long have you been here?"

"About a week."

"When are you planning to leave?"

"Tomorrow morning," she said with a smile. "Tonight's my last night."

"Could you show us your passport, please?"

"Claro, si," Carla replied, casually reaching for her purse, which was placed next to her left leg on the tile floor. She unzipped the bag and handed the elder detective her fabricated passport and authentic plane ticket. "And here's my ticket."

The two men looked over the documents. She knew that they would be unable to spot the forging. After all, like the real ones, the passport was issued by the government. After a few moments of study, the two men nodded at each other. The elder man handed her back the passport and the ticket while the younger man spoke. "Have a nice night, miss."

"Gracias," responded Carla, hiding her relief.

Soon after, the waitress came by to ask if she wanted anything else. Carla requested the check. It came quickly, and Carla paid with cash, plus a decent tip. The detectives were still talking to other patrons when she exited the restaurant. Carla walked the three blocks down the street to return to the hotel. She refused to look behind herself, lest the authorities add to whatever suspicions they may have had. Into the hotel and then up the stairs, strolling as if completely unconcerned, she entered her room without incident—and without an apparent police tail.

Carla removed her shoes and relaxed, turning on the television to view the evening news. It was there that she learned about the latest lead. Police were now convinced that the perpetrator was foreign-born. They were also convinced that person was a Latino. It made the most sense when trying to discover someone unfamiliar yet able to blend into their crowds. Apparently, by showing a passport confirming a different ethnic background, Carla prevented the police from thinking more about her.

Noticing that the hour was not too late, she took her phone from her purse and called her grandfather. She knew he would be awake; he was not one for an early slumber. Sure enough, after the second ring a voice answered. "Hello, Carla?"

"Yes, giddo, it's me. How are you?"

"Tolerable as always," he said light-heartedly. "And how is my favorite granddaughter?"

"I'm your only granddaughter."

"Like I said, how are you doing?"

"Fine, very fine," she began. "It's a beautiful country. You and Elnora should think about taking a vacation here."

"Really? I heard it was really violent. In fact, I saw on the international news the other day that a poor fellow was blown up at some college. Did you know that?"

"I heard about it," replied Carla, then provided faux outrage. "Hey, wait a minute! If you knew that happened, why didn't you call me to ask if I was okay?"

"Because I just knew you were. It's a gift."

"Of course, you knew."

"Well, you are obviously okay, are you not?"

"Yes, giddo, I am," said Carla with a smile. "Thank you for asking."

"No problem at all."

"Anyway, I will be back in the country tomorrow. I have a flight scheduled in the morning."

"Any chance you could stop by on the way back?"

Carla laughed. She knew he was kidding. "Oh yes, giddo. Of course. While I go from Central America to DC, I'll take a twelve hundred-mile detour."

"And all this for me? I am touched."

"Besides, you know once they finally build that new office, I will only be ten or fifteen miles away."

"Or even less if your husband becomes governor."

"Or even less if my husband becomes governor," she repeated in agreement. "Anyway, got to go. Love you, giddo."

"Love you, Carla."

II

Darkness was their ally. This went beyond it being nighttime. They were dressing for battle with shades of evening. Nondescript hoodies, bandanas, pants, all hued in charcoal, sable, ebony, and vesper. Black gloves and tightly laced military boots were worn by all, despite an inherent hatred for the concept of state-sponsored armed forces. Little skin was shown. Eyes were uncovered just enough for viewing their surroundings, the tips of fingers jutting from holed gloves. Drawstrings had been tightened over the head coverings. Some wore ski masks. Some had traces of red on their outfits, including the lead organizer. Yet otherwise the dark, otherwise the blackness.

Inside a terraced house that held multiple tenants, they gathered. Curtains were closed and the lights were off. The external sources of luminance, a pair of streetlights on the sidewalk, provided sufficient visual aid. Plenty of objects for the event were scattered around them. Several bottles were filled with flammable materials here, a half dozen flares there. In the corner of the room leaned a few flags. Two of the banners were divided into two triangles, one red and the other black. It was a widely recognized symbol of their cause. One had a tear from the last confrontation. The third banner was all red.

The light conversations decreased as the hour drew nigh. They were ready. A petite woman, dressed as the others, commanded their attention. Her hood was looser due to it covering a full head of dirty blonde dreadlocks. She wore a pair of fingerless gloves, each emblazoned with the circled red A, a symbol of anarchism. They all turned their attention to her. Those on the opposite side of the room struggled a little to see her over the heads of others. Hearing her was no problem as she projected well.

"Okay, everyone, we're about to meet the fascists," she explained. "For those of you who are new, let me just lay down some key points. First of all,

15

don't trust the cops. The most violent people are going to be the police. They have guns, Tasers, and cars. They're going to be worse than the Nazis we're fighting. Second, always go in a group. *No one* is to go anywhere alone. If you have to punch a Nazi, get a couple others to go with you. Third, don't remove your masks. At all. If any fascists recognize you, they might find you later. That can cost you your job, your life. Don't let people take your photo. If someone takes a shot of you with their phone, knock it out of their hands. Does everyone get it?"

Several nodded, several others verbally responded in the affirmative. They were of one mind. Hearing no dissent, she continued.

"Our contact at the university told Rudd and I about what was happening. Some alt right fanatic is headed to campus to speak. We're going to deprive that fascist of a platform to spew his hate. We're going to cause violence. We're going to cause anarchy. We're going to scare him and his white supremacist allies on campus. Are you all ready to spread some anarchy in the empire?"

Fervent shouts of affirmation followed. Cheering was brief, but unanimous. They were saving their fullest rage for the enemy. Another leader came forward. He was a lot taller than his peer, standing a little over six feet. With brown eyes, pale skin, a slim frame, his physical appearance was typical of the group. "Before we head out, one more important thing. If things get really bad, there's a church that'll be a few blocks from the campus. I'll point it out on the way there. I know the priest, he's sympathetic. He'll help if necessary. And what's more, he knows people who can pay any fines or bail. Got it?" There was less enthusiasm, but still an acknowledgement. "Now let's go kick some fascist ass!"

That brought more shouts and cheers. As people gathered their things, the two speakers each grabbed a banner; the third went to another member. She was not as charismatic as the other two, but she was just as committed. She was four inches taller than the woman who had spoken and had short, dark red hair. It was originally blonde, but she preferred the change. Covered by the long arms of the hoodie were a few tattoos, symbols of the cause. They led the dozen or so activists out of the terraced building unit, down the once quiet stairs, and into the evening along streets that led to the campus.

Cars were few as the hour was later. There were no checkpoints; apparently someone thought that they would not be required. As they drew closer, a domed Catholic church came into sight. Rudd Yansk did as he promised and pointed to the holy structure, reminding people that it was a figurative and literal sanctuary. Saundra Jaspers, the short leader who gave the opening remarks, did her part by pointing to some back streets and alleyways they could use to get away if the police closed in.

There was no question where they were supposed to go. Shouts and jeers were audible from some distance, easily reaching from the street where they walked. And they were getting louder with each step forward. They saw similar banners among some of the protesters. Smoke was already rising from the flares other people had lit. Police were starting to show up. Other masked demonstrators were facing down the street, where they knew the divisive speaker was expected. Soon they were in the chaos.

They were met by students and recent alumni as well as local radicals, some of whom were confident enough to show their faces. Visible countenances were in the minority, however. At first, the protest was more a rally. Authorities were still several feet away from the throngs of disagreeable people. There were nearly a thousand gathered around the campus entrance. The mass became more diverse at this point. Rainbow flags and the blue-pink-white striped banner were there. Men in drag, women in fishnets. Numerous African-American youths had donned outfits of red, green, and black, many holding posters of varying widths emblazoned with the declaration *Black Lives Matter*. Several Middle Easterners and Muslims were there too, Arabs both immigrant and native, wearing keffiyehs and some waving Palestinian flags. All that appeared to be missing from the progressive agenda crowd were environmentalists. Ironic, given that the scheduled guest speaker was planning to argue against climate change science and had virtually no statements on the record about his views on race.

"Jessie," said Rudd to his fellow banner-waving radical. "I don't see any Nazi protesters. I think we scared them off."

"That just leaves the cops."

"And that fascist speaker," added Saundra.

The trio broke off their conversation as chants cascaded over the masses. Fists pumped into the air, banners were swung side-to-side, long posters were shaken back and forth to convey the pulsing fury. More smoke wafted through the air from flares, though most of the incendiary items the radicals brought with them remained unused. Many took out smartphones to photograph and film the action, posting their experiences online. These were done with care, making sure to not tape the faces of those seeking anonymous dissent. Campus police did little to cause any ebb in the demonstration, even though no official permit had been granted. Local police were likewise ambivalent. There were still no fascists present.

"That's his car, isn't it?" asked Jessie, pointing at a vehicle flanked by police motorcycles.

Rudd nodded. "Yeah, that's him."

Others drew the same conclusion and were correct. The mob grew in its ferocity. Chants and screams amplified, a wave of sound rumbling along the street. Bottles lit and unlit were thrown in the direction of the approaching vehicles. Camouflage of night, crowd, and hood prevented an exact identification of who was responsible. Glass smashed against the pavement, small fires brightened the nighttime. Stoic police tried and failed to calm the crowds. The car with its motorcycles halted about fifty feet away. The protesters held their ground. Then, after a few waiting minutes, the three vehicles turned away.

Cheering engulfed the mass of people. Hugs and kisses everywhere, people were jumping with hands in the air as though the group was in a dance club. Chants of victory were uttered, yet few left the setting. There was a collective sense that this was not the end. Saundra received a text message. She did not hear the buzzing noise amid the popular cacophony, but she did feel the vibration against her thigh. Taking the device from her pocket with one hand while the other steadied a banner, she checked the message.

"Is he gone? It can't be that easy," said Jessie, readjusting her bandana around her face, as it was starting to drag low.

"No, he's not," affirmed Saundra, still looking down at the message. "According to Robespierre, the fascist is going to the other side of campus. A different entrance."

"Does he say which one?"

"Yes, Milk Street."

"Then we have to get to Milk Street," stated Rudd.

Saundra nodded and took the lead. She began to shout at the people around her, urging them to follow her and the others to the other side of campus. "The fascist isn't gone! He's coming in through Milk Street! The fascist is going to Milk Street!" Her declarations spread quickly. Many of the activists within earshot were acquainted with Saundra. They knew her well, both before and after graduation. Her word was accepted and soon hundreds of people were breaking away and heading across campus. A minority stayed behind, just in case the hated figure returned to the original port of call. Dormitories full of students looked out their windows to see the streams of agitated people going by. Some joined the masses; others objected, but kept their objections mum out of fear.

It took them several minutes to get there; trampling fields of grass and crowding the sidewalks. The first hundred or so, which included most of the people who had met at the terraced house near campus, arrived just as the car and its pair of motorcycles in escort was nearing the campus entrance. Molotovs were thrown to slow them down. All three machines halted their advance as sporadic fire got in their way. Hundreds rushed to the street, screaming and cursing and raging. The two motorcycles were joined by some campus police, who finally intervened though only to keep the car and the protesters apart. The motorcycles curved sideways along with a campus police vehicle, forming an impromptu wall. Radicals clogged the streets, barring entry yet again.

"No fascists, no pigs! No fascists, no pigs! No fascists, no pigs!" they chanted over and over again. Others shouted expletives, still others denounced Nazis.

They stood their ground once more. A half dozen police with arms stretched out in a halting pose behind the vehicle wall protected the guest speaker. Technically, the protesters had the numbers and the strength to overwhelm the small security detail. However, the demonstrators were of one mind to not take their outrage too far into the realm of force. Minutes went by. The crowd calmed a little, their outcries not as intense. Yet a great tension, a passionate objection, abounded still.

The car slowly backed away. Cheers started to emerge from the mass of people. Fatigue prevented the whoops and hollers of success to be too vociferous. The vehicle veered backwards to the right, then turned left to go forward away. And it kept going. It did not circle around, it did not turn either direction. It only kept going straight. The mob did some more celebratory chanting, then started to gradually break apart. Students and others posted at other campus entrances texted allies, confirming that no sight of the car had been found. Finally, Saundra received a text message from her source. She smiled when she read it.

"He's gone."

"Gone?" asked Jessie. "As in, *gone*-gone?"

"Yup."

"All right," stated Rudd with a smile and a nod.

"Back to the apartment?"

"Back to the apartment."

* * *

Alfredo Hernandez was at National Mall. It was a beautiful day. The weather had been a little hotter than normal going into the week. However, sheets of heavy rainfall the day before had washed away the high temperatures. That evening, the nation's capital had an elegant glistening gloom. The following day, the sunlight lacked the brutality of days before. Had it been sweltering, Hernandez likely could have managed. He was used to tropical climates due to his work overseas.

"Excuse me, sir," said an overly formal voice. "Do you have any immigration papers to prove you're legal?" Hernandez turned to see his friend from the Federal Bureau of Investigation.

"So sorry, me speak no English," he replied before laughing. Michael Zambo was about to shake his hand. "Come on, you know a handshake is never enough." Zambo laughed and the two embraced.

"No, seriously, show me those papers."

"Viva la raza," he deadpanned.

"All right, all right," said an amused Zambo. "Have you had lunch yet?"

"Nope."

"I saw some food trucks on my way here."

"Anything good?"

"Kebab, Mexican, Chinese, or maybe it was Vietnamese."

"You had me at kebab," said Hernandez with a smirk.

Alfredo and Michael walked side by side along the large rectangular sections of green grass. On one end was the Capitol Dome, the other the Washington Monument. People were moving and talking all around the pair: a few joggers, some cyclists, lots of people in suits and dresses having an outdoor lunch break, a huddle or two of tourists. Like most of the folk around them, the two men were in business casual, slacks, ties, and collared shirts. Zambo had a lanyard around his neck denoting his credentials.

"By the way, I heard about Alva getting married," began Michael with a sense of pity. "Hope you're holding up well."

"I'm doing all right," he responded with a smile. "It is better that way. She was never coming back to me."

"Indeed."

"Besides, she ended up marrying a Guatemalan, so I claim partial victory."

"Sure thing, bro."

The two reached the bright-hued food truck serving kebab. After a few minutes in line, they approached the window on the broadside of the vehicle. It did not take long for them to order. "Oh no, let me pay for it."

"You sure?"

"Sure, I'm sure. After all, you paid last time."

"I did, didn't I?"

"I remember. You did," Alfredo agreed. The two men walked off to the side of the truck to wait for their orders.

"So, what else is going on?"

"The new office is going on."

"Oh, you mean the one in the Rust Belt?"

"Now, now, not so loud," stated Alfredo with mocked caution. "You know they can get very sensitive about that label."

"I'm sure we're safe here. So tell me about it."

"Well, as you know, the Agency is looking to recruit a lot of folks with Middle Eastern and North African backgrounds. A lot of folks from Somalia, Middle East, etcetera, they ended up in that part of the country. You know, Dearborn, Minneapolis, Detroit, what have you. So, as the old politically-incorrect cliché goes, we're trying to bring the mountain to Muhammed."

"Pun intended."

"Maybe," said Hernandez with a smile and a quick bow of the head. "Construction has already begun on the facility. Scaffolding, foundation work. I'm no expert, so I don't know the details. The day laborers were on the other side of the family."

"I knew that," replied Zambo, acknowledging Alfredo's dry humor. "So, does that mean you'll be moving out there?"

"Most likely."

"Might be a nice place to end up. No hurricanes, after all. And fewer bugs than the DC swamp. Got to love that idea."

"Winter will be awful."

"Well, then schedule all your covert operations for December to March."

"I might do that," said Hernandez, who was about to add to his comment when the food truck worker called their order up. Each giving gratitude to the server, the two government employees walked a short distance before finding a park bench to sit upon for their meals. "So, what is happening on your end? How's the Missus?"

"She is doing just fine," replied Zambo, who smiled with fabricated outrage. "Hey there, you trying to start something?"

"Perish the thought."

"Good," said Zambo between bites into his kebab sub.

"So what else is happening? Anything exciting at the Bureau?"

"Every day at the Bureau is exciting."

"Are these days more exciting than normal?"

"They're busy, I will cede that."

"Is it more election issues?"

"Some of that, yes," nodded Zambo as he took a swig from his bottled water. "You know how it is ... death threats against candidates, political extremists plotting disruptions, militia groups trying out new territory, a militant cult here and there, and of course those dreadful antifa chapters. Lots of fun to go around."

"It's not too much work, is it?" inquired Hernandez as he finished his first strip of kebab, consuming meat and vegetables alike.

"Overall, we're doing okay. But there's this one possible case, it's just a bit out of our ability to seriously pursue."

"A *possible* case?"

"I call it possible, because I think there is something really bad just waiting to happen with it, but I don't have enough information."

"I'm intrigued, tell me more."

Zambo took one more bite into his sub and he crumpled up the paper it came in. "Well, there's this one antifa group out in California. They do their share of protests and disruptions. They indulge in violence here and there, been hauled off a few times. You know the type."

"Pretty familiar. Yeah."

"Well, sources in the area say that they are planning to do something more. Some unknown source seems to be guiding them. An unknown person of interest. He's readying them. Training them and leading them. And he's going to do something big. And when I say big, I mean *really* big."

"Really big?"

"Indeed."

"Sounds big," quipped Alfredo before finishing off his kebab. "So why isn't the Bureau looking into this more?"

"Well, the reason is because it's all speculation. I don't have anything concrete. What's more, I don't have anybody I can spare to investigate the matter further."

"You said you had sources."

"True," said Zambo as he and Hernandez both got up from the bench and threw their remnants into the nearest public trash can. "But these sources are unable to get any closer. They cannot infiltrate. Partly because they are too familiar to radicals in the region. They have gone as far as they can on insider info."

"So why not get someone from elsewhere to go undercover? Grab an agent from another part of the country, an FBI fellow unknown to radicals, and work from there."

"And that's the problem," stressed Michael as the two walked back to National Mall. "I don't really have anyone who fits that. Everyone is busy or not qualified. And higher-ups do not believe it's worth extra effort."

Hernandez had an idea. He stopped as they got to the walkway beside one of the big rectangles of grass. "You know, Michael, I think I have the perfect person for you. Someone who is off the books, has experience with radical elements, and who is currently on vacation and thus between assignments."

"Really?" Zambo perked up at this bit of information. "Sounds like an idea. As soon as possible, I would really like to meet him."

Hernandez bowed his head and smiled. "*Her*."

* * *

"You deserve a better state," declared Josiah Sharp, pausing to let the large exuberant crowds applaud and cheer the statement. "You deserve something better than the old violent ways." Another pause, more vocal support. "I am running this campaign to make sure that our state is better than it was. Not simply better than the current administration. Not simply better than the administration before that. I need your help to make a better state than we have had since the new millennium began. You can help me make this a reality." His tone got louder. "So tell me, are you going to help me make a better state?"

The crowd matched his increased volume with a great outpouring a support. There were around two thousand in attendance, so the noise was able to reach grand levels. People there represented a nice survey of the masses. They were an hour's drive away from the capital, with rural and urban folk alike gathering for the campaign rally. Three rows of young people stood behind Sharp, behind them a large American flag. At both ends of the elevated stage, there were three state flags on poles.

Amid the crowd were many cameras pointed toward the stage, a host of journalists both broadcast and print listening to his every word. Some recorded just the audio for later transcription, other used smartphones or professional film cameras. Many posted to social media immediately, putting up the inspirational quotes for their followers and critics alike. There was also security, both obvious and unobtrusive. The detail had a pair on the peripheries of the stage, in the event that one needed to take a bullet for the beloved gubernatorial candidate. Several others were in the crowd, dressed to blend into the typical, ordinary, attendee.

"We must rebuild," declared Sharp. "This rebuilding has to come through a mix of public policy, economic investment, and self-examination. We are bringing civility back to politics. I take great pride in running a clean campaign, and I thank each of you for contributing to this effort to drain the vilest aspects of politics out of our culture. With your help and with God's blessing, we will continue. We will *win*." The applause and cheers mixed together to again dominate the audio waves. "God bless this state, God bless all of you, and may God bless the United States of America."

Patriotic music was piped in through the multipurpose room's sound system. One last round of passionate support, and the crowds began to slowly disperse. Several reporters made their way toward Sharp from the press area, weaving through the shifting seas of departing people as he shook hands with those who had purchased special tickets for the event. He did all the proper candidate actions, engaging in brief gratitude for their support, taking the occasional selfie, signing the occasional piece of campaign literature, even hugging the occasional senior citizen. The fourth estate soon followed, a gaggle forming at the point after which Sharp concluded socializing with his fervent fans.

"Mr. Sharp! Mr. Sharp!" they called, each begging for a quick dialogue. They zeroed in with cameras, microphones, digital voice recorders, and at least one smartphone. Josiah was used to this attention. Political party operatives had trained him well, and he brought his own experience of dealing with the press when he was a lowly assistant district attorney. They had crowded just as much when interviewing him last year about his investigation that led to the destruction of the Cicero Organization, one of the worst home-grown terrorist organizations in the state's history. The woman who helped him destroy that cruel group, who killed its leader and gave him the necessary evidence to lock away the remaining members, was waiting for him behind the stage.

"Mr. Sharp!"

"Yes," he said, pointing to the reporter.

"How does it feel to know that the most recent polling puts you twenty points ahead of Senator Pearlstein?"

"I feel great," Josiah responded, knowing that each entity was figuring how to properly lede with his words, especially the journalist who made the query. "It's great to see that the good people of this state want to have a better future. They want economic revival, they want civility back in politics, and they want a more moral society. I appreciate all their support and hope this only continues come November."

"Mr. Sharp," said a reporter to his left. He looked at her and nodded. "We know that Senator Pearlstein initially claimed he was suspending his campaign, only to later back away from those comments. Yet there are still rumors that he has basically quit. What is your opinion of the rumors that Senator Pearlstein is purposely overseeing a weak campaign because he secretly wants you to win?"

"It would be best to ask Senator Pearlstein about those rumors."

"How do you respond to those who feel that your platform threatens the rights of women and minorities?" asked one reporter who wrote for a progressive blog. Sharp was familiar with the person and responded calmly.

"First, I would note that this type of extreme rhetoric oversimplifies complex agenda ideas and wrongly vilifies large numbers of well-meaning people in this state and nationwide. Second, I would note that I am either leading or in a statistical dead heat with Senator Pearlstein in nearly every voting bloc, regardless of race or gender. People understand that the partisan rhetoric doesn't match the facts. As an assistant district attorney, I have a history of helping all kinds of people, regardless of gender or race or creed. That desire to help has not disappeared because I am running for governor."

A few more harmless queries were answered, then an aide tapped Josiah on the shoulder. He bade farewells to the reporters, getting some additional unanswered questions thrown his way while he headed behind the curtain. They had their stories. While not sharing many of his political viewpoints, the news media remained largely sympathetic. They saw him as civil, intellectual, and well-meaning even when in disagreement. Small wonder his poll numbers were strong across the board.

Upon entering the backstage area, he saw the few people who had been watching his speech on a flat screen television. All but one of them immediately stepped forward and offered their compliments. Josiah knew many of them and gave those individuals brief social responses. All present understood that he was most interested in the one person still by the screen. As people went about their various duties behind them, as stage crew showed up to take down the campaign impedimenta, he approached her. Carla saw her husband and the two embraced, happy again to be in each other's company.

"How'd I do?"

"Not bad," she replied when they slowly loosened their mutual pleasant grip. "Maybe your best yet."

"Thank you."

"Of course, this is the first speech of yours I have actually paid attention to, so ...," she said, trailing off as he laughed.

"What high praise," replied an amused Josiah. "Shall we go?"

"Sure."

"What's the time?"

"A quarter until six."

"So we might get to your grandfather's place in time for dinner," spoke Josiah with optimism as the couple went toward the nearest black SUV.

"We might be a little late, but he told me they can be patient."

"You know, it seems like ever since I married you I have been that much later to things than in the past," he said as they got into car.

"My grandfather calls it 'Arab Standard Time,'" she explained as she shut her door.

"That must be it," agreed Josiah while shutting his door, the engine sound igniting and the vehicle taking off into the fading afternoon.

* * *

It was a good meal and a good time with family. Elnora had cooked chicken with a mushroom sauce and rice pilaf. Warm rolls and butter along with a small salad were the sides. She was complimented by the other three for her restaurant-quality dinner. As usual, Carla said grace to start the occasion. She and her husband Josiah were only a few minutes late. Elnora quipped that she was getting used to it, with her husband George al-Hassan being a great help in that endeavor.

At this point, the meal was nearing its conclusion. George was having two more rolls, weathering the judgments as he lathered the four halves with butter. He had a cane resting on the top of his chair, its long staff hanging along the back end of the frame. To his right sat Elnora, drinking a cup of coffee. Opposite Elnora was Carla, who, like Josiah, was drinking a soda after the meal. Josiah was to her right, opposite the man who gave away the bride at the wedding earlier that year.

"My grandfather has not had any accidents, has he?" Carla asked Elnora.

"I said I have been accident-free," insisted George in his Syrian-accented English.

"I want an unbiased source," his granddaughter countered with a smile.

"George tells the truth," Elnora assured Carla. "He has yet to fall since going from wheelchair to cane."

"That's good."

"Although he did have a few close calls, if I recollect correctly," Elnora began, being lightly tapped on the arm to encourage her to be quiet. "Oh come on, George. She should know about the times you almost fell."

"Okay, okay," he consented. "The important thing is that I have not fallen all the way down to the ground."

"Yet."

"Now, Carla," said Josiah. "Show some optimism."

"Besides, we all fall down eventually."

"That is true," added Josiah to George's comments. "As a very, very new translation of the Bible would put it, 'let he who has never tripped and fallen cast the first stone.'"

George pointed at Sharp with approval. "Now that is a man after my own heart."

"So what's new on the campaign trail, Josiah?"

"Any scandals yet?" jokingly asked George.

"Hey! I thought you were on my side."

"I'm fickle."

"I can tell," said Josiah with a laugh. "Things are going well. All the polls show me way ahead. Pearlstein isn't even bothering to debate me, and best of all, no new assassination attempts."

"Not bad, not bad," said George. "My country could use a lot more of that."

"Elections or no new assassination attempts?" queried Carla.

"Maybe both," replied George, amusing all at the table.

Carla's phone went off. The buzzing vibration caught both her attention and her husband's. She took out the mobile device and checked the alert. Alfredo Hernandez had sent her two text messages. Unlocking the phone, she checked them as the other three continued to engage in light-hearted conversation. The two bubbles were on top of each other, with no time elapsed between them. The first read "Very important update" and the second "please call me asap." Her demeanor changed, holding a trace of dread.

"What is it, Carla?"

"It's work-related, giddo," she responded as she rose from the table. "I need to make a phone call. Excuse me." While the two elder individuals returned to idle chatter, Josiah watched his exiting wife with concern before being reeled back into the pleasant socializing. Although he enjoyed the light humor, his internal thoughts simmered with what might be happening in the living room, where Carla called her handler.

"Hello?" asked the man on the end of the line.

"Al, its Carla."

"Ah, yes, of course. I should have known," he said with a light tone. "I'm not interrupting anything, am I?"

"Family dinner."

"Oh, well ... Um, sorry about that. You know how the world is: no rest for the righteous or the wicked. Rest only in the grave."

"What is the new update?"

"Oh, yes, that," he began while Carla stood in the living room, pacing as their conversation continued. "I have a new assignment for you, this one is stateside."

"Stateside? I thought the Agency was supposed to do its work overseas."

"This won't be an Agency job," said Hernandez with a breath. "I am loaning you out to the FBI. A buddy of mine works there and he needs someone to infiltrate an antifa chapter out in California." Carla was already feeling dissent as her superior continued. "My friend believes that the chapter is going to do something bad. Really bad, even by antifa standards. Problem is, Bureau staff are a little stretched and there is no one available for the undercover assignment who is qualified."

"So, that leaves me."

"Correct. You are as smart as you are beautiful."

"I don't know," protested Carla. "I mean, I just finished spending more than a month being undercover as a student in Central America."

"Which means you have plenty of fresh experience to work with. You'll be playing the role of a student radical. Join the antifa chapter, learn what you can for a few weeks or so, and if nothing comes up, then you at least get a free, state-paid vacation to sunny California. And if something does come up, then the FBI will handle the rest. This might actually be the least violent work you've ever done."

"Still, Al, listen," pleaded Carla, a headache throbbing into being. "There has to be someone else. I have never done an undercover job this deep."

"Trust me, Carla, you are the most experienced person for this job," assured Hernandez. "You spent years working for a domestic terrorist group. And when the opportunity came, you singlehandedly destroyed the cell. For the past year, you have done many assignments for the Agency, getting in and out of tense environments with impunity. Tell me with a straight face that this will not all be very familiar."

"I really do not know."

"I get it, I get it. You are a little drained. For what it is worth, the first few steps will be easy. Detective Zambo and I will be flying out to where you are to debrief you about the assignment. From there, you go out to California. We have all the details of your identity, some basic info, social media accounts, the works. And I assure you that after this assignment, you will get a long break."

Carla sighed. She wanted to keep arguing the point. She wanted to make another point of contention, as though it would serve some beneficial purpose. She wanted more time to think it over, to find some way to weasel out of this. Josiah had never liked her occupation, what she was doing. While his word was not final, his concerns echoed the lamentations within her conscience. However, as was often the situation for her life, there appeared no better solution, no higher nor purer path to sojourn.

"Okay. I will do it."

"Excellent," said an elated Hernandez. "I am always happy to work alongside you, Carla. And you will like my friend. He is very amiable and intelligent. I mean heck, if both of you were not married to other people, I would probably play matchmaker."

"You are pushing it."

29

"Okay, maybe a little," conceded Hernandez. "Regardless, have a good weekend and I and Zambo will see you Monday morning."

"Good night," Carla said, ending the call. It felt so typical. It felt like a repeat of history. It was a repeat of history. Knowing that she would again have to discontinue a normal life for her work. It happened earlier that year, she remembered, just as she was beginning to undergo more mainstream pressures and joys. Even as she tried to formulate her explanation for the family in the adjacent dining room, she was going back to that time not long ago when the dark work had last interfered. It always interfered, always drew her away from the ordinary, slow-moving vapor of a life.

III

"Nervous?" Josiah Sharp asked his fiancé. He was driving his compact car into the suburban neighborhood where his parents lived. His passenger was quiet, looking out the window at the passing world. Her focus on the commute was disrupted by the query. She shifted her body to face him.

"A little," Carla al-Hassan admitted. "You?"

"Me too, also," he responded. His parents had lived in the same home for nearly a decade. It was smaller than Josiah's childhood abode, which was too big for just two people. He knew the way, a byproduct of frequent visits. It was not a confusing route, even for a community in which every street kind of looked the same: green manicured yards, two-to-three story homes, concrete drive-ways, well-ordered light brown sidewalks, generic paint jobs for all the buildings, similar basic designs, similar cars. Yet Josiah eschewed his usual GPS crutch. "I have never gone this far before."

"Neither have I," she replied. "I did some dating here and there in high school, and college, but nothing serious."

"Same here." They halted before a four-way intersection. Josiah waved with permission for the SUV to his left to go ahead and cross in front of him. He smiled. "Who do you think is more nervous? Me or you?"

"You, no question," Carla stated flatly.

"No question?"

"Yeah," said Carla. "After all, if it is a total disaster, I do not have to see your parents ever again. You cannot claim the same."

Josiah looked at his fiancé briefly, seeing a faint grin. He reciprocated the expression before directing his eyes back to the road. "Anyway, I told them about your parents, so you don't have to worry about that awkward conversation."

31

"Thanks," said Carla as they reached the street before the street where the Sharp house was located. Her tone darkened. "Did you tell them anything else 'awkward' about me?"

"What do you think?" asked an amused Josiah. Carla simply nodded in response. Another left turn, another curvy, smoothly paved road. "Welp, we are almost there."

"So, you were not raised here?"

"Nope. My childhood home was elsewhere. But honestly, it looked just like this place. You know, low crime, middle class, upper-middle class ... dare I say privileged? Maybe 'spoiled' would be a better term."

"'Spoiled' sounds good," Carla agreed, smiling as Josiah looked at her.

"Here we are," said Josiah softly, slowing the sports car and turning toward the barrier between street and sidewalk. The two felt a faint nudge as the front passenger tire bumped the curb before the upward route became level. The driveway had two cars parked beside one another.

Carla examined the brick home for a moment. It was a little smaller than the other homes, which were owned by nuclear families. Sharp turned off the engine and the two got out of the car. Both were dressed in modest business casual. Josiah wore a tie, dress shirt, and slacks, while Carla had opted for a dark blue pantsuit and white button-up shirt.

"I think I'm ready," she said following a deep breath as the two went down the brick walkway to the front door. "At least I will not have to worry about being attacked with a knife."

"You have obviously never met my mother," deadpanned Josiah, who opened the screen door and rang the bell. Both could hear some noise behind the thick wooden door before the portal opened to reveal a kindly middle-aged couple. There was obvious happiness at his arrival, as Josiah hugged his mother and shook hands with his father. "And this is Carla." First Mrs. Sharp extended her hand and Carla shook it. For Mr. Sharp, Carla was the one who first offered a hand, which he accepted. As they were shaking hands, Josiah introduced his fiancé to his parents. "This is my mother, Rose, and this is my father, Terry."

"A pleasure to meet both of you," said Carla.

"I am so glad you could stop by," Rose added. "Please, come in." The two obliged, both still feeling a little nervous even with the kind welcome. The four made their way to the living room. A flat screen television hung over a seldom used fireplace, with a mantle situated between the two, supporting a row of family photos in different sized and different hued frames. Two large couches provided seating, each one placed parallel to a wall. A rectangular glass-topped coffee table was situated between the two couches. As Terry, his son, and his future daughter-in-law stood around the furniture, Rose instinctively went to the adjacent kitchen. "Would either of you like something to drink?"

"Tea would be nice," said Josiah.

"Same here," responded Carla.

"I'll have coffee, Rose."

The three who were still in the living room sat down. Carla found the family resemblance between father and son quite striking. Terry looked much like Josiah, save for the grayer hair, increased wrinkles, and different eye color. He also appeared to be a few inches taller. Otherwise, there was a strong resemblance, especially when he smiled. The couple implicitly thought it best to put some distance between them as they sat on the couch. It seemed like the best possible way to sit in front of a possibly hostile audience. Then again, if there was hostility, Mr. Sharp was keeping it well hidden.

"So how was your trip here, Joey?"

"It went well. Little traffic, with a little rain. But it all cleared up by the time I got to your neighborhood."

"Must be our anti-storm shield," joked Terry. He directed his attention to the new woman in his son's life. "So, what do you do, Carla?"

"I work for the government."

"I see," responded Terry, with a faint laugh. "You know, when I was younger, whenever someone said they 'worked for the government,' it meant they worked for the CIA."

Carla laughed with some nervousness. She knew she would have to be careful on the details. For the time, she did not feel too concerned and lightly replied, "Guilty as charged."

"Good to see some things don't change," he replied. "So, what kind of stuff do you do for the CIA?"

"Oh come on, Dad, you know their work is classified," interjected Josiah.

"My grandfather always asks me if I have toppled any governments recently." The trio laughed at her comment as Rose entered the room, carrying a wooden tray with four drinks; Two coffees and two teas.

"Here's your tea," she said, leaning the tray toward Carla.

"Thank you," she responded while taking the glass. Josiah thanked his mother as well taking his glass of tea. Rose then went over to the other couch where her husband was seated. He got his coffee from the tray as she placed onto the glass tabletop. She then took the remaining ceramic cup from the tray.

"So what was all the laughter about?"

"Just talking about how Carla works for the CIA, which means she topples governments for a living."

"Oh, I see," said Rose after taking a swig. "Just be sure to warn me if you have to topple ours, okay?"

"Sure thing," Carla lightly agreed.

"Josiah told me you were from Syria originally."

"I was born there, but I was raised here in the US. I must have left when I was, maybe two or three at the oldest."

"Have you ever been back?"

"Sometimes to see relatives. But not often. It's been a few years since I last went, what with all the violence. My grandfather did not want me anywhere near there."

"Still, an interesting place to be connected to," noted Terry. "I mean all the history, the biblical significance."

"Yes, I know," Carla agreed. "I have been to the Chapel of St. Paul in Damascus. You know, it was built from the same stone that was part of the gate St. Paul was lowered from to escape being killed for his beliefs."

Terry was impressed. "And to think, I know some fellow pastors who actually believe that the Orthodox don't read their Bibles."

"And that's when they aren't confusing them with Catholics. Right Carla?" Josiah remarked.

"Yes, exactly," she said, smiling at her fiancé's comment. "Of course, you know, being Arab, most of the time people mistake me for being Muslim."

"Well, to be fair, the whole not drinking thing does not help things," Josiah said to Carla.

"So, you're a teetotaler?" Terry asked.

"Well, I still take communion."

"And remember, Dad, other churches use wine for communion."

"I know, Joey," stated Terry, feigning annoyance.

The conversations between the four continued for some time. It was an amicable occasion. Josiah's parents appeared genuinely interested in Carla and seemed to be giving their approval. The younger pair became more relaxed, though they still retained some formality—especially Carla, who still worried about making a bad impression. By the time Rose brought in the second round of non-alcoholic drinks, Terry had requested to see his son alone. The two got up as the women remained on opposite couches. Carla learned about the substance of the dialogue between father and son later on.

* * *

Terry wanted to show Josiah the new work that he had done on the backyard patio. That was the stated reason for the men departing the scene. Carla knew the real reason. Still, she put on her best diplomacy, continuing to socialize as she and Rose enjoyed their respective drinks. Josiah expressed no subliminal fears to Carla as he got up to follow his father through the kitchen and outside to the back yard. She was not going to keep an eye on them, for she knew it would appear improper.

Josiah and Terry exited the house, the father at the lead. The day was still beautiful, the sun with some clouds amid a large blue sky. Neither had a drink with them, kindly putting their respective cups in the sink on the way out. The mood was still easy. Terry pointed to the parts of the patio that had recently been redone, giving his son brief descriptions as though leading a tour of some historic site. Josiah offered little comment during this moment, simply nodding or giving brief verbal affirmations that he understood what was done. He was not particularly nervous; the small gathering was going well.

"It will be interesting," began Terry, finally beginning to get around to the obvious conversation, "I wonder when your mother will bring up her little story about how she almost traveled to Syria back in college."

"I was surprised that she hadn't already brought it up."

"Yes."

There was a pause. Josiah felt some anxiety mounting. His father seemed to be waiting, like a spider for a fly. Then again, perchance this was all in his head. *It had to be*, he thought. Josiah broke the silence, just in case: "So, what do you think of her? She's amazing, isn't she?"

Terry bowed his head, then eased into his response, "She seems nice. Decent ... and a Christian who knows her Bible, that's definitely a plus."

"There's no 'but' here, is there?"

"Thing is," began Terry, briefly upping the angst in his son. "Joey, your mother puts on a good face, but we are both a little worried about the speed of all this. I mean, how long have you known her?"

"I met her over a year ago," Josiah stated defensively, omitting the several months in which they did not contact one another. "We have spent a lot of time together. You and mom only knew each other for a year or so, right?"

"Two years."

"Two years," conceded Josiah. "Two years after you met, you were already married. That included months of engagement."

"Why so fast? Why not wait until after the election?"

"Carla and I just feel it should happen soon. She works a lot overseas and usually only gets short notice for when she has to go. Besides," added Josiah in an effort to lighten the mood, "it will do wonders for my poll numbers."

Terry smiled weakly. "That might help. But still, Joey. I just want to make sure you know who you are marrying. I mean, what if it turns out that she's a serial killer?"

"Daaaaaad," stated an annoyed Josiah, keeping the facts to himself. "I think the CIA would have found that out before me."

"There is that."

"I get where you are coming from. If Carla and I were teenagers, I would get you being worried about our decisions. But we are both in our thirties. We have matured, trust me. And we know what we are doing."

"Well, okay, okay," said Terry with hands raised, his son jubilant at the concession. "I will respect your decision. And honestly, she does strike me as an excellent choice."

"You and mom raised me well."

"I mean, I was never really worried that you would bring some depraved Jezebel to our doorstep, but your mother always had her doubts."

"Well, I'm glad that I could prove her wrong."

"Likewise," said Terry. "It will be my pleasure to officiate your wedding."

Josiah's angst levels went up again. "Um, yeah, Dad, about that." His father looked at him with a melting smile. "I guess I should tell you now that the wedding will be happening at her church. That's what she and her family want."

"Joey, Joey," protested Terry. "How can you agree to that? I performed the weddings of all your siblings. And many of your cousins. It's a family tradition."

"And her family's tradition has it that all the weddings are done in her church. Their church, that is. I did not know you would care. After all, like you said, you have already done the weddings for all my siblings and most of my cousins."

"Is she firm on that?"

"Pretty much, yes. In fact, we're scheduled to meet with her priest next week."

"Which church is it?"

"St. Paul's Orthodox Cathedral. Its located in the capital, downtown."

"Yeah, I think I am familiar with it," mused Terry, who tilting his head upward to think for a moment before returning his sight to his son. "Yeah, actually, I know the clergy there. We have done some ecumenical charity work in the city."

"So you're okay with it, right?"

"You are pushing it, but I think I can live with it."

"Thanks, Dad," Josiah happily declared, as father and son embraced.

"I guess we should see how your mother and Carla are doing."

"Yes, yes we should," agreed Josiah as the two men made their way back into the house. Josiah held the door for his father, who nodded in gratitude as he passed through. From there they went through the kitchen and back into the living room.

As both men entered the living room, they gave each other a look of tacit amusement as they heard what Rose was saying to Carla: "You know, when I was a student, I almost went on a study abroad trip to Syria ..."

* * *

It all went well, despite all the fretting over something—anything—going wrong. No one tripped during the procession, no candles were dropped to the cathedral floor. The wedding crowns remained on the heads of the bride and groom. Friends and family celebrated the new wedded couple, with no dramatics. From there, came the reception. George al-Hassan gave a heartfelt speech, with even the relatives he had issues with applauding his words. The dance floor opened soon after, and the festivities continued for hours.

The last of the guests were gone, returning to their hotel rooms or homes. The Sharps went back to Josiah's place, which was no longer his alone. A single unremarkable vehicle followed, containing a security detachment. They relieved another security detachment, which had been at the home of Josiah for several hours. A chauffeur dropped the couple off in front of the domicile. They said their goodbyes, with Carla instinctively reaching for a tip only to realize that her dress had no pockets.

For the ceremony, Josiah had worn a tuxedo with bowtie. He had had his hair tamed with product and combing, making it remain still for most of the evening. His sisters had wanted him to wear contacts, but he overruled them. He had great trepidation over one of them falling out. Carla wore a modest white wedding dress, covering her arms and back. She opted for flats instead of heels, having never been particularly good at walking in the latter and not wanting to trip during the sacred event. Makeup artists had painted her face with great detail, delicately punctuating the eyes, cheeks, and lips.

Nearing the door, the two were well past their prime appearance. Josiah's tuxedo was not as polished and his bowtie seemed to be irreversibly looser than before. Carla's makeup was wearing off, the cheeks being less rosy, the lines defining the eyes faded. They were weary from all the attention. Josiah had the keys, a benefit of having pockets. He also had his phone present; Carla had left hers at a friend's place.

"Now, before we go in," began Josiah, "you know that we have one more little wedding ritual to do."

"Which one is that? I feel like we did them all."

"You mean you don't remember the 'carrying over the threshold' part?"

"You sure you have the strength for it?" she asked, prompting Josiah to look at her in bemusement as she grinned.

Josiah opened the door. "You wait here and I will set up the phone. I will put it on video so we can pick a still or two to send to family."

"Sounds good," said Carla through the opened front door, a screen door being the only divide between them. Josiah leaned the phone against his Bible so that the front camera faced the doorway. He tapped all the necessary buttons on the screens and then the phone started the recording.

"Okay, we are in business," he said as he walked toward the entrance. "Now I just need to fix this screen door and we can begin." The task was an easy one, Josiah pushed the stopper along the bar on the door, forcing the screen to remain open. He took a deep breath, his shoulders going up and down. "Okay then, you ready?"

"Just don't drop me," she quipped.

While Josiah was not a muscular figure, it turned out he was strong to carry the average-sized Carla in his arms and across the barrier. They held their position for a few seconds, smiling in the direction of the phone screen. After about ten seconds, they agreed to halt the pose. Josiah gently let go, allowing Carla to ease back to a standing position. From there he went back to adjust the screen door, closing it and the main door. For her part, Carla stopped the recording and eventually handed the phone back to her new husband.

After that, the two finally began to relax. Carla took off her shoes and put them by the couch, not really knowing where else to put them. Josiah removed his jacket and took off his bowtie, then unbuttoned the top two buttons of his shirt. "You know, this has to be the longest I have ever worn a tuxedo."

"Really," said Carla as she sat down on the couch at the center of the room. "What about other weddings?"

"Never wore a tux for those."

"I see," Carla said, pressing her palm against her face, which made some of her makeup blur and end up on her hand. She noticed it quickly. "You know what? I need to get this stuff off my face. Is your bathroom still where I remember it?"

"Yup," said Josiah as Carla walked by him to the small tile-floored room. She closed the door behind her. For his part, Josiah sat down on the couch. He leaned back and stared at his ceiling, his thoughts pouring over the significance of what happened. His mind went through the sacred and the profane, the spiritual and the carnal. There was no one else, there was no better time. There was nothing wrong. He knew it.

"So glad to get all that stuff off my face," said Carla as she came from the bathroom.

"You look better without it."

Carla smiled.

"You know, how fitting it is that we're here," explained Josiah, his attention no longer at the ceiling but rather focused on his wife. "This was where we first met."

"It was," she nodded. "I was running away from a failed bank robbery. Yours was the only place I could think of going to."

"I remember you pretending that some criminal was stalking you or something."

"I was technically telling the truth," Carla pointed out as she neared the couch. Josiah nodded in concession. Carla laughed. "It seems so scandalous that I was here for days on end."

"Let 'em talk," said Josiah, rising from the couch and standing before her. "We both know we did nothing immoral."

"Very true."

"I mean, we didn't even kiss," said Josiah with a laugh.

"You are right, we did not."

"We only hugged."

"We only hugged," repeated Carla as Josiah's hands slowly came to grip her shoulders. Words stopped. Suddenly, it was all touch. The breathing, the implicit knowledge. And then the kiss, a second kiss, a third kiss, more embrace. More touching. All sense of the misery of the outside world blurred away. Nothing was happening beyond their mutual comprehension, their mutual passion.

* * *

Five loud knocks awoke her. Whoever was outside pounded on the door with such force as to be heard through the bedroom door. Carla Sharp stirred and grudgingly left the bed, her spouse still unconscious. She put on some sweats so as to be decent, brushing her black hair out of her face. *Maybe it was a dream*, she thought groggily. Then the five knocks came again. It was not a dream. Yawning as she walked from the bed, she opened the door to the living room just as another volley of knocks were fired.

"I'm coming! I'm coming!" she shouted in the direction of the knocker, annoyed. Agitation sharpened the tone of her voice. She held no concerns over who might be on the other side of the thick wooden barrier. A gubernatorial hopeful in a state where politics had a history of recent bloodshed, Josiah Sharp had a security detail outside. Furthermore, a professional assassin would hardly be so arrogant as to attack a defended target on a sunny morning by boldly knocking on the front door. At least the knocking had stopped.

Carla unbolted the door and opened it, seeing a smiling Alfredo Hernandez holding a large bouquet of flowers. He wore a dark brown tie, white shirt, brown pants, and a jacket. Carla quickly noted that the bouquet, with its bright, wide open petals and long stems, were artificial in nature. There was a dozen or so sweets tucked into the arrangement, covered with gold-hued paper wrapping.

He also had a manila envelope clamped under his right arm. She remained sedate at his presence.

"Congratulations!" he said as though he worked for some delivery service. "What God has joined together, let man not tear asunder." Carla said nothing, but simply stepped aside to let an all-too-peppy Hernandez enter. He quickly found a table to put the bouquet on. "I made sure to get one with chocolates, because they are tastier than real flowers."

"Thanks," she said with a soft voice.

Hernandez was quick to realize that his company was not at full strength. He placed the manila envelope beside the bouquet, hesitating at first to speak. "Would you like me to make you some coffee?"

"The machine is over there," said Carla, her voice a little stronger than before. Her arm pointed in the general direction of the kitchen. Fortunately, the maker was clearly visible on the counter. Hernandez found the packets and poured in the water from the nearby faucet. The instant coffee was beginning to percolate as he went back to the dining room table, where Carla was sitting on a pulled out chair, her hand balancing her head while she slowly blinked a couple of times. Hernandez approached.

"I am sorry, Carla," Hernandez said as her superior looked at the arrangement he had delivered. "I assumed that by coming later in the morning, you would be well-rested."

"You also assumed that I slept last night," she replied, prompting Hernandez to look at her. She had a weak but contented smile.

"Yes, well ... um ..." Hernandez was interrupted by the beeping of the coffee maker. He raised an index finger to make a point. "I will be right back." A minute later, he returned to the table with two mugs full of the dark brew. "I must admit, I do not know your drinking habits, so I didn't add any sugar or cream or what have you."

"Thanks," she responded, carefully taking the mug and sipping its contents. "So, what are you doing here?"

"You mean aside from offering my congrats in person?" He could see her mild irritation, so he got to the point. "Yes, Carla, I am here to notify you about your next assignment." She quietly drank more of the coffee as Hernandez stood there, expecting far worse. Having no interruption from her, he continued. "Anyhow, the finer details are, of course, in the envelope there, but just to give you a bit of a summary, we need you to take out a cartel operative. He

41

is working at a university down south. He's recruiting youngsters to organized crime and also getting others addicted to drugs. All sorts of bad actions."

"Why don't you go to the cops?"

"Because none of our evidence is admissible."

"Ah," she spoke in a soft tone of faux epiphany.

"So since our evidence is inadmissible, our solution must also be inadmissible."

"Okay."

"Like I said, the details of the cover and the overall assignment are in the envelope. You will not have to leave until next Tuesday, so you have plenty of time to rest, relax, enjoy married life, and do whatever else married people do. I've never been, so I don't really know."

"I know," she replied as she took the envelope and opened it.

"Anyway, um ...," added Hernandez, who still felt guilty over the timing of his arrival. "You know what? There is a doughnut place a mile from here. Let me get you and your husband a dozen doughnuts. It will be part of my wedding present."

"Thanks."

"Be back soon!" said Hernandez, with an inoffensive smile. He darted back out the door and into his car before she could reply.

Carla sat there, thinking. She was not surprised. For years, shadowy work had disturbed her civilian life. Whether or not it was government sanctioned, it came. A text message here, an email there. Life seemed to be divided between the normal and the abnormal, the civilized and the cruel. They came as day and night, wake and sleep, hunger and fullness. The idea that any potential plans with Josiah were to be suspended was expected. They did not even bother to schedule a honeymoon. Him for the campaign, her for the Agency. She recalled offering no real protest to Hernandez. Candidate Sharp had offered only mild protest, a concern over what the government was making her do, but little else. Maybe even he was starting to adjust, to adapt to the normalcy of covert interference.

"It's another assignment, isn't it?" asked Josiah, both on the morning after their wedding and at that moment at Elnora's place.

"It's different this time," she explained. "I will be working for the FBI. Apparently, Alfredo can send me over to them at will."

"What will you be doing?"

"Undercover work. Out in California. It is probably best if I do not give you more details. Honestly, I know little more than that."

"Why am I getting used to this?" asked Josiah, fingers rubbing his forehead. "Why am I letting them use you as a weapon?"

"This might be different, Josiah," she assured him, coming closer to grip his arm. "It's with the FBI, undercover. It's possible that all I will do is just report things. They will do the rest." Josiah expressed little confidence in her assurances. But he turned to face her and gave her a deep embrace.

"When I get elected, I am going to find some way to get you out of this."

"Josiah ..."

"I do not know what it will be, but I will think of something. Somehow."

"Josiah ..."

"What is it?"

"I love you."

The statement halted his speech. The two embraced and kissed before joining George and Elnora at the dinner table. They acted as though nothing serious had just happened. They always seemed to keep things from the ones they loved. Neither Carla's grandfather nor his wife knew of anything ominous. Only that their granddaughter was going to be on the West Coast for work for an extended period of time. She hoped to be back by Thanksgiving.

IV

Professor Holton Fillerhouse was in a grumpy mood. His haggard, middle-aged appearance made the emotion plain to see. He had gray hair, with pale skin and prominent lines on his face and neck. His face tended toward a scowl, a smile being a rare expression for those stony features. His students considered him too strict; he wondered if he was being strict enough. Always tilted toward proper attire, he wore a button-up collared shirt, tie, slacks, black dress shoes, and a sweater, despite the current temperatures. A plump belly and thick limbs gave him a mountain appearance as he waited.

Beside him was Mack Channing, a man who made the pair a study in contrast. He was in his late thirties, much slimmer, with a youthful sparkle and a personable demeanor. He stood slightly above average height and was often seen jogging or cycling along the campus before class. His was a more contemporary style of dress. Mack was rarely seen with tie or jacket, generally working with sleeves rolled up and sneakers his preferred footwear. It was not uncommon for him to take his graduate students out for beers following the last class of the semester. Students rated him highly online, describing his courses as laidback, easy, and understanding.

Despite differences of personality and politics, Fillerhouse and Channing presented a united front while they waited in the provost's office. Academic publications and college-centered magazines were available for reading and a few awards given to the university were framed and hung on the walls. A student secretary manned a computer at a desk facing opposite the two inhabited chairs. She was balancing her time between monitoring the office's inbox and social media chat.

"Come on in," said Provost Juana Marciela. Opening the door to her office, she bestowed a welcoming gaze of familiarity upon the two men she had known

44

and worked alongside for some time. Channing rose quickly and took a slight lead over Fillerhouse, despite the latter being the instigator of the meeting. A small tan woman who always wore heels, Marciela returned to her desk as the two men entered and sat down. She directed her remarks to Fillerhouse. "Thank you for taking the time to meet with me. I got your email about last week's disruptions, but I thought it would be better to talk in person."

"Likewise," nodded Fillerhouse, shifting in his seat. Channing leaned back in silence, his arms folded. "So what is being done about it?"

"I just want to point out that I think it is always important to respect the rights of the students. I think we can all agree that students have the right to express their opinions, especially if they take issue with a controversial speaker."

"No one is disputing that," grumbled Fillerhouse, who had heard this lecture before. "However, let us not forget that plenty of students wanted to hear John Murray speak, but were deprived of that because of violent protests."

"Now, now," cautioned Marciela. "Few of the students actually engaged in violent behavior. Campus police told me that there were around two thousand students and others present, but only a handful of outright violent actions were taken."

"And only a minority of Southerners belonged to the Ku Klux Klan," countered Fillerhouse. "Does that mean the Old South was engaging in acceptable resistance?"

"Listen, please," replied the provost with a calming voice. "The point is, we need to always approach this erring on the side of students' rights to express their opinions. You are right; it is wrong that some people took to preventing him from coming to campus. Campuses should be a free market of ideas, regardless of political opinion."

"Thank you," stated the elder professor.

"But as you know, Murray is a controversial figure. His viewpoints were very disconcerting for many students, especially women, minorities ..."

"His issue was climate change," interrupted an annoyed Fillerhouse, hands moving back and forth with the words. "What does that have to do with race or gender?"

"I can answer that," spoke up Channing, halting an explanation from the provost. He shifted himself to speak with his academic peer. "You see, Holt, many have noted that climate change disproportionately affects the developing world. The developing world is mostly minority. Someone who denies climate change is more likely to oppose measures to fight climate change. A climate change that, as aforementioned, disproportionately affects minorities. Therefore, a denialist of climate change supports a status quo that, at least according to climate change believers, hurts minorities. Make sense?"

"In a way," he conceded. "Still, though, to label someone racist you should have evidence of a malicious intent. There is none with Murray. Besides, if we want to play the racism card like that, one could just as easily argue that climate change believers are racist. After all, they are demanding that developing countries approve various rules and regulations that could harm their economy. An economic harm that would disproportionately affect minorities. And so on and so forth until we are all racists and never knew it."

"Debating racism aside," interjected the provost. "Our university's police lack any ability to single out specific violent agitators. For all we know, none of the violent elements were students. They could have easily come onto campus at any point and joined the peaceful demonstrations that the students were holding."

"That's another thing I mentioned in my email," protested Fillerhouse. "What was the deal with campus police? They were supposed to *protect* Murray and make sure he got to the auditorium. Yet when all those radicals showed up, they barely did anything."

"Please understand, Professor Fillerhouse," implored the provost. "Police brutality is a major problem in the United States. And I was not about to turn Pacific Coast State University into a militarized police state."

"Still," Fillerhouse shot back. "Something has to change. This keeps happening. Murray is the fourth conservative speaker that faculty or students have tried to invite to campus to speak only to have tons of radicals show up and stop them. We even tried to be more covert about his arrival, but somehow the activists knew all about where he was coming from and when, and what route he would take if blocked off. Sad thing is, Murray's experiences were probably the least violent of the bunch."

"Meanwhile," Channing pointed out, "liberal speakers come and go without incident. With all respect, Juana, you have to admit, that that is far from fair. I can't ever see myself agreeing with Murray or the other conservatives who come to campus. But they also have a right to speak, to express their opinions. In our divided country, we need to do a better job of talking to each other."

"And what's more," added Fillerhouse. "You need to think about what the alumni are thinking about all this. The state is expected to cut education funds even more next session. We rely on a lot of charitable giving. Many of the folks who give us money would be disgusted to see the University callously disregarding intellectual freedom."

"I know, I know," said the provost, looking down at her desk. She thought for a moment before responding. "Do you have plans to invite any more speakers this semester?"

"Yes," replied the elder professor. "There is a conservative writer named Charles Lewis. He is planning to speak on the strategies to consider if we have another war in the Middle East. It will be based off of an essay he wrote earlier this year."

"Sounds controversial."

"And that liberal speaker Burke hosted last spring, the one that said 'Republicans hate black people,' that wasn't controversial?"

"Point taken," conceded the provost. "All right, all right. Here is what I will do. I will make sure that Lewis gets as much campus police protection as necessary. I promise that if trouble comes, people will be arrested. I will even make sure that security checks people before they get to enter the auditorium. Good enough?"

"Yes," an unsmiling, yet content Fillerhouse stated firmly. He stood up, prompting the other two people in the room to do the same. "Thank you for your decision."

"Thank you for bringing me your concerns," she responded. "Have a good day."

"You, too," said the troubled professor, flanked by his younger ally. The meeting had ended in pleasantries, with both sides feeling a level of relief as to the resolution. Fillerhouse still held his grudges about the disparate treatment and the recognition that no one was going to be made accountable for the furor. However, he had never really expected anything of substance to be done. He spoke with Channing as the two professors exited the office. "Thank you for coming to help. I feared those crazy people were going to win."

"No problem," Channing replied. "Anything to stick it to censorship."

No one else was in the waiting room. The student secretary was especially curious about the conversation between the two leaving academics. Exiting out of social media but keeping the office inbox up, she left her post and walked into the provost office through the open door. Marciela looked up and smiled at her receptionist, who was curious: "What was all that talk about censorship?"

"Just some issues with a future event," the provost informed her secretary. "The professors just wanted to make sure that a speaker was protected when coming to campus."

"Protected?" asked the student in confusion. "Who would want to attack him?"

* * *

"Antifa," stoically pronounced Michael Zambo, detective with the Federal Bureau of Investigation. He stood next to a large screen, connected to a laptop. Before him were three rows of seats behind three long curved tables. It was a classroom setting in which only three people were present: himself, Alfredo Hernandez, and Carla al-Hassan Sharp. They were seated together, helping to narrow Zambo's focus. Carla paid attention, taking mental notes. Hernandez fought a minor urge to have a cigarette.

"Short for anti-fascism, correct?"

"Yes, Alfredo," confirmed Zambo. "They trace their origins back to over a hundred years ago with the rise of fascism in Western Europe. They were a loose coalition of far left entities: you know, your communists, socialists, anarchists. In nations like Germany, Italy, and even England, they fought Fascist groups in street warfare. A major fight of great symbolic significance happened in London in 1936."

"Not just significance, Carla, but 'symbolic significance,'" uttered Alfredo to his agent, who smiled in amusement.

"Children," commented Michael. "Please hold all comments until the end of the presentation."

"Yes, teacher," quipped Alfredo.

Michael smiled and nodded, clicking a button on his laptop that changed the image on the screen from a modern protest photo to a large black-and-white image featuring a great number of men, mostly in suits, with arms raised in protest. "The Battle of Cable Street. 1936. A large protest featuring as many as twenty thousand antifascist activists in a predominantly Jewish part of London. When a group of British fascists attempted to stage a rally there, they were met with fierce street resistance. Ultimately, the fascists had to call off their rally, making it one of the greatest victories of the movement. Following the end of

48

the Second World War, however, the movement weakened as Western Europe and the United States moved rightward in response to the growing menace of the Soviet Union."

"The Red Scare?" Carla asked.

"Correct, exactly," replied Michael. "Even labor unions in the United States purged their more radical elements in response to the new cultural climate."

"Hey, I thought we were supposed to wait until the end of the presentation," said Alfredo in feigned outrage.

"Her interjection was nicer. And more thoughtful."

"Shutting up now," commented Alfredo as Michael continued.

"Antifa lay dormant for some years, until gaining strength during the sixties as part of the overall rise of the New Left. You know, your campus activism, free speech movement, antiwar movement, et cetera, et cetera," said Zambo as he clicked the laptop and a new photo, showing opponents of the Vietnam War rallying on campus was placed on the screen. "The student activism component became the most pronounced. Also a broadening of the things they opposed. No longer was the enemy just those who overtly ascribed to fascism. Now, anyone who could be considered a 'fascist' in the broader sense. Which, of course, could include a whole lot of people who in any way leaned conservative.

"Again, the cause suffered setbacks after the end of the Vietnam War, as the United States once again moved rightward in the socio-political leanings during the late seventies until the end of the nineties. At that point, major domestic terrorist entities were largely part of the far right: your paramilitary groups, anti-government, compounds, and cults. Even with the resurgence of antiwar activism during the early 2000s, antifa was not quite resurrected." Zambo clicked and the image became sharper, a collage of high-definition photos of masked protesters from a few recent demonstrations.

"And then came the rise of Trumpism. The Trump Movement fueled increased fears among those in progressive circles that fascism truly was finally coming to America. From there, antifa reemerged and garnered much attention. They went back to focusing on college campuses and progressive metropolitan areas as the had in the sixties. They centered their tactics on disruptive protests and violent actions against fascists, both imagined and genuine. This century's Battle of Cable Street happened in Charlottesville, Virginia back in 2017. Large numbers of antifa activists descended upon the city during an alt right rally, meeting violent extremism with violent extremism. To be sure, they received their share of accolades as well, with more moderate liberals crediting them with saving lives. From there, they regained their status as an acceptable wing of the movement.

"Throughout its history, antifa has never been opposed to using violence. They have had an ever-growing definition of fascism, which for some includes anybody right of center. They have no central leadership, no true central fundamental beliefs. They are strongest in places like the West Coast, areas like Seattle, Portland, Berkeley, other college campuses. They are very paranoid of outsiders. Many are convinced that if their identity gets to the outside world, Nazis will hunt them down and kill them. This has made it a major challenge for us to infiltrate their ranks, let alone to connect dots, as they say."

"And here we are today," deadpanned Hernandez.

"Indeed, Alfredo," agreed Zambo, turning his attention to Carla. "I am having you infiltrate an antifa faction based near the campus of Pacific Coast State University out in Southern California. Indeed, they refer to themselves on social media as 'Antifa of Pacific Coast State' or 'PCS Antifa' elsewhere. Aside from that, however, we know very little about their leadership or their inner workings. But we know some of what they have been up to." Zambo clicked the button and a new collage of photos appeared, this time of various intense demonstrations in and around the aforementioned campus. "They have been stirring up a great deal of violent actions at Pacific Coast State. Scaring off conservative speakers, demonstrating against some businesses and politicians here and there. Most of the stuff has not been particularly high on the Bureau's list of concerns. Until recently, anyway."

"What happened?" asked Carla.

"A robbery," answered Zambo. "Specifically, a truck containing a great deal of explosives and firearms. They were confiscated in an unrelated police operation and were on their way to disposal. However, an unknown group of masked individuals hijacked the vehicle. Eventually the truck and the two passengers were found unharmed, but, the munitions were gone. The robbery happened within a few miles of Pacific Coast State."

"I see."

"What's more, what little ears we have on the radical elements of the area indicate that PCS Antifa is planning something. We do not know what, but I believe it is something that should concern a heck of a lot more people than it currently does."

"And that is where I come in, I assume. I am going to help you make sure that enough people get worried about this."

"Correct," nodded Zambo. "You will be known as Carla Wexler. You are from Minnesota. You transferred from the University of Minnesota for a graduate degree." Carla withheld her amusement, noting that in real life she still had not even gotten a bachelor's. "You transferred partly to get away from your parents and partly because school officials were sick of your activism."

"Okay."

"Now, our tech team has already photo-shopped you into a few protest photos, and a couple more agreeable activists have already spoken well of you on social media. Basically, we're giving the antifa chapter evidence that you have a history of agitation. We know they are holding an interest meeting soon near campus. We expect them to promote that meeting at various sites at the university. That is where you will make first contact and proceed to go in. As I understand, you're not for politics."

"I vote in most elections," she said defensively, "but yes, I normally steer clear."

"That can be a blessing," added Hernandez. "It means you will be more tolerant of hearing what will most likely be a constant barrage of extremist political rhetoric."

"But it also means that you'll have to study up. Get your hands on as much far left literature as you can. And I'm not talking Hillary Clinton left, I'm talking Bernie Sanders and beyond left. Basically, that will be what you really study when you go there."

"Just remember, Carla, what Aristotle said," cautioned Hernandez. "'It is the mark of an educated mind to be able to entertain a thought without accepting it.'"

"Trust me," assured Carla, "I already have plenty of bad experiences with domestic terrorists. I am not about to like one just because they have good writers."

* * *

It was a beautiful day at the campus. A part of the network of public universities, Pacific Coast State University of California was one of the newer academic institutions. It came into being to accommodate the growing number of people seeking a higher education, courtesy of increased government assistance.

The campus started with three buildings on a small tract of grassy land, with a single parking lot for pupils and professors. Over the years, it kept adding buildings, newer edifices to learning. The original student union, which was about twice the size of the average middle-class home, was eventually replaced by a larger entity that was roughly half the size of a football field and four stories tall.

The greatest transformation for the university was not so much the building density or the growing acreage. Rather, it was the emergence of an on-campus population that made the academic institution feel truly collegiate. Originally, all students were commuters. They drove or were driven to the campus, went to classes, and then exited the premises for home. However, many of the recently added buildings were dormitories. At first, this on-campus populace was a tiny fraction of those enrolled. Campus life reflected this trend, with few services available for those on site. There were only a couple of fast food restaurants nearby that closed by late evening and a small grocery store that did not operate on weekends.

As more and more students took to living on campus, the culture and its sustenance increased. More restaurants opened, including a fancy one at the new student union. Longer hours were posted for the other eateries, two convenience stores were built, and weekend hours were common for nearly every entity functioning for commerce. A student government was created, though it continued to struggle with awareness and action. More events of a recreational nature were organized, with numerous student orgs offering a deeper involvement in on-campus life. No longer was Pacific Coast State a desolate land at night.

Carla was not involved in any of these other student activities. As with her time in Latin America, planning out that assassination earlier in the year, she mostly kept to herself. As a graduate student, her semester's course load involved only a single class. She balanced her studies for that class with her continued studies on the far left. Much of her research came from the on-campus library, which had an exorbitant number of nonfiction books on a host of topics, or online at her apartment just off-campus.

That day was warm and sunny. Like many of the other young adults and older teenagers, she was taking to the outside for her study and leisure. Her current text was a manifesto on radical grassroots activism. The cover included an illustration featuring rows of silhouetted protesters with fists raised and bearing red banners. Carla jotted notes, not so much for her benefit but for the appearance of study. Occasionally, she looked around her to see the world of the university. There were other students reading and studying, some couples socializing or even kissing. On one stretch of grass, ten students—nine males and one female—played a game of soccer. One of the men, the chief organizer, had brought several small bright orange cones to mark the goals and the boundaries of play.

Then Carla saw a person of interest. A woman of average height who looked to be in her twenties, with short, dark red hair and pale skin. She had the look of a punk rock fan, with pierced ears, a small nose ring, and visible tattoos. Dark cargo pants, boots, and a dark sleeveless shirt made up her outfit. In one hand, she held a bunch of flyers while the other held a small roll of clear tape. She placed a few flyers around the area, putting them on outdoor tables and benches. Periodically, she stopped at a streetlight pole to tape one to the cylindrical surface. She carefully balanced the thin layer of papers as she took one from her hand, pushed it against the metal frame, and then ripped some tape off to secure it to the surface. Few sitting nearby or walking to or from class paid her much attention.

The person of interest was nearing Carla. Not on purpose, but rather because near Carla was an outdoor community bulletin board. Carla sat at that location hoping that it would get her close to someone posting signs. Sure enough, the activist moved closer. Her stack of flyers was getting thin. She approached the bulletin board, which was a great mess of papers and announcements, ads and inquiries. There were job offers, event details, memos about textbook sales, information on study abroad trips, and other student community matters. Nearly all of the documents were stapled. The activist apparently felt a little dismayed, as she did not have that stronger means available for her flyers.

"Hey there," said Carla, grabbing her attention. Carla offered a welcoming smile and a mini-stapler that she took from her backpack. "You need a stapler?"

"Yeah, thanks," she sheepishly responded. Carla handed her the office tool, getting a smirk of gratitude. The activist quickly secured three flyers to the board. Carla saw the revolutionary imagery, the calls to action against the forces of evil, the meeting details, and she knew that the group she sought was found.

"I see you are part of the resistance."

She smirked, a little nervous as she did not know what was coming next. "Yes, I am."

"I used to do my part up in Minnesota, where I am from."

"Really?" she asked, getting warmer.

"Yes. I attended some protests here and there. I really wanted to do more, but we did not have a strong presence there. Not enough grassroots, you know?"

"Yeah, I feel you," she nodded.

"That's a big reason why I transferred out here. I wanted to go where the revolution was. Where I could really stick it to the fascists."

"Well," stated a pleasantly surprised young woman, "it's good I found you." She handed Carla one of the flyers. "Come to the meeting on Friday."

"I will be there," Carla stated in confidence.

"Great," replied the activist. "By the way, my name is Jessie."

"Carla Wexler," responded the agent as the two shook hands.

"Anyway, I have to get the rest of these out. See you later," said Jessie as she waved and went her way on the campus.

"See you," replied Carla, who then looked down at the flyer.

* * *

It was once beautiful. And sacred. The church had been modeled after its elder cousins in the Old World. There was a vaulted sanctuary with stained glass windows and cut stone pillars. Two columns of wooden pews, with religious symbols carved into the aisle ends. Chandeliers hanging above the rows once contained candles. An elevated platform held an altar, font, and a pulpit. The choir area had its own seating on either side of the altar, a railing dividing that holy space from the pews and the aisle. This spiritual vessel could hold as many as four hundred plus clergy, ushers, acolytes, chorus, and crucifer. Many a past Easter Sunday it had.

Then time, demographics, and the rise of the unaffiliated dwindled their ranks. The bowed heads in the pews became grayer and grayer. A secular culture, a church abuse scandal, and many families moving away to other parts of the metropolitan area doomed the congregation. When word of its closure came from the diocesan officials, a fervent few refused to vacate the property. Still, no court order nor other public authority was capable of vindicating their pleas. Besides, even this devoted remnant was incapable of maintaining the costs and repairs for the facility. The last mass was held the year before.

Abandoned but not destroyed, the vacant space became the meeting place for a less holy group of people, although no less committed to a lofty cause. They also fought a wicked force, sought comfort in community, and feared persecution and marginalization from the outside world over their beliefs. As afternoon became evening, candles were lit in the sanctuary once more, glowing like little stars in the vaulted interior that directed the travelers who used memory or smartphones to locate the meeting area.

"Nice to meet you," said Saundra Jaspers, helping to greet the trickle of young people coming to the gathering. Rudd Yansk was on the opposite side of the opened double doors.

"You know, it's funny."

"What is?"

"When this was a church, there were people doing exactly what we are doing. Greeting people as they come in."

"Yeah," nodded Saundra. "Interesting."

"Seems like we have more people than last month."

"That's good," she said, both of them looking at the outside world rather than each other while they spoke. They were peering into the dusk, studying human movement, seeing if any of the pedestrians were coming their way. Few were out at that hour. That part of town was not known for its nightlife, making their meeting all the more secretive.

"Many young people. Students from Pacific Coast, I bet."

"Definitely."

"Jessie did a good job with those flyers."

"She usually does," concurred Saundra. A bearded young man and a short-haired woman who were walking arm-in-arm arrived. Pleasantries were exchanged as they passed into what used to be the narthex. It was easy to figure out that the meeting was happening in the sanctuary. All other parts of the building were dark. "However, we both know that it was not just Jessie's work that is making us stronger. It's Robespierre."

"Maybe."

"No maybe, Rudd," insisted Saundra. "Before he established contact with us, our efforts were only so noticeable. Then he started to tell us where to go, how to fight the cops, all of that. We are a force because of him."

"Yes, he's helped," said Rudd as he briefly looked at his peer before turning to face the street. "We have done a lot of good because of him. I do not doubt that. But ..."

"But?"

"The thing is ... I mean, what do we know about him?"

"Not much, but still. He has helped us a lot. His advice and his information have always checked out. You can't deny that." She and Rudd both shifted their attention to the next person to come toward the former church's open doors. "Hey there."

"Hi," said Carla. "The meeting is in the sanctuary, right?"

"Right," replied Saundra with a nod.

"Thanks." Carla went through the narthex and into the dimly lit sanctuary, almost crossing herself on instinct.

"You can quit looking at her now," said Saundra, causing Rudd to blush. He offered no verbal response. "Going back to our earlier conversation, I think Robespierre is a good person to help lead us to bigger efforts."

"Like that arms truck?"

"Shut up!" she hissed angrily, eyes widened. "The newcomers might hear you."

"No one is around now. They're all in the sanctuary."

"Still! The fewer people who know about that now, the better. When they are committed like us, then they can learn all about it. About the plans we have."

"Yes, Saundra."

"It's been hard enough keeping this under wraps because you had to let them live."

"They were workers," stated Rudd defensively. "They were the very common people we are trying to protect. They couldn't help what they were told to do."

"Maybe."

"Besides, you know how I feel about taking a life."

"You still throw a nasty punch," said Saundra, offering the comment as a peace offering.

"Point is, we should be careful about him."

"Agreed," conceded Saundra. "But remember that he is doing nothing but good things for us. The resistance needs to grow. And he can grow it."

"I hope you are right," cautioned Rudd. Moments of silence came as the two looked outside. No one was around. Yansk checked his smartphone for the time. "I think it's about time we began this meeting."

Saundra took out her phone to check the time and nodded. "Yeah, it's definitely time." Each activist took a door and closed them off. "Remember,

Rudd." Her words prompted his look. "The fascists must be destroyed once and for all. Robespierre has the way to do it. It will not be long. It will not be long."

V

For the past few weeks, the stadium had been used for high school and college basketball games. The paneled court with opposing nets saw its share of excitement and action, fast paced dribbling and long distance shots. A few times, operations crews had to add four additional hoops, two to each broad side of the court, for practices. No one school owned the stadium, so different teams used it at different times. No game filled the entirety of the interior, though men's basketball had a far higher attendance than their female counterparts. Social commentators continue to debate the reasons.

That evening, a campaign rally was planned. The operations manager called up several young folks to fill the shift. A few full timers were there; they were the specialists who actually knew what they were doing when constructing or deconstructing a stage or a court. Several were in the middle ground: on-call and yet aware of how to do a few one of the more complicated tasks assigned. Despite the many novices in a given shift, few injuries were ever reported—although a good number of close calls came to pass. It was a loud occupation, distracting to the first timer but normative for the regular.

Three men in business attire were seated in the stands, a hundred or more feet away from those taking apart the court. The hoops had already been wheeled off to the back and the large cubic score box lifted into the rafters via several thick steel cables. Attorney General Kyle Brown, the oldest of the trio, sat to the left of the candidate. He had salt-and-pepper hair and was clean-shaven. Once the work day had concluded in the capital, he would drive the hour and a half to get to the stadium. His journey did not pass in solitude, for he was accompanied by District Attorney James Colbert. Seated on the other side of the candidate, he had curly hair and was in his early thirties. Earlier, he had accidentally lost a button from his shirt.

The candidate they spoke to was Josiah Sharp. The son of a Methodist minister, he was an abstainer from alcohol who read from his Bible every day. A bit nerdy but ultimately charismatic and appealing to the broad population, he talked with the two men who had convinced him to run for governor months before. Election day was only weeks away. There had been one gubernatorial debate between himself and his main competitor. Few of his rallies had been disrupted by protesters. News reporters and analysts were already hailing this political season as one of the least violent races since the 1990s.

"You're going to love these polls," said a jovial Colbert, who look to his smart phone for further prompting. "We're talking fifteen points ahead of Pearlstein according to the Courier, seventeen points ahead according to the Times, and twenty-one points ahead according to the Post!" He smiled all the bigger, staying seated but slightly jumping. "This is going to be a blowout. I love it!"

"Same here," said a relaxed Josiah. "If I knew it was going to be this easy, I would have gone into politics sooner." The three were temporarily interrupted when one of the crews lifting the large rectangular pieces of the court dropped it prematurely onto a cart. Each saw that no one was harmed and returned to their discussion.

"Almost makes me wonder if Pearlstein is even trying."

"Well, there is some gossip from friends of mine on the other side that he actually kind of likes our Josiah," noted Colbert. "One gal I know from their campaign even told me that Pearlstein thought about dropping out when you secured the nomination."

"Or maybe she was just leading you on, like young women often do to gullible single men," responded Brown, further lightening the mood.

"If you saw what she looked like, you would let her lead you anywhere," said Colbert with a grin. "I am *so* single." The three laughed.

"Speaking of which, Josiah," asked Brown. "How is your wife doing?"

"She's doing okay. She has an assignment in California."

"So, she's missing all the fun? A pity."

"Just as well. She was never one for politics."

"But to be clear," asked Colbert suddenly serious, "she will be back in time to vote for you, right?"

"She already voted absentee."

"Okay, okay, that still works," replied Colbert. The other two looked at him with varying degrees of incredulity. "What? Never underestimate the need to get all the votes you can."

"All right, fair enough."

Brown's phone buzzed. The two younger men looked at the workers before them as the attorney general checked his new message. Professionals were seated or kneeling on the floor, using cordless tools to remove the bolts that connected each of the rectangular pieces of the court. Once loosened, a team of four individuals, usually young men, showed up with a cart and lifted an individual piece onto the cart. They then slowly moved the cart forward a few feet and repeated the action. This continued until a whole row of rectangular pieces had been stacked on the cart. From there they were moved to a storage area underneath the rising rows of seats on one of the two longer sides of the stadium.

"Good news, Josiah," said Brown, returning the attention of the duo back to their political ally. "I just learned that you will be going to the governors' convention to serve as a speaker."

"Really?" Josiah asked, shocked and largely thrilled.

"Just got the email," explained Brown. "You still have to win the election, of course. And if you don't, they have a backup. But as it stands, you are the chosen one."

"That's amazing."

"They explained that your story, your taking down of the Cicero Organization, your youth and vigor, your image as the future, all this makes you far too appealing not to give the stage to."

"Glory to God, indeed. So when is the convention?"

"The week before Thanksgiving," noted Brown. "Organizers like to have it before the holidays to give people an excuse to leave work early. You know the type."

"Do I ever. My father used to tell me how back in the day for Thanksgiving week, people only got Thursday and Friday off. Problem is, nearly everyone would skip on Wednesday. So the powers that be added Wednesday to the holiday week. The result? Nearly everyone started to skip on Tuesday."

"Not me," chimed in Colbert. "My teachers were cruel and always scheduled a test on the Tuesday before Thanksgiving."

"You were probably the better for it," countered Brown, receiving no resistance.

"Still, I am amazed that they want me."

"Enjoy it now, because you never know when it will go away."

"The humble will be exalted and the exalted will be humbled, as the Good Book puts it," said Josiah, getting a nod from his peers. "So I will enjoy it now. But I will also make sure it doesn't interfere with the focus on my speech tonight."

"Good to hear," agreed Brown.

* * *

Candles were blown out, small streams of smoke floating toward the vaulting. The clandestine group calmly departed the sacred building, people going their own ways through the eventide hour. Most walked, some drove, a few cycled. Carla had taken public transportation most of the way there, having to walk five blocks from the stop. She lacked an automobile; it was considered contrary to the image she was trying to portray. However, Jessie Phelier asked Carla if she wanted a ride with her and Rudd Yansk. It was his vehicle, but she asked as one who had authority over who could join the carpool.

Carla said yes and Rudd offered no complaints. It was a modest used car with a black paint job, several scratches, and a few dents, but otherwise in good condition. Rudd took the wheel and Jessie sat in the front passenger seat. Carla had the back all to herself. The sense of solitude was a deception, as she and the other two occupiers of the vehicle were in constant communication.

"Thanks again for the ride," said Carla. "I am new to the area, so I do not know the bus schedule this late."

"They barely come," replied Jessie. "That's why Rudd and I take turns driving here for meetings."

"Ah. So you own a car, too?"

"Yeah, but I don't use it much. Only for grocery trips, going to meetings that are far from campus, some of the protests we do off campus that's far away."

"Like that one workers' rights demonstration we're going to in a few weeks," chimed in the driver. "Jessie and I will both be using our cars to get people there."

"Makes sense."

"You don't own a car, Carla?" asked Jessie, who smiled a little extra at her own phrasing.

"Nope. Not for years. I was never much of a driver. And the whole idea of giving to big oil always turned me off."

"It bugs me a little, too," conceded Jessie. "But, you know, I take comfort knowing that we're using their gas to fuel a revolution."

"Good point," said Carla with a smile.

"So where are you from, Carla?" asked Rudd.

"I was born in Detroit, but my family moved to Minneapolis when I was a kid. I guess they got sick of looking at what capitalism does to a city."

"Amen," stated Rudd.

"Carla told me a few days ago that she came out here to be part of the movement. Join up with a strong anti-fascist front."

"So now we have a national reputation? That's awesome."

"Yes," agreed Carla. "You and the people at Berkeley always made the headlines. I knew transferring here was the best thing for me."

"Well, let me say I'm glad you're here," stated Jessie as the car neared the backseat passenger's apartment.

"Likewise," said Rudd as the vehicle slowed to a halt. "According to my GPS, this is your place. Is it right?"

"Yes, it is," responded Carla while she unbuckled her seatbelt. "Thank you again for the ride. Do you want any gas money or something?"

"No, no that's okay," Rudd replied, waving off her suggestion. "You have a good night."

"Thanks, you too!"

"Good night, Carla," said Jessie as the backseat passenger exited the vehicle. Carla waved before turning toward her apartment building. Jessie looked at Rudd, who was paying close attention to Carla as she entered the apartment complex.

"Like what you see?" teased Jessie, breaking Rudd's focused. He blushed.

"My momma raised me to be a gentleman. And a gentleman always waits until the woman enters the building before he drives away."

"You are so advancing patriarchy," Jessie stated with little sincerity.

"In a vile world like this, I think I'm being considerate."

"Yeah," Jessie grudgingly acknowledged. Soon after, Carla was inside the complex and Rudd pulled away to take his other passenger to her place. "Saundra told me you were looking at her quite a bit when she first showed up."

"Maybe."

"Don't be evasive with me, Rudd. You're a bad liar."

"Okay, so I'm interested. The fascists haven't banned that, have they?"

"Probably not. However, if you want her, you've got to be more proactive than just looking at her a lot when she walks away."

"Of course, I know that," he said as the car stopped before a red light. "I will gladly accept all your advice on this, um ... issue."

"Issue."

"Getting to know her is important. I know that."

"I want to get to know her, too."

"Really?" asked a surprised Rudd, who briefly looked at his passenger before putting his eyes back to the night road. "I didn't know you rolled that way."

"Oh shut up, Rudd," stated his annoyed yet somewhat amused passenger. "I mean, I want to learn more about her background. You know, just in case."

"Just in case," nodded the driver. "I understand."

"I mean, she seems nice, passionate, experienced."

"But?"

"But I want to make sure. We can't have just anyone meeting Robespierre, knowing more about what is being planned."

"Yes," said the driver in an ominous tone. "Yes, you're right."

"Carla Wexler," said Jessie, pausing to yawn. "I'll look her up when I get back to my place. See if she exists online. See if she has a history that predates a few days ago."

"Tonight? You seem a little tired to do all that research."

"It's called coffee, genius."

"Coffee, it is," he agreed as he slowed the car before her place. "You see, I didn't even need the GPS system to find your place."

"I'm already scared," she sarcastically commented. "Thanks for the ride." She quickly unbuckled her belt and opened the door.

"Jessie?"

"Yeah?"

"If you find anything wrong with her, let me be the first to know. If she is a fascist, the sooner I get over her, the better."

"Gotcha," Jessie agreed. She slammed her door shut and waved good-bye. As with Carla, Rudd waited until she disappeared into the security of the apartment building walls before driving away.

* * *

She opened the door to see the darkened interior of her apartment. Only the small lights from outside offered any illumination to the cavern-dark space. The imagination allotted many flights of fear about what was inside the shadowy veil, from the supernatural to the all-too-human. A burglar, a killer, a psychopath of some strain, poisonous bugs, pestilent rodents, all could possibly be scampering unseen in the night-coated corners.

Yet Carla entered sans trepidation. Her adult life was punctuated by entrances into darkness of a literal, figurative, and allegorical nature. The unknown held little dominion over her fretting. She left the door open as she entered, going to the corner of the combination living room-kitchen to the nearest light. Once on, she returned to the entrance, closing and locking the portal.

Removing her shoes and leaving them by the door, she tossed her purse onto the couch. No television was present. Detective Michael Zambo thought that having such a device was incompatible with the kind of person she was pretending to be. A similar argument came for the car question. And the formal clothing question. At one point, Carla asked Zambo if this had less to do with making her cover believable and more to do with a lack of budget from the Bureau. Zambo declined to answer.

It was a small apartment. One bedroom, one bathroom, and a living-room with kitchen attached made up the floor plan. Carla had to use the laundromat provided on the basement floor. Fortunately, the landlord was kind enough to make the machines free for tenants. Like others in the basement floor, for wash day she brought a book with her to study while the clothing went in circles. An elevator went all the way down to the basement level, but Carla purposely carried her basket up and down the two flights of stairs. She wanted the exercise and knew that her cover prevented her from the usual avenues of fitness.

Her laptop was powering up in the corner on the floor. Carla unplugged the machine from the outlet and carried it to the couch. A few pillows had been tossed to one side of the couch, which Carla leaned against upon sitting down on the furniture. She balanced the laptop on her legs, swinging the screen half upwards to turn it on. A password was required, but she knew it by heart and quickly gained access. An application for communication was selected and double-clicked. With the system running, Carla selected a favorited number and called it, getting a face on the screen.

"Agent Carla Sharp?" asked Zambo, whose face occupied most of her laptop screen.

"Detective Zambo."

"I take it you are alone."

"Just me in here."

"Good," he replied. "How's your progress?"

"I attended their interest meeting tonight. They meet at an old abandoned church about a mile and a half from campus."

"Just like the Jacobins," commented Zambo. "Any talk about the stolen explosives, major terrorist attacks? Other suspicious things?"

"Not really," said Carla. "They talked about who they were, what they do, and spoke about some planned protests they have for the next few weeks."

"What were they?"

"Well, details were still pending, but they included some alt right demonstration scheduled to take place at a dockyard a couple of hours away. There was some conservative writer who was invited to Pacific Coast State and we are going to counter him somehow. But again, nothing specific."

"And nothing about explosives?"

"No."

"Guns?"

"No. None of that."

"Damn," Zambo said to himself. "Well, keep at it. Attend the meetings, befriend the leadership, take part in the protests." The agent was interrupted by a buzzing noise. It was loud enough that Carla could hear it. "Hold on." Zambo took out his smartphone and read the message. His laughed a little before returning his attention back to Carla. "I just got a message from our IT guys. Apparently, there has been a spike in the number of online searches for the name 'Carla Wexler.'"

"Interesting."

"Well, at this rate, we'll know how well you fooled them by tomorrow morning."

"Yes."

"I will keep you posted on that, as well. One of the interesting things about antifa is that while they get headlines for their offline activities, the fact is that they do a lot more online. Research, trolling, social media posts, the like."

"I see."

"Anyway, like I said, I'll keep you posted and you keep me posted."

"Yes, sir."

"No salute?" asked Zambo with a light heart.

"My apologies," said Carla raising two fingers to her eye brow, quickly thrusting them forward. "Sir."

"That's the spirit," he said, smiling. "Good night."

She waited for him to sign out before doing the same. She checked the time. It was late, but not too late. Even adding the two hours of time difference, it was not yet midnight where he was situated. His was the first number she had marked as a favorite. A double click and the call was made. It took a few rings before a familiar face appeared. His was older and far more pleasant than that of Zambo. It was the man who had raised her, greeting her with a wrinkled smile. She reciprocated the smile upon seeing him.

"Hey, giddo. How are you? I did not wake you, did I?"

"Oh no, Carla, you did not inconvenience me at all."

"That was not what I asked," she said with a smile.

"Yes, you are right. Always as smart as you are beautiful. I was only resting in front of the TV. I was about to sleep, but then you called."

"Ah, okay. So not quite."

"Correct."

"So, how are things back home?"

"They are going well. Elnora has been getting more clients. This afternoon, she brought a couple of 'leasing now' signs into our place."

"That's good. She said she was having problems before."

"Yes, but with the jobs expected to come here, people are moving in."

"That's good," nodded Carla. "How is Josiah doing?"

"I see him on the television every night. He gets a lot of attention."

"Is he doing okay? Have you talked with him?"

"A little. Like you, he's on the move a lot these days."

"I see."

"But if the television and the Internet can be believed, he is doing just fine."

"That's good. I think I miss him, you know, a lot."

George al-Hassan grinned. "You know, this reminds me of when I was in the Syrian army. When I left on my first assignment after marrying your grandmother, I felt absolutely miserable. Like I was trying to quit smoking."

"How did you handle it?"

"By seeing her as soon as I got back."

Carla smiled and said nothing.

"How are things in California?"

"Good."

"Have you been to the beaches?"

"Giddo," she said in faint annoyance. "I am on assignment."

"Like the Syrian army?"

"More or less."

"Well then, good and beautiful soldier, I hope you win the battle."

"Me, too. And soon."

"Likewise."

"Well, giddo. I know it is late where you are and it is getting late where I am. You have a good night, okay?"

"Okay."

"And tell Elnora I said hello."

"Of course," he said with a pleasant grin. "Good night, dear Carla."

"Good night, giddo," she said, kissing her own fingers before she held said fingers in front of the screen. Both signed out at almost the same time. Carla was then alone in the night. And she felt very alone at that.

* * *

Saundra Jaspers and Rudd Yansk were casually seated in the apartment at the terraced house that held multiple tenants. As was typical, the curtains were closed, beams of mid-afternoon light streaming through the gaps. Both were in comfortable clothing, each occupying a different couch, with laptops open and operating. They had several radical objects around them, a few book shelves with filled subversive literature, some empty bottles that had once contained various types of alcohol, and containers filled with flammable materials. There were also a few flares and three revolutionary flags on poles leaning in a corner. Otherwise, the décor for the living space was Spartan in nature.

Fingers pounded the keys with passionate political activism. Saundra was the better typist, but both were fast with their alphanumeric actions. They were engaged in search and destroy, a bloodless hunt to expose and eliminate the enemy. Their dual efforts involved them entering the darker corners of the Internet. Hateful message boards, bigoted chat rooms, and fringe blogospheres; truly the most rejected and vile of human nature, vomited upon webpage after webpage. If ever there was evidence of the existence of the fallen nature of man, it was plastered on each entry in those cruel conversations.

Rudd sifted through the heap of dehumanizing literature with its many grammar errors, inflammatory memes, racist gifs, profanity, slurs, and conspiracy theories. He shook his head at the contradictory horror of people claiming there was no Holocaust only to later complain that Hitler didn't finish his job. The fears of white genocide, Deep State secret killings, the need to kill one black for every one white murdered, banks being part of some one-world government, celebrations over the latest news of police brutality, demands to abolish just about every federal government department, calls for militias, rape gangs to attack feminists, cross-burners for the next Black Lives Matter rally, and more.

"You got anything, yet?" Saundra asked Rudd, bringing him closer to the real world of the bland apartment. She was getting impatient.

"Almost," he assured her.

"You said that five minutes ago."

"I know," Rudd conceded. "But this time, I'm close." Punching more keys, tying together more evidence, like a detective, his eyes never left the screen.

"The sooner you tell me, the sooner I can tell everyone."

Rudd smiled. "Got it!" Saundra leaned forward from her couch, opposite the one that he was seated on. Rudd turned his screen to show her the personal information of the man who they were targeting.

"Good," she replied. "Send it to me now."

"Sure thing," he acknowledged. He opened an email document and pasted in the links, a couple of screengrabs were taken and attached as well. Plenty to convict in a court of law, more than enough to convict in a court of popular opinion. Saundra's email address came up in its entirety after Rudd typed only the first two letters. All finalized, he sent it her way. "You will get it all right ... about ... now."

Saundra nodded. She took the information Rudd accrued, the evidence of the poster's real identity, and splashed it all over the chat rooms of like-minded people. The note was the same that she had written plenty of times before, urging action against an extremist keyboard warrior by showcasing their name, and, more importantly, current residence and source of employment. Saundra took pride in the fact that her efforts had cost at least two dozen white supremacists their jobs. She regretted not knowing the exact tally. Little time elapsed before others were liking and sharing her comment.

"That makes four so far, today, right?" asked Rudd.

"Three."

"Three fascists held to account for what they post online. Three fewer bigots getting away with it. So far, so good."

"We'd have more if Jessie were here."

"Perhaps. Very likely."

"Where is she, anyway?"

"A theatre meeting, I think."

"Seems to be going a little long, don't you think?"

Rudd shrugged. As the two got back to work hunting down cyber-enemies, they heard a noise coming from the other side of the apartment door. They gave it some attention, always wondering in the back of their mind if it was the enemy paying them a visit. These paranoid thoughts were stronger in the vesper hours whenever such noises were heard. This time, it was who they expected it to be. She came in wearing casual clothes, with boots, and had a laptop carrier slung over her left shoulder. Rudd looked up and nodded before getting back to work. Saundra gave her ideological ally a judgmental look.

"You're late."

"I know, sorry," Jessie apologized as she walked around the back of the couch to sit beside her critic. "My players group meeting went longer than I thought. A lot of debate over which play we should produce next."

"So are you going with *Spartacus* or *Caesar?*" asked a genuinely interested Rudd.

"*Caesar*," replied Jessie as she removed her laptop from its case, opened the top, and turned it on. "Just as well, we did *Spartacus* last year."

"Although, everyone liked it."

"Can we focus more on the important efforts, please?" interjected Saundra. Jessie nodded in response, taking out the small black box that held her reading glasses. Once the spectacles were on, she took to the laptop with a similar typing ferocity as her peers. "I sent you a couple posters I want doxed."

"Yeah, I see," affirmed Jessie. Her focus channeled onto the screen, the lines of code and html flowing through her consciousness, processing and compiling, going through the system as though she herself was a program. Her lips began to move, though only silence escaped. Rudd divided his time between his own research in the viler corners of social media and looking at the determined computer geek, afraid to say anything lest he break the determination of the woman who was sociable moments ago. A few minutes later, Jessie tapped the shoulder of Saundra and directed her to take a look at her handiwork.

"That's more like it," Saundra said with approval. "Send me their contact info and I'll post it everywhere."

"You got it," nodded Jessie quickly tapping the keys to make it so.

Saundra did her part, though not with the speed of her peer. It was not long before the phone numbers, email addresses, home addresses, credit card information, and employment information of the offenders were made public. In the days to come, those targets found themselves inundated with hate. One of them lost their job, while another was temporarily suspended and denied a promotion. And then there were all those messages, written and vocal, hurled their way. Sometimes Saundra was one of the ones sending vicious texts or leaving angry voice messages. Jessie sometimes did it as well, using her theatrical abilities to make the voices come with different accents.

"I think it's time for a meal break," said Rudd several minutes later. He got no dissent as he put his laptop on standby and rose from his couch.

"Will it be the usual sandwich place?" asked Jessie.

"Yup," he replied, his legs a little iffy due to sitting with the weighty device on his legs for so long. "So if you give me your orders, I'll pay."

"You know my order by now," stoically replied Saundra.

"This time, I think I'll try the Greek salad sub. But the same chips as before," said Jessie as she removed her reading glasses and instinctively placed them in their box.

"Got it," said Rudd, taking his mental notes.

"You're not having a BLT again, are you?" Saundra asked with arms folded.

"Of course, I am."

"Rudd, you need to change your order."

"Heck no! None of you care if I eat a BLT, do you?"

While Jessie tacitly agreed, Saundra pushed a little more. "Eating meat contributes to global warming, animal rights violations, and it turns off some of the people who we march with."

"How about this, Saundra?" proffered Rudd. "You find me lettuce that tastes just like bacon, and I will change my ways." Saundra replied only to his challenge with a wry smile. "Anyway, be back soon!" Both women said their goodbyes as the door closed and was locked.

"I should stretch my legs," commented Saundra as she rose from the couch, wincing in faint pain from the excessive amount of time sitting down. She walked to the back of the couch as Jessie put her laptop on sleep and then put it back into its case. "So, Jessie?"

"Yes?"

"Have you looked into the backgrounds of the new activists we met last night?"

"Yes," she said, leaning back more as she now had the couch all to herself. "And they all checked out. Nothing suspicious."

"All of them?"

"Yes," she restated.

"Even that Wexler woman?"

"Yes," she stated, defensively. "Why do you ask about her?"

"She's different from the others," noted Saundra, slowly pacing alongside the couch, her hand gently gliding along the back. "Coming all the way out here, as though there weren't plenty of antifa chapters where she was."

"She checks out," assured Jessie. "Her social media, the photos, some veteran activists out East. And her bank account has been active for years."

"How so?"

"Nothing weird. You know, deposits, withdraws, big purchases, small purchases, bill paying. You know, normal stuff."

"Nothing weird?"

"Nothing. Except one thing."

Saundra stopped her pacing and stared at Jessie, who laughed. "It's nothing really that serious. It's just that it seems like a couple accounts were under a different name. But that could be for all sorts of reasons."

"Marriage, divorce, gender transition," listed Saundra in agreement.

"Exactly, though I'm about a hundred percent sure she's cisgender."

"Would you say that she is woke enough to meet Robespierre?"

"I don't know enough to say yes just yet."

"Very well," said Saundra, returning to her pacing. "I will make the final call on that matter. We will see how good she is."

"Yes."

"And when he meets her, he will decide if she can be trusted."

"And if she can't?"

"Do I really need to tell you?"

"No. No, you don't."

* * *

It was one of the many modern yet generic classrooms at Pacific Coast State University: white walls, long light brown desks put in three rows, cushioned rolling chairs for the pupils, an alabaster marker board with a few markers and erasers laying on the gray metal ledge directly underneath it. A single door with a rectangular glass window served as entrance and exit. This was located at the front of the classroom. On the opposite corner was a podium, which had a set of buttons to operate a few lights and a viewing screen tucked away in the ceiling. Between the podium and the single door was a desk with chair, a beige hue and like the other desks, rectangular.

Professor Mack Channing eschewed the chair, preferring to lean on the front of the desk instead. He talked with his hands during the period, coordinating discussions both banal and provocative with his students. They varied in fashion, skin color, nationality, religion, age, shape, and political leanings. This particular course was an interdisciplinary class, combining fulfillment in requirements for history, sociology, and philosophy. The educational debate was both timely and timeless.

"Blame," Channing stated. "Collective and individual. Examining the topic with the assigned reads for this week, that of homophobic violence in both the late twentieth and early twenty-first century United States, we see this debate over collective or individual blame. When you read about Matthew Shepard, Lawrence King, the Pulse Nightclub shooting. You see the same dynamic, the same debate ..." he explained, rising to a standing position and pacing in front of the main desk. "You should be well-versed in the arguments by now. So what do you have to say about them? Do we blame all people who hold negative views of homosexuality for antigay violence? Any takers?" A twenty-year-old woman, one who still looked more like a girl, raised her hand. "Madeline?"

"I say blame them all," she said without reservation.

"Care to elaborate?" asked the probing academic.

"They created the monsters who did the awful violence. They gave them the justifications. They did everything except the crimes themselves. The guilty parties wouldn't have done what they did without the upbringing. So I say, they are all culpable."

"I see. A collective blame," observed Channing. He turned his head to see a teenage student wearing a sweatshirt with the school logo on it raising his hand. "Nathan?"

"If we blame them all, we have to punish them all. That makes no sense. That would mean tens of millions of people would have to go to jail as accessories. Including those who condemned the violence. That does not sound fair or just. I mean, do we really want to criminalize a viewpoint? I mean, how can our civilization survive?"

"True, it can be dangerous to ban an opinion," conceded the professor, walking a little closer to Nathan and the two students sitting on either side of him. "However, there are plenty of countries, like Canada, Sweden, the United Kingdom, that ban negative opinions all the time. Hate speech laws are what they are called. Surely, they are still 'civilized' nations." Nathan raised his hand again, getting a nod from Channing.

"But they do not have our Constitution. Our First Amendment says we can say what we want. An opinion cannot be banned just because someone thinks it is bad. If an idea is to fail, then it must fail in the market of ideas."

"Or as former Secretary of State John Kerry once said, in America we have a right to be stupid," acknowledged Channing as another hand went up, this one in the back. "Qasim?"

"I say they are still to blame. Even if they do not like the violence, they should know better. They know that whatever they say to bash gay people will be used to hurt gay people. So yeah, charge any of them that are outspoken, you know, *flamboyantly* antigay."

"Flamboyantly antigay," commented Channing. "I bet those two words have never been put together before." Some sounds of amusement rose from the classroom. "Still, though, Qasim, given your background, would you not be saying that your family should have their rights curbed?"

"They are not, well, not 'flamboyantly antigay.'"

"They keep it to themselves?"

"Yeah."

The door gently opened, getting the attention of a few students seated closest to it, but little else. An older man, Professor Holton Fillerhouse in fact, slowly entered the classroom. Channing saw him from the corner of his eye, briefly turned to nod, and then continued with the class discussion. As he returned his gaze to his pupils, a Latina student who wore a rosary around her neck raised a hand. "Martina?"

"What about the other people?" she asked in dissent. "I mean, there are plenty of crazy people who attack conservatives. I remember how the readings discussed that shooter who tried to massacre the Family Research Council group, that other shooter who tried to slaughter Republicans at a baseball practice, and those churches in North Carolina getting vandalized. Why can't we use those hateful acts as proof that all LGBT activists and allies and politicians can be thrown in jail as accessories?"

"Exactly!" declared Channing, much to Fillerhouse's amusement. "Every cause has its bad people. Every movement has its extremists. Every organization has its flaws. If we can blame all fundamentalist Christians for a homophobic act of violence, then why not blame all liberal homosexuals for the FRC shooting? Why not throw them all in prison? Force them to live in community. That might be the best solution of all." Channing looked at the clock behind the last row of students. "Okay, that concludes today's class." The simple sentence generated a rustling and bustling, as the young adults gathered their things, put away books and notebooks, closed laptops, shut off tablets, and zipped backpacks. Channing shouted his reminders as the students departed. "Remember to do the assigned readings for next week, plus I expect an essay topic emailed to me by tomorrow at noon." As the last of the pupils exited, Fillerhouse approached his fellow professor.

"Hey Holton, how's it going?"

"Doing fine."

"I am surprised to see you. Thought your class period went for another half hour."

"It would have, except none of the students read the book," explained Fillerhouse as he got closer. "I told them that I would waste neither their time nor mine and stormed out of the classroom angrily. I think they are still wondering if I am coming back."

"They're probably afraid you're waiting in the hall, ready to give an F to the first student stupid enough to leave."

"Now that's an idea," replied Fillerhouse with faux openness. The two academics laughed at the idea.

"So, any update on the whole Lewis event?"

"Yes, yes," replied an optimistic Fillerhouse. "It will be two weeks from now, on a Friday, at the main auditorium, with campus security stationed to guarantee entry, and to search folks as well."

"That serious, huh?"

"Freedom is never free."

"Correct, it must be fought for."

"Thanks again for helping me with the provost," said Fillerhouse. "A part of me thinks she would not have given me much thought if you had not been there."

"I was only too happy to help," responded Channing. "I may not agree with Lewis on a lot of issues, but he should be able to present his ideas. And students are free to offer their disagreement."

"It is like going back to those finer fundamentals of higher education. That is what we need: debate, discourse, critical thinking, and intellectual development."

"Yes."

"Reason must prevail."

"Truly."

VI

Both of them had class before they went into action. For Carla, the course was in history. She learned of the mass organizing taking place among the working class in Guatemala before and during the Arbenz administration. Next week, the class was focusing on the repression that took place following Arbenz's overthrow. For Jessie Phelier, it was a women and gender studies course. The professor continued the previous class discussion on the presence of the male gaze in modern movies, with the depressing claim that even in the 21st century, this toxic masculinity remained.

They met at the student union for lunch, each carrying backpacks that included their course materials as well the flyers they were planning to post throughout the campus. They chatted about nonpolitical things while in the crowded food court. Their options were diverse, despite the limits placed upon the school having a contract with only one food service provider. Jessie and some of the others with the antifa chapter had joined demonstrations by students demanding that Pacific Coast State University end its contract, accusing the provider of a host of bad actions. The administration responded with their usual condescending commendations of students for their passionate feelings, but did nothing more. At this point, even Jessie had entered a state of complacency on the matter.

Jessie was a vegetarian by principle, while Carla was a vegetarian to blend in. Jessie ate a salad while Carla ate a pasta dish. Finding a drink was a moral dilemma for them. Both rejected any of the sodas or other big corporate brand name products. After all, these entities were committing gross violations of workers' rights abroad. Or so the various blogs and websites they followed charged. Yet many of the smaller business products, those who adhered to better worker standards, came with ingredients wrought through questionable treatment of the less fortunate. Worse, many of them came in non-recyclable containers, plastic bottles, or included attached straws. Eventually, both agreed to bend on their principles and picked a pair of bottled waters. They would repent of their actions later through activism, not only on campus but also elsewhere in the state.

"We would like to post some of these flyers around the student union," Jessie spoke in kind formality to a student employee at the information desk. Carla stood beside her while the person at the desk, a young woman, examined the propaganda papers. She wore the uniform that many student employees donned for work at the University: a green button-up collared shirt with short-sleeves and light khaki pants.

"Okay, sure," responded the apathetic desk person. The student employee took out a small device and stamped each of the ten copies of the flyer, imprinting a circular red seal on the lower right hand corner of each piece of paper. "No more than two of them per board, don't cover-up other posters." She handed them back to Jessie while continuing the formal recitation of the rules. "They will be taken down by the janitor this coming Sunday between one and two PM, so if you want keep them get them before then."

"Okay, thanks," said Jessie as she and Carla walked away from the information desk area. Jessie handed her a few of the stamped copies. "Just liked we planned, you do the second floor of the student union while I do the first."

"Sounds good," said Carla with a smile, nodding as she went to the nearest stairway and ascended. Upon getting to the second floor, Carla encountered a lax study environment. There were large tables, their centers lined with outlets for laptops and other electronic devices. Many brought their lunches up with them, eating and drinking as they searched the Internet, checked emails, read documents for class, messaged friends on social media, or watched videos with headphones keeping the noise to themselves.

The central part of the floor was opened up, allowing people on the first floor to see the ceiling of the building. A three-foot tall railing lined the edge. Next to the railing were small square tables, each with two plush rolling chairs. Some of these pairings had been broken up, as chairs were rolled to the larger study tables or to other smaller tables lining the rails. Among the tables were several rows of books, organized by topic and alphabetical order of author names.

Carla found the four display boards on the floor with ease. The bigger challenge was finding space to staple the flyers. Many announcements had crowded the limited display area. Some were technically violating the rules by obscuring other ads and info on student club meetings. With some effort and with little attention from others on the floor, Carla found some blank canvas for the flyer. She had her own mini-stapler with which to pound the paper into the display board. To be sure, she was covering a few of the other items somewhat, but no worse than most of the other sheets.

The papers she was posting were provocative in nature. They took a few quotes from a recent opinion column by conservative writer Charles Lewis, maybe not in the most accurate of context, and called on students to show up to the event later that week and make their opinions felt. Taken by themselves and with the narrative pushed, the quotes sure made Lewis look like a fascist war-monger. Carla had not bothered to read his work for herself; there was no upside to her expressing a nuanced understanding of what the man she was supposed to hate actually believed.

In addition to the large open study space with tables and book shelves, the second floor also had two hallways with various offices and meeting rooms. Carla made her way down one of the halls, going toward the Department of Women & Gender Studies Office. Despite receiving taxpayer money and officially being for educational purposes, the department bore more resemblance to an advocacy group headquarters. Pro-choice and pro-LGBT signs adorning both the outside of the office and its interior. There were also posters with inflammatory statements from feminists of old.

"Hi, can I help you?" asked a teenage receptionist who was also working on a bachelor's degree in gender studies.

"Yes, I am Jessie's friend and I am dropping off these flyers," said Carla. The receptionist nodded with familiarity.

"Of course, Professor Curtis-Stray told me to expect you. You can go ahead and place them here. We'll see about getting them handed out."

"Thank you," said Carla with a smile as she gently placed about a hundred flyers on the empty corner of the desk before exiting. "Good-bye!"

"Take care," said the receptionist before returning her attention to the computer.

Carla walked by two of the display boards before descending the stair case, mainly to make sure that no one had removed her flyers. Jessie had told her earlier about times when rightwing students went by and tore down their sheets. In one incident, Jessie recalled a male student who followed her around just so he could remove her posters. By the time she had realized he was doing this, she had had nearly thirty posters promoting a campus protest had been thrown in the trash.

Fortunately for Carla, the flyers remained where they were. Furthermore, she noticed while walking by that a few students were taking a genuine interest in what was being advertised. A couple of them bore concern about the idea of a genocidal lunatic speaking at their campus. Fire was emerging in their eyes. Walking down the staircase, backpack slung over her left shoulder while her right hand held the railing, Carla saw Jessie waiting around. She turned to see Carla and smiled.

"How'd it go?"

"Just fine. No one followed me to tear them down."

"And the Gender Studies Office?"

"They welcomed me with open arms."

"Great," said Jessie. "Next stop is the outside." Jessie walked toward the main doors for the student union, with Carla quickly catching up and walking by her side. "The free speech zone is a great place to post stuff."

"That's good," agreed Carla as the two left the building, with Carla expressing passing gratitude as Jessie held the door for her. She looked at her wristwatch. "At this speed, you will even get to practice on time."

"Yeah, I know," she said with a laugh. "I bet you still can't believe I act, huh?"

"Well, to be honest, you do seem a little shy for the stage."

"I'm only shy when I am playing myself," explained Jessie. "When I am pretending to be someone else, it gets easy. Very easy, in fact."

They got to the plaza area designated for free speech. The concept was a product of last century, when faculty were frustrated by student activists constantly disrupting classes to protest the Vietnam War. The compromise reached was to section off a portion of campus, away from the places where learning was supposed to happen, and use that for people to express their outrage, beliefs, and outrageous beliefs. The activists switched from staplers to tape, with each carrying a small roll to use. Rain was in the forecast, but not until later in the week. Jessie told Carla that hopefully, by then, the message will have gotten out.

As they went about adding flyers to poles and an outdoor display board, Carla was doing research.

"So how did you hear about this event?"

"I didn't," admitted Jessie, looking at the flyer she was taping to a pole.

"Oh, my mistake," said Carla as she secured a flyer to another pole. "I guess I thought because you are a student, you must have heard about it first."

"No, I didn't," Jessie reaffirmed, taking out another flyer. Both finished up adding flyers at the free speech zone and walked toward their next destination. "I learned about it from Saundra."

"Saundra is not a student, right?"

"She graduated two years ago," explained Jessie. "She told me that she heard about it from Robespierre."

"Who?" asked a sincerely perplexed Carla.

"Robespierre. You know your history, right?"

"I know the eighteenth century Robespierre."

"Well, here in the twenty-first century, Saundra and Rudd get text messages from Robespierre. He tells them stuff."

"Like stuff about events on campus?"

"Yeah, stuff like that," nodded Jessie. They neared a building that mostly contained social science classes and academic offices. "He usually tells us stuff about fascist speakers on campus, when and where their events will be. That way, we can coordinate with like-minded students. Saundra told me he texted her days ago and told her all about the Lewis event."

"Have you ever met him?"

"Once," Jessie recalled. "It was at that old church we meet at. He stayed in the shadows, so I couldn't make him out. I think he's a professor here, but don't quote me."

"I will not include you in my report," Carla said with a smile.

"Saundra and Rudd have met with him more often. Yet they don't tell me too much."

"Really? That seems weird," said Carla, as she returned Jessie's earlier favor and held open one of the doors to the academic building for her. She ended up holding it for two more students running late for class. Jessie waited in the hallway for Carla to catch up. The two then walked side by side down the hall.

"Yeah, I know. They're very secretive about Robespierre. Few people get to talk to him in person even once, let alone a bunch of times."

They soon made it to their last stop, the office of the Black Student Alliance. This was not to be confused with the office for the Department of African-American Studies, whose décor and demeanor were centered on exclusively academic pursuits. The BSA was more geared toward community activism, organizing things ranging from blood drives and clothing donations to political protests and hosting their provocative speakers without incident. Jessie and the male receptionist exchanged pleasantries.

"We will definitely be sure to let people know about this," he said to the two women standing before him. "Thanks for letting us know."

"Sure, no problem," said Jessie. "We're trying to get as many woke students as we can."

"Have you thought about talking to the Young Democrats? I bet they would be happy to help out," posited the receptionist. Carla was about to speak up with an openness to the idea, but Jessie cut her off.

"Democrats aren't much better than Republicans."

* * *

Carla was standing perfectly still. Trees were everywhere, but it was not quite a forest. They waved their silhouetted branches, winds moving them yet not touching her. She felt nothing, nothing but dread. Dread emerged, welling inside of her gut and spreading to every atom of her frame. Rocks were everywhere. She did not notice them at first. They just came, appearing ex nihilo. It felt like a circus, with a central sandy area where she stood. Not a ringmaster, though; her clothing was typical street attire. No audience. Just rocks and trees and fear. The skies were reddish, seeming to go from a solid crimson to a cloudy matted moving canopy of angry charcoal..

The rocks became people. Shadowy, silent, menacing. They seemed to go toward her, yet always stayed the same distance away. Walking in stasis. She wanted to run, but her legs stayed at attention. The rocks were hoods. Some looked like ghetto hoodies, others like the cowls that her former superiors in the Cicero Organization used to wear. Few faces, just hoods, hoodies, cowls, capes, overcoats. Yet she sensed their stares, their piercing eyes all focused on her. Noises in the background, weird noises. Like a mixture of drone and scream, scream and drone. It was getting stronger, multiplying in the reddish clouds.

Carla tried to run, tried to look at her pursuers. Then she saw them. Faces finally emerged. They stood in front of her, each of them at various sides. Rudd,

Saundra, others. Faces she met while in California. Faces at the campus. Antifa faces. They were all of the same group. They all stood, silent, staring, nervous. Her dread was matched in their expressions. They were ashamed of her, judgmental, angry, sad, depressed. She tried asking them if they knew. Did they know who she really was? They seemed to say yes. It was all mental. They kept looking at her, more afraid of her than she of them.

Suddenly her arm raised up, hand gripping a pistol. Carla was more surprised than they. Before she could contemplate the sudden emergence of the weapon, she fired at Rudd. She saw her own hand firing a few shots into him, blasting bloody holes into his body. They were not quite real, like some paper target range image. His expression had not changed. Still the look of shame, sadness, anger, all reserved and fueled from within. Suddenly she turned without her body changing its lethal pose. There was Saundra, standing still as Carla, despite her best efforts, fired more shots, blasting holes in her as well.

It kept happening, the screaming moans in the background punctuating with each fired shot. Carla shouted for it to stop, trying to keep her finger from pulling the trigger. Nothing worked. Her aiming body swung around to another angle, seeing another activist, shooting more holes into them like they were paper targets at a firing range. The crowds around them did nothing. Just watched, seeing the macabre entertainment and offering neither outrage nor cheers. Just there, just witnessing the gunfire.

Carla swung a quarter of a circle to face Jessie. She was the most hurt of them all. Her negative showcase of emotions skewed to the sadly betrayed. Her eyes were so big with requested pity. She seemed childlike, begging with her expression. Carla could see her finger tightening on the trigger. She tried everything, willing it to not move closer. The surrounding screams were getting louder. She wanted to warn her of the firepower, to tell her to get out of the way. To move, to leave. Nothing seemed to register, no sound reached Jessie's ears. Carla could not resist any longer; the gun fired again.

Yet it was Carla who received the wounds. Each shot led to another spray of blood from her chest. Carla looked down, finally able to move her body. She did not feel pain, but the wounds were clearly gaping. Her fingers went along each of the holes in terror. She looked up again and saw Tiffany. Her old friend from her days in the Cicero Organization. She was standing right where Jessie had been. The same facial expression dominated her face. Then Carla found herself aiming a loaded gun at her head. She could not resist, the finger was pulling back on the trigger.

And then Carla awoke, nearly screaming as she entered the conscious world. She rose to a seated position in the single-sized bed. Gasping, she pushed her black hair from her face while she gathered herself. Carla's breathing slowed and heart rate reduced as her internal self regained the stability of a saner surrounding environment. Sheets still covering the lower half of her body, Carla reached for her wristwatch on the small mantle beside her bed. She pushed a tiny button in the corner of the watch to light up its face. She sighed when seeing that it was too late to go back to sleep yet too early to get ready. A few minutes later, she finally got up from the bed and began to get ready, finding it preferable to the risk of being late for class. Preparations for the day went without incident.

By the time she was ready for the campus, her phone buzzed. A quick check of the screen revealed that the federal government wanted to talk with her first. There was plenty of time for a fast update about things before she needed to walk to campus for class. Putting her backpack on the couch, Carla went to the corner of the living room where her laptop was charging on the floor. She unplugged the device and turned it on. From there, she went to the communications app and called up FBI Detective Michael Zambo. He responded immediately, his formal countenance looking from the screen.

"Good morning," she said.

"It's lunch time here at the office," he replied. "But it's the thought that counts."

"You needed to talk to me?"

"I have some good news and some bad news. Which do you want first?"

"Surprise me."

"Then it's the bad news," began Michael. "One of our techies found out that a Neo-Nazi group might be trying to target Antifa of Pacific Coast State. In other words, the group that you are a part of. As in, they will try to go after you."

"Why? How?"

"Apparently, a couple of them just got fired from their jobs because your antifa chapter told their bosses about their afterhours activities. So they want revenge. They are going to stake out a place named Harper's that apparently a lot of the antifa types go to."

"It is a restaurant. Usually, when we have dinner together, a couple members will get carry-out from there. We rarely eat there, though."

"Well, you should eat there less."

"Fair enough."

"And if your antifa comrades are as tech savvy as we think they are, they are going to find that out and tell you as well. They look after their own a lot, after all. Which actually is a perfect segue to the good news."

"They think of me as one of their own?"

"Most likely," said Michael. "Also from our tech people: searches for 'Carla Wexler' have decreased to virtually zero. They must have finished investigating you some days ago and have been content with their findings."

"Maybe this undercover work is easier than I thought."

"Well, not to be 'that guy,' but you *are* dealing with amateurs."

"And I am thankful," said Carla. She asked the next question with some nervousness. "So does that mean I can now return to contacting family?"

"No."

"Why not?" she protested with some anger brewing to the surface. "If they have stopped investigating me, it must be safe to call my grandfather and my husband again."

"I'm sorry, but we cannot take the chance. That Phelier woman you have befriended knows how to navigate the Internet. And to find targets. Just the other day, a tech guy contracted with the Bureau tried to hack her files and got a virus download for his troubles."

"You contact me," Carla pointed out.

"The Bureau has a secure connection. Your friends and family do not."

"All right, I see that," Carla grudgingly acknowledged.

"With our tech guys effectively blocked out, you are our best source of information on these people."

"Which means I am still stuck here."

"Yes."

"Have I told you how much I hate this?" she began, taking an exasperated breath before continuing. "I mean, I cannot talk to the people I care for, and the people I am making friendships with are waiting to have me betray them."

"I understand. Undercover work can be very draining," Michael said in a calm voice. "I appreciate what you are doing and the personal sacrifices you are making. If I did not think something big was here, I would not keep putting you through this."

"Okay," said Carla. "I will try to keep it together for at least another week."

"That should work. By then, my superiors will be demanding something tangible on my end. And if I have nothing, then I have no choice but to end your misery," he said, smiling, getting a weak smile from Carla in return. "So, what's next on the agenda?"

"Tonight, we are protesting a speaker on campus."

"Sounds fun."

"Yeah."

"My advice to you, Carla, is to release your current frustrations at the protest. It can only make you feel better."

"I will think about it."

"Anyway, enjoy your classes," he said as a parting remark.

"Thanks. Bye," she said, as the connection ended.

* * *

Jessie worked at a computer lab part time. She did so to have money for groceries and to pay for a few living expenses, as well as the occasional luxury purchase, like new clothes or beers with friends. Rent for her off-campus apartment, books, and tuition were paid by her parents. Jessie's relationship with her mother and father was tenuous, to say the least. They knew she was a radical, a rebellious offspring who, unlike her more wholesome religious older sister, left church and convention back in the teen years and never returned. Nevertheless, mutual familial love still remained. Jessie wondered how much that fragile bond would remain if they were fully cognizant of her activism.

The lab was off campus. It was operated like a library, with patrons expected to remain largely quiet when present, reverently keeping phones off as they surfed the web or worked on some document. It was an easy occupation whose greatest burden was the long hours of inactivity. Another employee checked people in and out. Her chief responsibility was to help with any technological problems, answering any customer queries, among similar obligations. While often in a room with several people at a time, Jessie could go hours without talking to a single person.

Fortunately, Jessie came prepared. Her weapon against boredom was her copy of Sir William Shakespeare's *Julius Caesar*. Her company had decided to do the classic play, though with a twist of some kind. They always did twists. When performing a play about Spartacus last year, the production set the story during the American Civil War. Spartacus and his slave army were black, the Silesian pirates were the Union blockade, and the elite force that defeated them was the Army of Northern Virginia.

"Excuse me, miss." An old lady disrupted her reading through the play. Jessie looked up and gave a customer service smile. "I am sorry, but I am having an issue with a picture. Can you please help me?"

"Yes, of course," replied Jessie, putting a piece of scratch paper in the book and closing it before getting up. She was wearing her reading glasses for the book and kept them on when following the elderly woman back to the computer. "What seems to be the problem?"

"Well," said the gray-haired woman, pausing to laugh. "Well, I am trying to save it onto the computer and then send it to my grandson, but it isn't saving."

"Okay," noted Jessie, who stood behind the seated patron. "Let me see if I can save it."

"That's the photo, there," she said, pointing to a family picture on the screen. "I've saved photos like this on other computers, but ..." Pausing again to briefly laugh. "But this time, it isn't working."

Jessie right-clicked on the photo and then tried to select copy, so that she could paste it on the desktop, yet, the option did not appear. Studying the alternatives, she saw that the normal save option was also unavailable. "I see what you mean, it is not letting me copy it the usual way, either."

"So did I break the computer?" she asked with a laugh.

"Probably not," assured Jessie. "Some websites are very strict about people saving documents off of their pages. They have means to stop people from taking stuff from their site. So, this might be another example."

"Okay."

"Let me see if I can screengrab it," Jessie said, thinking aloud. As the old woman watched, Jessie pressed the print screen button. A window came up asking her if she wanted to queue the image for the lab's printer. Jessie knew it would come up and exited out of it the moment it popped up. From there, she went to the start menu, selected the proper program, and then upon opening the program, pasted the screen capture in a document. Jessie cropped the image to include just the family photo, and then successfully saved the document on the desktop. "That should do the trick."

"Excellent, thank you," the customer said.

"No problem. Need help with anything else?"

"No, I think I can do the rest by myself," she replied with a laugh.

"Okay, good. Well, let me know if you need any more help."

"Sure thing."

Jessie walked back to her desk. She looked around the other computers, most of which had people situated in front of them. No one was looking up to ask for assistance with their eyes. All was back to normal. Seated back at her desk, Jessie opened up the playbook and continued to read. The characters were overwhelmingly male, but her company had done plenty of gender bending in the past. She was playing Cassius, one of the conspirators. Reading and re-reading the lines. As any stage player, she found herself being absorbed into the character, maintaining her distinct individual self while also subsuming some of their attributes, their thoughts, their great and terrible inclinations.

"Jessie!" A projected whisper from a surprise arrival broke her concentration. It sounded like a sergeant ordering a private, a manager summoning an employee. She flinched in her chair, looking up to see Saundra Jaspers standing there.

"Damn, Saundra. You scared the hell out of me."

"I would have texted you, but I remembered the lab rules."

"What is it?"

"We're going to a different restaurant tonight before we head out."

"Okay."

"I didn't want you to accidentally forget to check your phone and go to the wrong place."

"Well, thanks. Not sure it required you to come here."

"Yes, it did," Saundra firmly stated. Her demeanor unnerved Jessie.

"What's the problem?"

"We need to talk alone. Now."

"Okay," she said with unease while rising from her seat. The two activists walked toward the front. Jessie stopped briefly to talk with her coworker. "I need to step away for a few minutes. Are you okay?"

"Yup," said the coworker without looking up from his smartphone.

"Good," Jessie responded and then left the lab to go outside with Saundra. They went to the alleyway between the lab and a neighboring office building.

Oblivious pedestrians went by the narrow space as they talked. "What's the problem?"

"You can't go to that restaurant anymore."

"Harper's?"

"Yes, Harper's."

"How come?"

"It's not safe."

"Wait, what do you mean, 'not safe'?"

"This morning, I was looking at alt right chat rooms and there was a lot of talk about Harper's. They mentioned it a *lot*."

"Are you saying the restaurant is in bed with Neo-Nazis?"

"I don't think so, but that's not the point. They were talking about watching it, looking at it. Scoping it out. You know, like a sting operation or something."

"A sting operation?"

"They're using it as a trap," stressed Saundra. "If any of us show up and they recognize us, we could be attacked."

"Surely, they can't know what we look like."

"They might. You know they might."

"I get it," conceded Jessie. "I'll steer clear."

"Good."

"Anyway, I'll see you tonight at the apartment, right?"

"Right."

"Okay."

Saundra breathed out relief as the two walked out of the alleyway. "I am glad you got the message. Everyone else was texted, but I knew you might miss it."

"Thanks for caring," replied Jessie, smiling.

"We have to care for each other. You should know that."

"Yes."

"Anyway, like I said, see you tonight."

"Sure. Bye," replied Jessie as her fellow radical walked away. She struggled to focus on her reading for the next couple of hours as fighting to suppress the idea of violent fascists coming to other places she frequented. By the end of the workday, with the customers gone and the coworkers closing shop, she returned to stability. She kept the emotional angst locked away for later that night, when she would be the aggressor.

* * *

Fewer than two hours remained before the start of the Lewis event. At certain parts of the campus, student activists were gathering in small groups in anticipation of the big protest. Some were at the free speech zone, standing with signs, demanding that the University stop the march of fascism. Security were already positioned at the main entrance to campus, as well as at certain points from the parking lot to the auditorium where operations staff were testing the sound equipment and cleaning the aisles.

Several activists were in the terraced house at that one apartment. Folks sat on the couches, in chairs, and many on the hardwood floor. A two-foot wide circular trashcan was placed in one of the corners, a few spare bags laid out by its side. Multiple conversations were happening as people trickled in. There was no official ceremony, no opening remarks. Just young folk coming together for common cause, eating what was ordered, some offering financial compensation, and staying for the eventual rallying by the antifa chapter leadership. From there, they would go to the campus.

"Hey, Carla," said Rudd, noticing the newer member of their group when they both ascended the staircase. She smiled as they walked beside one another.

"Hi, Rudd."

"Looks like we're a little late," he concluded as a third person ahead of them opted to keep the door open for them to enter.

"Yeah," she said as both of them said their thanks to the person who let them in. Each said their hellos to their respective people and then made their way to the kitchen, where the orders were put. Jessie and a couple of others drove up to the restaurant to pick up the five large bags of food. She felt some nerves when picking it up, wondering if the online enemies had also figured out that place. However, as they drove away from the new place, Jessie's nerves calmed when nothing happened. By the time they returned to the apartment, she was fine.

"I guess we both have bad habits of being late."

"Looks like it," Carla said with a faint laugh. Periodically, she would make a joke about "Arab Standard Time" when caught in this situation. Yet her current persona had no expressed Middle Eastern heritage and she feared that a revelation of it may complicate the trust she was forming. In that one moment, she felt colder, remembering yet again how much of her true self and true intentions had to be suppressed.

The two found a place to sit on one of the couches. Earlier, a trio of teenagers had taken to the space. But they had just finished eating and were taking a smoke break outside. This left their unreserved seating open to the two early-thirty-somethings. Lacking table space, which was taken up by others, Carla balanced her unwrapped food on her lap. Thinking nothing of it, she silently said a brief grace with the motions. With her eyes not fully closed during the quick supplication, she saw Rudd doing something similar. Both crossed themselves after tacit remarks, each reflecting their respective churches.

"You know, you did it wrong," Rudd said lightheartedly. Carla was perplexed at first, but then quickly realized what he meant.

"I was about to tell you the same thing," she replied with a grin, getting a brief laugh out of the activist.

"I say you're both wrong," interrupted Saundra Jaspers without a hint of amusement.

"She must be a Protestant," said Rudd to Carla, both amused at his remark while Saundra gave a wry smile.

"We'll talk about it later," stated Saundra.

"Talk about what?" asked Jessie as she walked by, giving fleeting but kind hellos to Rudd and Carla. "Like I said, talk about what?"

"Religion, as usual," explained Rudd.

"Oh, I thought she was finally going to set you right about women's issues."

"Now, Jessie, you know full well I am perfectly fine on women's issues."

"What's this whole 'women's issues' problem?" asked Carla.

"Great, Jessie," said Rudd in faux annoyance. "Now I'm going to have to make a bad impression on Carla."

"Hey, you're the one who holds those beliefs."

"And they are consistent beliefs," said Rudd with a finger raised at Jessie, before turning his attention to Carla. "You see, I support life. I hate killing. So I am antiwar, anti-death penalty, anti-gun, anti-euthanasia, and anti-abortion. It's consistent."

"Sorry you had to hear that, Carla," explained Jessie, hand on her shoulder. "We keep trying to enlighten him, but he just won't budge."

"That's okay," said Carla. "To be honest, I'm a little anti-abortion myself."

"We used to be friends," said Jessie playfully while going toward the trash-can to toss from used napkins and a paper wrapping.

"Something I said?"

"She'll get over it," assured Rudd. "You know, I'm accepting."

"It does sound like it."

"Life all the way."

"Life all the way," affirmed Carla, the two giving a mock toast with their bottled waters.

"Except when it comes to Neo-Nazis," added Jessie as she walked by.

"Deal!" declared Rudd with raised bottle.

That was most tense of the conversations for those gathered at the terraced house apartment. Many spoke nothing of politics or religion while feasting on the carry-out dinner. Some struggled to eat, their internal fretting bearing hard on the stomach. Others were disappointed to learn that it was a dry occasion; the beers were reserved for after they came back from the event, assuming they were not arrested. While diverse, they were united in their hate, despising the speaker with little knowledge of where he stood on any issue, foreign or domestic. They were told by those who knew and those of like-mind on the Internet that he was bad, and they believed it.

Saundra checked her smartphone and saw that it was a little over an hour until the event was scheduled to begin. Putting the phone back into her pants pocket, she got up from the couch and walked toward the side of the apartment where the windows showed the street. A few blocks off from there was Pacific Coast State University. Rudd and Jessie understood the significance and also rose from their respective seats, standing alongside their shorter peer. Carla did not join them, but she paid close attention.

"All right everyone, listen!" Saundra announced, getting a few heads to turn. She projected her voice more. "Listen up!" The rest ended their conversations and turned toward the de facto leader. "It is an hour until the event begins. We're going to head over now. But before we do, I want to remind you about the rules." Saundra raised an index finger. "First, no action until we get to the auditorium and the speech begins. Once Lewis starts his propaganda, we all stand and turn our backs. I've talked with other groups planning to go, and they agreed to do the same thing."

Saundra's middle finger joined the index to form a V. "Second, no masks and no violence. There is going to be security all over the place. They will give you problems if you wear a mask. Other student leaders have met with the professor behind this event and the provost. They promise no violence. But keep your smartphones ready. If something goes wrong, you need to record it and get it online ASAP." Three fingers were raised. "Finally, there is supposed to be a Q&A after he speaks. If you want to say something, do it. Hell, if you want to boo the guy, do it. Everyone get it?"

A series of affirmative statements and nodding heads came in response. Saundra turned to Rudd, who nodded, then spoke. "When the event is over and we have held that fascist accountable for his propaganda, we come back here. Don't go straight home. We want to make sure everyone got back safe. Understood?" The nods and yeses were less enthusiastic, but present. "Also, we have a ton of beer that needs to be drunk tonight, so ..." Some laughs and many smiles came in reply to that comment. Even Saundra expressed some amusement at his quip. Tacitly, he handed focus back to her.

"All right then," she said with rising power. "Let's show this bigot what it's like to have the people shut down hate speech!" Everyone, Carla included, shouted back their approval of the declaration. From there, they piled out of the apartment and into the night.

* * *

Carla was inside the building, nearing the entrance to the auditorium. Before her were a pair of security personnel, wearing body armor and holding scanners. A small table was placed nearby where students put any packs or purses and had them checked. Everyone got the same treatment, as school officials feared that the slightest disparity would lead to rioting. As such, the lengthening line took a while to get people through it. She had time to look around and see folks of varying colors, creeds, and clothing standing around. The attendees ranged from people like her, wearing cargo pants and a T-shirt, to mature-looking youths wearing ties and sports jackets. A few wore hoodies, a few others wore hijabs.

There was no speaking between Carla and the security. She had no purse nor backpack, making her experience with the duo of guards fairly fast. Arms stretched out, they scanned her for a few seconds and then gave her thumbs up to go into the auditorium. The entrance involved going through two propped-open double doors. It looked like a movie theatre, with its lack of windows and a box shape. Aisles divided up three columns of seats, the middle column having twice the number of seats as the two other ones. Despite the simmering crowd, she found her party at once.

CARLA: THE END OF REASON

"Got through okay, I see," commented Jessie. She was standing in the right aisle, hand resting on the seat at the end of a row that was ten ranks from the stage. Saundra, Rudd, and a few others were already seated in that row.

"Yeah, no problem."

"Good," said Jessie. "You want the aisle seat?"

"If you would rather have it, that is okay with me."

"Then I'll have it," she said, Carla walking by her and finding herself sitting next to Rudd. She leaned past Carla and Rudd to speak with Saundra. "Anyone else have problems?"

"No, not from what I can tell," reported Saundra.

Carla looked around. Security flanked the stage, armed with guns and wearing badges that reflected in the stage lights. There were numerous chattering conversations going on. Many were about other things, a way to pass the tension. Her sight glided along the world behind her seat, seeing fewer and fewer empty chairs. They were still coming in, one at a time. A half dozen people were waiting around the entrance for friends to get through security. She recognized many of the people sitting behind her, not so much by name as by face. They had been to meetings of the antifa chapter, and they had brought friends tonight.

"They always start late," said Rudd to Carla, drawing her attention.

"Really?" Carla checked her wristwatch. "Yeah, a few minutes after eight."

"Maybe he knew what he was in for and left," Jessie suggested.

"You don't really believe that, do you, Jessie?" asked Saundra.

"Not really."

"And ruin all the fun we had in mind?" asked Rudd.

Professor Holton Fillerhouse entered from off stage and walked to the lone object on the elevated platform: a podium with microphone. By this point, the number of people entering the auditorium had dwindled and nearly all had taken seats. Unlike a theatrical performance, the house lights remained on, albeit dimmed. The stage was a little more illumined. Lacking make-up outlining his features, Fillerhouse's face was a bit blurry when a photographer from the campus newspaper took a few shots.

"Good evening, everyone," said Fillerhouse, hands gripping the sides of the podium. The chatter calmed to quiet. "I am Professor Holton Fillerhouse of the Economics Department here at Pacific Coast State and I welcome you to tonight's lecture by Dr. Charles Lewis. The title of his lecture is 'An End to

Quagmires.' It is based off of an essay he had published last year. Dr. Lewis is a scholar, author, and writer. He has a bachelor of arts in history and a masters in political science. He has spoken about Middle East issues at several colleges and universities, and is widely considered an expert on foreign policy." The audience remained silent through the introduction, many itching to act. Carla herself was feeling a little antsy. She had never done something like this before. If things went violent, she was trapped in a crowded, enclosed space without a weapon. "So without further delay, it is my esteemed pleasure to introduce writer, speaker, and intellectual extraordinaire, Dr. Charles Lewis!"

Fillerhouse led the audience in applause, turning to face the side of the stage Lewis entered from, clapping as he got closer to the podium. About a third of the students in attendance also applauded, most of whom were seated near the front. Most kept their peace; a few, unseen by the speaker or the security, flipped him off. Fillerhouse and Lewis shook hands before the former walked off stage. Carla beheld the target, seeing a small old man with thick glasses and puffy gray hair. She held some guilt; she did not know whether the man on the stage was a particularly awful person, but she was going to make his night miserable anyway. She reminded herself of the obvious: she had done worse to other targets.

"The historian ...," he began. That was the cue. Carla, Rudd, Saundra, and Jessie joined over half of the audience in rising to their feet and turning their backs to the speaker. Carla's view went from the lit stage and its observant security to the backs turned by scores of her peers. She could hear Lewis hesitate for a moment in his words, but he kept on with his speech. "The historian is meant to draw lessons from the past. He, or she, seeks to learn from the mistakes of those who came before, and to tell others those lessons before they make identical mistakes ..." The initial rattling from the audience displeasure was gradually overcome as he continued, drawing contrasts between the World Wars and the Gulf Wars.

Minutes passed as he continued to give his speech. The various activists and dissenting students felt a collective sense of disappointment. Yes, they unnerved Lewis by their public stance of immediate disagreement. Yet still he persisted in his words. His apologia for total war and laissez-faire capitalism were getting to the hearts of those standing in rows. Silent protest was not enough; there had to be more. As he started to argue in favor of the total war model for the next possible Middle East intervention, the protesters started to boo. A few at a time participated at first, then more joined in the fun.

"We, um ... We are told we have to respect different cultures," said Lewis, his voice lost among the jeering. "Even if those values include smoking hookah, chanting death to America and Israel, and blowing up their own children to send them to their Allah."

"Bigoted pig!" shouted Carla, getting some cheers for her and some more boos directed at Lewis. Carla could not believe she said it. Like the Holy Spirit moving through a gathering of Pentecostals, the partisan hate was inspiring her declarations. A few others joined her remarks, shouting the label at Lewis for the next minute or so.

It was becoming harder for the speaker to be heard. The more conservative students started to heckle back, cheering Lewis at each of his points and offering loud applause as well as hollers of support. Carla and the others responded, drowning them out on most occasions with their vociferous opposition. As he mentioned the need to remove Islam's influence on Middle Eastern nations, a few of the protesters turned around just long enough to give a mocking Nazi salute to the embattled speaker.

"Sig heil, fascist!" shouted Rudd, being one of the audience members to raise his palm in insult to Lewis. Carla joined him to do the same a moment later. Saundra started to think about Carla in a more positive light, seeing her taking on a leading role in some of the popular backlash to the lecture.

After an hour of speech and audience feedback, the speech finally concluded. The Republican and Libertarian students gave an applause while the dissident majority offered a chorus of boos and remained standing with backs turned. Few of the neutral spectators knew what Lewis' main arguments were, having heard little due to the upheavals. The main protest objective was largely successful. An annoyed and frustrated Lewis took a few steps back as Provost Juana Marciela walked from off stage left to address the crowd. Seeing it was not their target, most of the audience opted to sit down. Her steps were easily heard due to her high heels striking the elevated surface.

"All right everyone," said the provost. "I am Mrs. Juana Marciela, provost of Pacific Coast State. I appreciate your attentiveness, your respect ..." several on both sides openly laughed at the statement. "... and your passion for this subject. We are going to do the question and answer session now. If you could just tone it down a little bit and use this time to explain your issues with Dr.

Lewis, it would be very much appreciated. Thank you." Marciela exited the stage and went straight home. She passed by Fillerhouse without looking at him and ignored his request to answer him.

Once Lewis returned to the podium, those protesters who had sat down rejoined their brethren in the back-turned showing of disdain. Students and other attendees were lining up before the two microphones, one placed at each aisle. Still inspired, Carla slid past Jessie to get to the nearest microphone. A few other students spoke their questions and declarations, the dissenting ones getting cheers from the protesters. Lewis' responses were becoming heated as well, with half of his answers beginning with "I didn't say that ..." Carla got her turn at the microphone and stated her declaration.

"You claimed that we need to remove Islam and make it more secular, you talk about the need for the next war to be really horrible. You are demanding that we exterminate people. That makes you worse than the terrorists. How can you say we are better when you are demanding Nazi-style genocide?"

"I'm not advocating for genocide," declared Lewis, "I am saying we must defeat the enemy when we have a war. We cannot restrict our tactics in the name of political correctness."

"That's genocide!" stated Carla, getting some cheers from the standing pro-testers. She directed her microphone-amplified voice to the crowd. "Isn't that genocide?" An even louder statement of support came from the dissenters, espe-cially the antifa members who she knew by first name. "We oppose genocide. We oppose bigotry. We oppose you!" As Lewis tried to reply, his voice struggled to be audible over the cheering for Carla. She did not care; she walked back to her seat with the right people supporting her.

VII

Two time zones away, yet the same evening that Charles Lewis was hounded by the radicals, a very different gathering of souls was taking place at the headquarters for Josiah Sharp's gubernatorial campaign. While not as crowded as that university auditorium, the space was still well-populated. Around 50 folks connected to Sharp either politically or personally were enjoying refreshments, socializing with peers, standing, sitting, and watching the big screen that was set up along one side of the large white-walled room. The feed for the news updates came from a laptop connected to a projector. An expert in information technology held vigil near the machine in case it faltered.

For those many people at the campaign headquarters that night, the mood was joyous, relaxed, and easy. Few doubted the results of the statewide election. Since the polls closed and the ballots were being counted, the popular vote had been in Sharp's favor. County after county went his way, with only the occasional regional sector going for his opponent. Attendees of the party cheered and applauded when the stoic anchors reported another county going for Sharp, and expressed light disappointment for the few that went to Pearlstein. Many only somewhat paid attention to the news channel, confident enough in the decision to come. Going into that night, no poll had Sharp behind. A handful of local reporters were also present, on assignment and waiting for the big news to come.

"And now we can report that Hillsdale County has gone to the Sharp campaign," said the anchor, professional in attire and neutral in tone. His face was supplanted by a graphic showing the county turning red, the color representing Sharp's political allegiance. "As you can see with the overall state map, Sharp continues to lead Senator Pearlstein in counties roughly two to one. While the Pearlstein campaign has yet to officially concede, it appears as though, barring some unforeseen performance in the northern counties, this race is looking close to being called for Sharp ..." His subsequent words were drowned out by cheers from the younger folk present. Cameramen for the local TV news programs panned over the crowd, capturing their elation at the growing realization that their man was set to become the next governor.

The screen bearing better and better news occupied much of the wall that faced the glass front of the structure. Those transparent walls were mostly covered with campaign posters of varying colors and sizes. The other two white walls were lined with rectangular tables placed end-to-end, adorned with white table cloths and topped with numerous foods and drinks, as well as tons of napkins, small plastic plates, and plastic utensils. The cubicle maze that existed in the center of the space, where campaign staff and volunteers campaigned and coordinated for Sharp, were cleared away and replaced with numerous circular tables with folding chairs. George al-Hassan was at one of them, his cane hanging on the back of his chair. Sharp broke away from some others to approach him.

"Hey, George," Josiah said, getting the pleasant attention of his grandfather-in-law. "How are you doing?"

"Fine, fine," he said. "Quite the party. Not as good as some of the ones I attended in my youth in Damascus, but still quite the party."

"Yeah, Carla has told me some stories."

"All good ones, I hope," he said with a guilty smile.

Sharp laughed. "Of course, why not?"

"Let me just apologize for Elnora not showing up," began George. "She had a last-minute tenant meeting she could not miss."

"I understand," said Josiah, looking down briefly before continuing. "It's Carla that I miss. Here I am about to have the first and biggest victory in my political career and I cannot even send her a text message."

"I am sure she is very happy for you."

"Yes, I think so, too."

"Anyway," said George, lifting his semi-filled wine glass. "I bet you need to keep working the room. If I need a refill, I will let you know."

"Yes, sir," laughed Sharp as he patted George on the shoulder and walked away. He went only a few more steps before encountering his parents. They had been sitting with George at first, but left the table when Sharp felt an obligation to introduce them to some of his notable campaign supporters. Rose and

Terry saw their son coming and offered him their attention. Both were drinking sodas, with Terry holding an almost finished second plastic plate of food. "Are you having fun?"

"Just like an after-church picnic," his father replied.

"Except with more wine," chimed in Rose, getting a nod of agreement from her husband.

"We keep watching the screen and every time we look up, you have won another county. I think if we keep looking away and then looking back again, you'll win the whole state."

"A simple majority will suffice," said Josiah.

"Anyway, I think we'll go back to the table," suggested Rose. "I fear George thinks we have abandoned him."

"He will be happy to see you."

"You know, Terry," said Rose to her husband. "I haven't yet told George about that one time when I was a student and I almost took a study abroad trip to Syria. He would find that amusing."

"I'm sure he will," agreed, humoring his wife. He gave his son a look of amusement before the couple made their way back to the circular table. Josiah laughed to himself at the thought of his mother's storytelling when Attorney General Kyle Brown called his name.

"Josiah!" he said with a welcoming inflection. The two shook hands, Brown careful to put his wine glass in his left hand before offering his right. Greeting concluded, the glass returned to that hand.

"So far, so good, right?"

"Oh yes, very right," said Brown with a smile.

"I cannot believe this is happening. I mean, if you told me as a kid that I was going to be governor ... I mean, praise be."

"You haven't won it just yet," cautioned Brown. "But you are very close." More cheers were heard closer to the big screen, drawing the attention of most of those in the room. "And you got another county."

"Gladwin County, to be exact."

"My home town is in Gladwin," observed Brown, turning his eyes back to Josiah and lowering his voice. "That might be the first time I have ever been proud of my birthplace."

"Oh, come on," Sharp lightly countered. "They seemed nice enough to me when I showed up."

"That's because they knew you were leaving by afternoon."

"Ha," deadpanned Josiah. "So I guess this means my chances of speaking at that governors' convention later this month are all but secured."

"Just about."

As they were about to engage in idly plotting additional political plans, District Attorney James Colbert rushed toward them. His mixture of walk and run began in a private room located to the right of the big screen. Few paid him heed as they directed their attention to their own discussions or the latest update that kept Sharp in the lead. Sharp and Brown kept their peace, awaiting his arrival. Colbert initially tried to convey his message in words, but upon failing took Josiah by the arm and urged him to follow.

"What is going on?"

"Just come with me," Colbert finally stated, grinning with excitement. The two entered the smaller, more private space. Inside the room the walls were decorated with campaign posters and bumper stickers. A lone desk and chair were in the corner, with a landline phone attached to the wall and resting on the desktop. Sharp was quick to note that the receiver was laying on the desk as well. Someone was on hold. Colbert held both of Josiah's shoulders briefly, smiled, and stated "You'll want to take that call." Then he left the room, closing the door behind him. Sharp approached the phone and picked up the receiver.

"Hello?"

"Mr. Josiah Sharp?"

"Senator Pearlstein," he said with reverent surprise.

"How are you doing?"

"Pretty well, actually," replied Josiah. "I just won another county. Though the pundits say you still have a chance."

Pearlstein laughed. "No, I don't."

Sharp remained silent, his excitement jumping in intensity.

"You did a very good job, Mr. Sharp. I may disagree with a lot of what you stand for, but I very much agree with what you symbolize. Our state needs a better union. It needs someone who symbolizes a departure from the violence and vitriol that plagues our body politic. If we want our system to survive, it is better that you win. Simply put, ten minutes after I hang up I am announcing my concession. Congratulations."

Sharp breathed hard in exasperated joy. "I—I ... Thank you, Senator. Thank you for the challenge, thank you for the concession. I cannot wait to work alongside you next session."

"And to butt heads, I'm sure."

Sharp laughed. "Yes, that also."

"Anyway, good job."

"Thank you, Senator. Thank you. Oh, and as the old hymn puts it, 'God be with you till we meet again.'"

"Take care," said Pearlstein, who then hung up the phone. Josiah took a few seconds to do the same. He felt an immense lifting of spirit, a great ecstasy calmly channeled through his disciplined self. He remained there a moment, in silent prayerful contemplation over the great victory. He was interrupted several minutes later when his supporters and family cheered voraciously at the headline appearing on the news channel.

* * *

Back at the apartment in the terraced house, Carla and her fellow antifa activists held a celebration over their actions at the university auditorium. The disruption was a success. They had mostly drowned out the speaker. Not one of them was arrested or physically attacked. Lots of laughter, drinking, talking, boasting, and happy sadism went on over what they put the speaker through that night. Many of the drinkers were underage. Carla was among the few who shied away from the alcohol. Such refusals were welcomed; it meant more for those who wanted to indulge. The environment was lax, the compliments and recollections many in number. Most came for just a drink or two before saying their good-nights and returning home. No one left alone. Despite the carefree elation, there remained an assumed fear of reprisal. With just two leaving at a time, there was a sense of greater succor.

"Oh, how I loved it when he tried to shout and we—and we—and we STILL booed louder than he did," Jessie said, laughing as she talked. She was two-thirds of the way through her second beer. "It was beautiful."

"Or how about when he practically had a heart attack during Q&A?" said Rudd, barely through his first and only bottle. "I thought he was going to explode." Many laughed, including Carla, who sipped the contents of her soda bottle from time to time.

"It was amazing! Absolutely amazing!" exclaimed Saundra Jaspers with a big smile. The alcohol had removed her usual straight-laced demeanor. She was intermittently patting the shoulders and backs of the activists seated on either of her. They had taken several chairs and placed them by the couches for a circle of enjoyment. "And Carla ..." she said, pointing with her latest opened bottle, grabbing her attention, "I loved how you stuck it to that asshole. You knocked him down. Seriously. Knocked him down with your words."

"To the power of words," declared Jessie Phelier, lifting her beer. Others did the same, a couple repeating her statement. After she finished her drink, Jessie checked her smartphone. "Whoa, it's getting late. And I have to study for exams, and for *Julius Caesar*." She got up from the couch, stretching while keeping a good grip on the glass bottle. "You all have a good night, I got to head out."

"Nick, you go with her, okay?" Saundra asked a teenager seated beside her. He nodded, got up, and said his goodbyes before he and Jessie left. Jaspers took another drink and then grimaced. Her fingers touched her forehead before brushing back some of her dirty blonde dreadlocks. "I am going to have one super-massive headache tomorrow morning." Then she laughed. "Good thing it's my day off." Then she chugged the remainder of that beer before getting up to look for another one.

"You know what? I should probably study for my classes tomorrow. I have one that starts around ten," said Carla.

"All right. Good night, Carla," said Saundra, looking for another unopened bottle in the refrigerator.

"Mind if I walk you home?" inquired Rudd.

"Not at all," she replied, eliciting a smile from her fellow radical.

"Good night, everyone," Carla announced, getting positive responses from the few who remained. Those they left behind ended up spending the night at the terraced house apartment.

Rudd held the doors open as they went from the apartment to the hallway, down a couple of flights of stairs, and then from the hallway to the outside world. Carla uttered a soft "Thank you" in response to each chivalrous action. The night was cool but not cold. Dry also. It had not rained the entire time that Carla had been in California. They walked casually from the terraced house, Rudd taking the side of the walkway closest to the street. He smiled a lot as they socialized, putting his hands in his pockets as they went toward her place.

"Got to stress it, you were amazing tonight."

"Thank you," said Carla, brushing her black hair to the side behind her right ear. It was a nervous action; she sensed his feelings for her, yet she needed to learn more. "I just felt that I had to say something. And say it loud."

"You did," agreed Rudd. "I wish I had done as much."

"Well, you did the Heil Hitler salute, so that was something," countered Carla. "I found that to be great."

"Thanks."

"I hope he learned a lesson: that if he ever comes back, he will get more."

"Yeah, definitely," Rudd agreed. The pair stopped in front of a busy street. On the other side, a signal was visible that told them how many seconds they had until they would be allowed to cross. "I mean, I'll be honest ... I am not very fond of Islamic terrorists, or some of those regimes over there. But still, you're not going to make things better by carpet bombing people and telling them their religious views are stupid. Even the worst of the terrorists is still created in the image of God. Even they have a sacred worth, you know?"

"Yeah," said Carla with a nod. The signal for pedestrians to cross flashed on, and they walked across the street without incident. She decided to probe further. "If you don't mind me asking, Rudd, I'm curious. Can I ask you a personal question?"

"Um, sure."

"You seem, well ... different from the others. Why is that?" inquired Carla, quickly adding "I promise not to judge!"

"Fair enough. You want to know how a guy like me—Catholic, pro-life—ended up fighting alongside people like Saundra and Jessie."

"Yeah."

Rudd took a deep breath. "Well, radicalism and Catholicism have been in my family for generations. They usually take turns holding sway. My grandparents were super-Catholic, while my parents were radicals."

"Which is why they named you after that Weather Underground figure."

"Correct!" he said, removing a hand from a pocket to point at Carla. "For a time, I was straying from their guidance. I found and still find great solace in the Church. For a long time, I thought that was the only cause I would fight for."

"What happened?"

"Well, about a decade ago, when I was in high school, there was a shooting on campus. Some crazy person with an assault rifle started firing at people."

"That is horrible!"

"Just to be clear," he said, hands raised to caution her not to misunderstand to his words, "this wasn't one of those awful ones. I mean, no one was killed. But still, it galvanized me and a bunch of other overly optimistic teens to rally for gun control. I became a bit of a public face for a while, getting interviewed by local media, et cetera. That was when things got bad." He laughed with cynicism. "You see, I thought that if I conveyed my concerns eloquently, was civil, and presented evidence, that the mature adults would accept my concerns and change the laws. But, boy, was I wrong! Very wrong."

"Something tells me you got a lot of hate from the fascists."

"That's right. It was awful. Right wingers would harass me after school, an alt right cyber-lynch mob bombarded me with hateful messages on social media, and the news pundits claimed I was brainwashed and paid by some guy named 'George Soros,'" Rudd explained, implying that he still did not know the identity of the billionaire figure. "It was hell. I felt horrible. I thought I was going to die."

"I am sorry you went through all of that," Carla said in sincerity as they crossed another street without having to wait for the signal.

"Then antifa showed up," said Rudd, his voice lifting. "They fought the harassers on campus. They doxed most of the social media trolls, leading some of them to lose their jobs. They were there, doing things, when everyone else did nothing or only offered lip service. I owe them. I owe them my efforts. We have the same enemy. A powerful enemy that is okay with people being killed. An enemy that hates life."

Carla was impressed by his story and felt even more melancholy because of it. He was so sincere, so earnest. All she could do in response was lie. Even the authentic expressions of respect and friendship were linked to falsehood. It was also apparent to her that he was interested in her, beyond a platonic friendship. Carla felt all the worse knowing that if she had not been married, the idea would have been appealing. Rudd had a lot of amiable qualities, one of which was understanding.

"This is my place," stated Carla as they stopped before the main entrance of her complex. "Thank you for keeping me company."

"It was a pleasure," he said, moving in a little more. "You know, this may seem a little abrupt, but, I have to confess ... I like you. I like you a lot. And I want to know if it would be possible—"

"No," interrupted Carla, not wanting him to continue entertaining the impossible. He was taken aback by the sudden rejection. Carla felt guilty about it and immediately went about trying to heal the wound. "It is not you. Really, it isn't. It is just, just ..." she hesitated, but again went toward deception. "I just ended a really bad relationship. A very, *very* bad relationship. It was one of the reasons I moved out here."

"I see," replied Rudd, folding his arms.

"I am not ready to get into a new one right now."

After a pause to absorb her statement, Rudd gave her an accepting smile and unfolded his arms, raising up both hands so that the palms faced Carla. He took a couple of steps back as well and nodded. "That is okay. I respect your need for space."

"Thank you."

"And when you are ready, you know where to find me."

"Yes, I do," she said, smiling. "Good night, Rudd."

"'Night, Carla."

* * *

Professor Holton Fillerhouse was still in the mood he had felt after the Charles Lewis event had concluded. He was disappointed, angry, furious, and frustrated. His dour sentiments had ebbed during the weekend, a time of emotional recovery. Most of Saturday went to grading papers and watching TV with his wife. Sunday was filled with church and social gatherings. He found solace in the amiable company.

Monday was when the anger returned. Following his morning classes, he had a meeting with the provost. He wanted accountability, and justice; none occurred, of course. Fillerhouse had invited his peer and longtime sympathizer Professor Mack Channing to the meeting as well. Yet, for the first time in their time together at Pacific Coast State University, Channing refused to attend. This added bewilderment to his list of negative feelings. His steps were practically stomps as Fillerhouse went down the hallway toward the classroom where he knew Channing would be. Under his right arm he carried a few printed out pages, stapled together to the upper left corners.

He arrived just as the last of the students exited. The final youth to leave the room thoughtfully held the door ajar until the fuming professor could hold it steady. A brief nod and the student went away. Fillerhouse beheld his colleague, seated at the desk between the door and the podium that controlled the projector. He was leaning down, looking over a few papers handed in by his departing pupils. Channing briefly looked up to see Fillerhouse, pink in the face with frustration and with fists clenched. Most would be intimidated by his thick frame. Channing remained unconcerned.

"You missed my class," Channing deadpanned. "And we had such an interesting conversation."

"Mack, where the hell were you? Why didn't you show up?"

"I had other obligations. Besides, there was no way Juana was going to cave in to your demands. And that was your problem."

"My problem?" asked an exasperated Fillerhouse, lumbering closer to the desk where Channing sat. The younger seated academic kept his eyes on the student papers.

"You spoke about free speech and free expression, about people getting to say what they believe without being censored. And that is exactly what took place last week."

"That was not free speech," declared Fillerhouse. "That was a mob. They shouted him down, censored his lecture with their boos and jeers, and then had the balls to say that Lewis was the fascist!"

"Lewis had a microphone. One could argue that was an unfair vocal advantage for his side. To say nothing of no second speaker to balance the presentation."

"Balance the presentation?" Fillerhouse struggled for a few moments to form words. "Stop treating me like one of your students! This is about more than one hostile crowd at one event. Free speech is under attack and we must defend it. Ideas need to be exchanged. And above all else, something needs to be done about this." Fillerhouse tossed the stapled papers so that they landed on the desk. The thrown document finally broke Channing's focus on his students' papers.

"A petition," said Channing matter-of-factly.

"This 'petition' is a tyranny. It is totally against reason. It calls for banning conservative speakers for the foreseeable future. This is wrong. And yet it has been circling through the faculty, staff, and student body and, worst of all, it's getting a lot of support."

"I see."

"Have you read it?"

"Of course I've read it," said Channing, maintaining his emotionless tone. "I wrote it."

Fillerhouse's eyes widened and his mouth gaped open. As it closed, he shook his head in disbelief. "Mack, what the hell? We are professors. Men of reason. And you go on and do something like this?"

"Reason," Channing deadpanned. "Reason." He put the papers on the desk and slowly rose up from his seat. "Reason. Reason." He started to laugh. "Reason." He laughed more, Fillerhouse perplexed at his colleague's behavior. "Reason." His gaze became sinister and his voice darker. "Reason." Another laugh. "Reason? Reason." Then the guttural roar. "Reason! You give me the plea of reason? This great and glorious goddess of reason!" He glared at Fillerhouse with a fury. "Get out of here. Now!"

"Mack, what the ..."

"Fine," he declared, hastily gathering his things. "*I* will leave." He stormed passed Fillerhouse, intentionally bumping into his left shoulder on the way out.

* * *

Carla and Jessie were studying at the student union. They took advantage of an empty study room, which could not be reserved by any student or student group. These facilities were designed for academic pursuit. With the door closed, they blocked out most external noises. Each one had its own marker board with markers and erasers, simple décor, and ergonomic chairs meant for long periods of sitting down. One of the few distractions was the large window along one of the walls.

Carla sat on the side of the table facing said window. It was her preference, just in case. Jessie sat with her back to the window and the closed door. Carla used the traditional tools of study: a paperback textbook, pens, and a notebook. Jessie had a small laptop with which to do her coursework. The book she was required to digest before class next week had been downloaded onto her device in digital format. She typed up notes from time to time as she scrolled through the document. She wore glasses, the small case for them placed beside the laptop.

"So, what are you studying?" asked Jessie, taking a short screen break by gently pushing her laptop to the side.

"The Sandinistas," replied Carla.

"I thought you were covering Guatemalan history for your class."

"It is radical politics in twentieth century Latin America. We finished up with Guatemala two weeks ago, we did Chile last week, and now we are on Nicaragua."

"Sounds like a cruise."

"Yeah," responded Carla with a laugh. "But I have to read about how the Sandinistas took control of Nicaragua through violent uprising, only to lose power through an election."

"They should not have held the election," stated Jessie. "If there was even the slightest chance that the far right could have taken power back, then they should have done more to stop them. Even if it means missing an election or two."

"That seems to be the argument of the author," noted Carla. "What are you studying about? Another book from that Women and Gender class?"

"Yup," said Jessie, using both hands to turn the laptop screen so Carla could read the digital text for herself. "This one is about the 'male gaze.' It's all about how our entertainment always comes from the perspective of straight white men, which helps to enshrine the various oppressions that keep them in power."

"Wait ... So, even now, when we watch TV shows and movies that are written with female main characters or even by women, they are still influenced by a white heterosexual male bias?"

"Apparently."

"So, wait," added Carla skeptically, taking the slight risk of offending a friend who saw herself as a radical feminist. "Even if the TV show, or movie or play or whatever, paints women and minorities in a positive light, it is still corrupted by a male gaze?"

"Well, I think if it is done by a person of color or a sexual minority or a female, then it is probably free from that harmful bias. It undermines patriarchy and racism."

"I might not understand it," admitted Carla, "but it almost sounds like the author is saying that white males cannot create entertainment that is beneficial to society. Like, intrinsically. If that is true, that almost sounds, well, honestly, a little bigoted."

"I know what you mean," said Jessie, being surprisingly tolerant of the critical viewpoint. "I mean, I am a woke person, I am aware of all these covert and overt oppressions, but I still enjoy Shakespeare. I have enjoyed it since I was a kid. And my play company, everyone supports rights for all and we still do Shakespeare."

"Like *Julius Caesar*, right?"

"Exactly," nodded Jessie as she turned the laptop screen back around so that it faced her. "We put some spin on his stories to make them more acceptable. A couple years ago, we did a *Taming of the Shrew* adaptation where the shrew was a man and the tamer was a woman."

"Nice."

"By the way, you bought a ticket to the show next week, right?"

"I bought two," countered Carla. "I think it will be interesting to see how different your performance is between opening night and the following day."

"Was the other ticket for the matinee showing?"

"Matinee?"

"The Saturday afternoon one."

"Oh, yes."

"Then you'll have fun, because that will be our joke performance. The one where we don't take ourselves too seriously."

"*Julius Caesar* as a comedy. That will be interesting. So, is anyone else from the group showing up?"

"A few folks. As you know, Rudd will be there. I think he likes you."

"Yeah, I know. I told him I need time."

"And he respected that, right?"

"Yes."

"Yeah, he's like that," said Jessie. "Always respects borders. It almost makes me want to bring back that the old chivalry stuff. Almost."

"Yeah," Carla agreed, amused by the remark. "Saundra's not going?"

"Saundra hates theatre," Jessie replied with a sigh. "She thinks it's a waste of time."

"Even when a portion of the ticket sales go to the cause?"

"Even then," Jessie confirmed. A buzzing noise came from her smartphone, as well as a brief pop up message in the lower right-hand corner of her laptop screen. She knew what it meant, and checked to see the new email that had arrived. Jessie was amused. "Speak of the devil and she shall appear."

"Saundra?"

"She just emailed me and a bunch of other antifa members details about tomorrow's action. You know the one at the dockyard?"

"Yes, I remember. I am carpooling with you, if I recall correctly."

Jessie scanned the message and took a deep breath. "Sure enough, they got confirmation. An alt right group will be there. Apparently, our usual barrage of online threats was not enough to sway them this time."

"Good thing I already turned in my paper."

"Good thing I have an understudy."

* * *

It took about an hour to drive from the campus area to the location of the demonstration. This was due to distance rather than traffic. They boarded their vehicles on that early Saturday morning, already in their battle gear. Each of them, regardless of gender, wore a similar uniform: hiking or military boots, cargo pants, hoodies, and bandanas of varying designs, either red or black. Everything else was some shade of black. A few brought flags and banners, either all black or all red.

Barricades had been erected by local authorities all around the dockyard demonstration. They were privy to the possibility that some hateful extremist might attempt to plow through the protesters. Those driving in for the spectacle parked blocks away. Antifa of Pacific Coast State and their allies were aware of the security measures, and had picked a spot five blocks from the protest site to gather. Saundra lacked a soapbox to help make her visible to those behind the first two or three rows of activists. However she maintained a booming voice and a commanding demeanor.

Beside her were others in the core group, including Rudd and Jessie. Carla was in the front row of standing listeners. By this point, most of them had put up their hoods and covered the lower half of their faces with bandanas. Many wore gloves as well. Saundra wore her fingerless gloves with the anarchist A symbol on each. Her red bandana was tied around her neck, her hood was down, so her thick, dark blonde dreadlocks remained visible for the time. As she spoke, she kept her right hand raised in a fist.

"Remember," she stressed. "We go as a group. No one, I mean no one, goes anywhere alone. If you end up alone at some point during this march, you will be in danger. Second, don't trust the police. They are not your friends. They will try to stop you from helping the workers. Third, we keep moving. Don't stop. If the cops block our way, move with the group to the right of them and keep going. We have to get there. If we don't show up, the workers and their allies will be helpless. Does everyone get it?"

Many, including Carla, shouted in the affirmative. Others nodded. Many were nervous; for about half of the dozens of antifa present, this was the first time they were going to encounter opposition that might actually fight back. Since moving to California for the assignment, Carla had gotten her own pair of fingerless black gloves to wear for these protests. Her hair was in a ponytail under her sweatshirt, the hood covering most of her head. A bandana tied around her face concealed her features below her eyes. Saundra ordered everyone to begin the walk toward the barricades, moving her bandana so that it concealed her face from the nose down. Jessie marched alongside Carla, and had done likewise.

"Here we go," Jessie told Carla with a nervous breath. "I'm ready."

"I believe you," Carla assured her friend.

"Good," replied Jessie. "Now I just need to believe myself."

They marched on a beautiful day, with a sunny, bright blue sky overhead, a gentle breeze, dry ground, and a mild temperature. A few perspired under their extensive coverings, but none dared to remove anything for fear of being recognized by authorities. Only a few took photos with their smartphones. This was because such efforts were frowned upon by the activists, again fearing discovery and thus exposure to hate-filled violence or state-sponsored repression. The first barricade was an easy conquest, as it was unguarded. None of the cement obstructions in their way were a challenge to walk around or even crawl over. Their purpose, which was successful, was to prevent automobiles from entry.

The first real challenge came two blocks away from the demonstration. A pair of police officers on bicycles showed up. They were patrolling the outskirts, more to alert others than to impose their will. Both officers halted their cycling on a small grassy hill to the left of the marching column. After one of them radioed in the news of the antifa presence, they both cycled down the hill and halted on the street, about thirty feet ahead of the moving column. They dismounted their bikes and turned them sideways, placing them end-to-end to make a new barrier, which complimented the cement one adjacent to them. Saundra and Rudd were at the front of the group when this happened.

"Do we push through or do we move right?" Saundra asked Rudd.

"There are only two of them," Rudd noted. "And about fifty of us."

"So we push, then."

"No, we shouldn't," Rudd thought aloud. "We can bypass them by going to the right." He pointed to the flat grassy space east of the two police. "But we'll have to be fast."

"We can be fast," said Saundra. They were twenty feet from the cyclists when she rushed a few steps ahead of the group and turned around, briefly walking backwards as she shouted instructions. "We are moving that way, to the right! Run to the right!"

The crowd obeyed and nearly in unison picked up their steps. Like a basic training company, they jogged as a group, veering past the barricade and the pair of policemen, who tried and failed to get in front of them. After several seconds of running, Saundra again turned to shout at the group to walk once more. To their relief, the cyclists did not pursue; they had realized that their efforts were futile. While the protesters expected more police to appear on their way, few showed up. A pair of pedestrian officers with a squad car parked to the side stood indifferent as the activists marched into the dock area.

There were no ships at the site; safety concerns prompted captain after captain to conclude that it was optimum to go elsewhere. Aside from a couple of police cruisers, there were no cars, as the barricades prevented new arrivals. Local inhabitants, fearing private property destruction, had moved their vehicles the day before to other parts of the city. Demonstrators rallied and marched in a large oval on the broad open graveled space usually reserved for parking and handling cargo.

Getting closer, Carla observed the demonstrators. Mostly Latino, immigrant, and working class, many had been working at the dockyard for several years. Others were the children of those who had worked there. Most of the non-Latino workers demonstrating on that Saturday morning were African-American, descended from many families who fled the South before the 1960s to escape Jim Crow. Other student activists were there as well, wearing clothing more appropriate for the weather. There was also an interfaith group. They were mostly Caucasian, about equal numbers of men and women, and included mainline Protestants, a few Catholic priests, one Orthodox clergyman, and a trio of rabbis. Their leader, a black Baptist minister, wore a suit and a stole.

Many of the dockyard protesters carried signs, chanted in English and Spanish, and had even brought young family members. Several of the clergy were among the marchers, though the Baptist leader was speaking through a microphone system. He demanded what they demanded, namely better wages, a better union plan, expanded healthcare benefits, and an end to alleged workplace harassment. From time to time, another clergyman or community leader spoke with the amplifying aid of the microphone. One of the speakers, a Latino immigrant, rallied the crowd in their native tongue.

And then *they* came. They blared loud metal music riddled with lyrics of supremacy, genocide, race war, and the Third Reich. A dozen bright red banners with white centers showcased the swastika. From there the group came into fuller view, about fifty of them chanting and shouting invectives. They ranged in age from adolescence to early forties. Some were skinny, some fat, others muscular. Many of them had shaved heads and wore black military boots, black or camouflage pants, sleeveless shirts showing muscle and nationalist tattoos. A few had even had their eyeballs tattooed to look more demonic. They raised palms and fists alike with their shouts.

Others looked disturbingly normal. Button-up collared shirts, khaki pants or slacks, hair kept short and combed to a conservative style. For every mongrel with tattooed eyes, there was a sophisticated looking fellow with a Windsor knot around his pampered, clean-shaven neck. They came from working and middle classes. Some had never finished high school, while at least two of them had doctorates. A few had lost jobs or had bank accounts hacked because of the keyboard terrorism of the antifa members, doxing their accounts or contacting their supervisors. Ignorant of the physical manifestation of their cybernetic enemies, they took to funneling their rage at a more traditional target.

Anger, hate, rage, vile. It all foamed over in their presence. As they got closer to those workers who rallied for a better future, a few policemen with body armor protecting their chests, arms, and legs moved between the two groups. The local government knew about the Saturday rally and forecasted reactions. However, they feared police brutality almost as much as a riot.. Thus, the official security for the dockyard protest was reduced to barricades and a dozen personnel. County and city authorities hoped that better angels would emerge.

Students, workers, and clergy stopped their actions and stared at the alt right mob headed their way. The microphone where clergy and civic leaders were giving protestations and demands went silent. Workers and their friends and families, along with students and other volunteers, halted their circumambulation with trepidation. Children gripped their parents' hands, asking what was happening. Who were these people who came shouting profanity and slurs, who demanded that they leave the country or die? Some wanted to run away. Adults and children alike stood unsure of their next action.

Voices on the other side offered an alliance. "We're on your side. We're going to stand up to them," said Saundra to one surprised citizen. "We're with you."

"We're here to stop them," said Rudd to a few others, echoing similar comments found from many of the masked antifa figures. By and large, their group was going along the right side of the demonstrators, but there was some overlap on their flanks.

"Estamos contigo," Carla assured several of the Latino workers. She offered encouragement. "Marcha para sus derechos. Continuate a marchar para sus derechos."

"I didn't know you spoke Spanish," Jessie said as she walked by her friend.

"I picked it up while working for a maid service," said Carla, stating a true fact of her employment background that she assumed did not compromise her cover.

Carla and the others gave the other protestors encouragement. The intimidating mystique of the vocal supremacists was wearing off. The circumambulation continued, and the declarations by the Baptist minister restarted. Several of the younger, abler students and workers joined up with the antifa protesters. They were nearing the Neo-Nazis and their peers, who by sheer numbers and audacity, rather than direct physical contact, pushed the police back. Soon the two groups halted, forming up wide lines seven to eight feet apart from each other. Policemen kept their arms out, trying to keep the two mobs separate.

"Blessed Lord Jesus, hear us in the midst of this present trial," declared the minister in supplication, the sound system projecting his voice in the background of the standoff. "Have mercy on those who look after the poor, the weak, the vulnerable, the helpless, and the stranger in our midst." Each sentence he preached was followed by a few "Amens" from his audience. "Forgive them, O Lord, please forgive the hateful men who have come here today to attack those created in Your Divine Image. Forgive, Lord, as You forgave on the cross, for they know not what they do."

"They know not what they do," repeated Carla under her breath, lips covered by a black bandana. Those few words briefly touched a nerve inside her as she surveyed the young men in front of her. The glimmer of their eyes, the fear undergirding their hateful exterior. They were so frightened. Fearful of the future, fearful of being replaced, fearful of oblivion. How probable would it have been that she would be assigned to infiltrate their ranks instead? It would be a slight challenge, as she would have to prove her racial purity. In a typical setting, she could pass for white and often did. Though their fanatical standards might make them too paranoid to believe that she was part of their so-called master race.

Yet if she did pass the entrance exam, if she found herself gathering information on them as she was doing with the antifa community, how welcoming they would be. If she went shoulder-to-shoulder, helping and socializing, attending meetings, forming friendships. Would they not see her as one of their own? They would think nothing of inviting her to their homes, their apartments, their social gatherings. Surely, she would party with them after a successful protest, or help battle it out in chat rooms and dark sites. Then they would be the ones she sympathized with, they would get her help. For a moment, she felt pity for them, sorrow at how much they had been poisoned growing up.

Carla had to shake the sympathy off, however. This was not a time for understanding. Even if it was, as someone pretending to be committed to a cause that met hate with hate and violence with violence, such emotions would be far too out of character. Besides, she soon realized that they had weapons. No guns, thankfully, but ax handles, bats, brass knuckles, and wooden planks were accounted for. One man, in his early forties with a dark goatee and mustache, shook a long gray chain with malice. Some on her side had brought similar items, minus the prized knuckles. Some had picked up one of the many hard wieldable objects from the surrounding dockyard. The arms race continued as police stood in the middle.

None of the antifa members brought their heavier artillery, the explosive cocktails or fireworks. There was concern that while driving there, someone might get pulled over and with that, the whole march would be endangered. Peaceful in their original intentions, none of the younger workers or students had brought such items, either. Not even the ones who tracked the threat of white supremacists on social media. However, one Neo-Nazi at the event, a man who could have passed for a scholar on a public television program, had brought firecrackers. He got close to the front where the two sides were kept at bay by a thin uniformed line, lit them, and then hurled them toward enemy lines.

Their explosion was felt the worst by a teenage antifa member, a freshman at Pacific Coast State University, who received minor burns and a ringing in her ears due to the blast. Still, the echo, the noise, and bright terror of the firecracker aided in the collapse of order. The supremacists saw it as the signal to push forward; angered antifa members saw it as proof that they had to fight back. The small number of police in between the two masses were overwhelmed as the two sides charged into each other like some medieval battle on the plains of Western Europe.

All was violence, even as the minister a few hundred feet behind them implored for the peace that transcends all understanding to come down and heal the land. Fists flew, legs kicked, people tackled people, and weapons were used. A Neo-Nazi and his friend beat down a young antifa activist with ax handles, while nearby a prone white nationalist was being struck several times with a wooden beam. A few were struggling for possession of one of the Swastika banners, with the antifa folk trying to steal the prize. Meanwhile, an anarchist was using the flag pole to pin down an alt righter.

Rudd overpowered one of the larger enemies, punching him several times before he cowered to the ground. Another tackled him from the side, leading the two to grapple for some time. Saundra was punched in the face and then grabbed by a young nationalist. Holding no scruples, she jammed her knee into his groin and pushed him aside. Many others were punching and pushing, grabbing hold of weapons their enemies held before they could be slammed into their bodies.

One of the police urgently called for reinforcements. Sirens in the distance were rapidly coming to the scene. Meanwhile, the struggles continued. One Neo-Nazi struck Rudd on the lips, causing him to bleed. Two other young men, both Latino, tackled the Neo-Nazi and started punching the hated figure into semi-consciousness. Through the pushing and fighting, retreating and advancing, Jessie suddenly found herself peerless. Three skinheads came toward her. She pushed off one before another pushed her with such force that she lost her footing and fell backwards onto the gravel.

Before he could act, the man next to him was taken down by Carla. The lead skinhead turned to face Carla just in time for her to strike him in the kidneys, grab his arm, and then toss him over her body, causing him to land painfully on the ground. Jessie watched as the third man who had tried to hurt her attacked Carla, only to be swiftly kicked in his stomach and then given a spinning kick to the head, knocking him out. The other two struggled to stand as Carla approached a rising Jessie. "Are you okay?"

"Getting there," she responded. Soon after she spoke, the noise of the sirens brought flashing reds and blues. A small army of armored police officers came onto the site. Both sides tried to run. Some got away, many did not.

VIII

Carla felt like a prisoner of war as she waited with many of her antifa peers in the holding cell at the police station. A grid of iron bars on three sides with a fourth side of concrete prevented her from leaving the facility. There was one bench along the concrete side, on which the worst of the injured were given to rest. That included one teenaged member who, they would later find out, had suffered a concussion when struck with a bat by an alt right protester. Saundra Jaspers leaned against the bars, nursing a headache. Others with visible wounds had been patched up during processing.

Their enemies had a roughly equal number of belligerents held captive elsewhere at the station. Many of them also had cuts and bruises, though a couple had worse injuries. One was bad enough that he was sent to a nearby hospital under guard. One of the skinheads was still in battle mode, striking at any policeman who came near. He was handcuffed during his travels through the station, occasionally spitting up blood from a bad cut he got on his upper lip received during the brawl.

Hours went by as officials came in from time to time to the holding cell area, taking antifa members one at a time to an interrogation facility. Most of them offered mild resistance to the presence of authority, struggling to express their displeasure, though avoiding the menacing brutality from the dockyard. Mostly, it was words: lambasting their captors, accusing them of totalitarianism and inhumane treatment. Some wondered if those taken would ever come back. Or if, upon coming back, they would be dragged in by uniformed men, having survived an intense bout of torture. Nerves ran amok.

None of these dark fantasies came to pass. Every activist taken to interrogation came back without physical harm. A few with wounds had been bandaged up. Those who left without scars came back without scars. When the lunch hour came, they, along with their enemies in the distant holding cell, were given sandwiches and water. Bathroom trips were allowed. The concussed youth was eventually sent off to the same hospital as the injured skinhead. As the far right extremist was heavily sedated, it was agreed to put them in the same room at the facility, albeit under police guard.

"What a waste of human flesh," stated one of the cell guards to another. They were lax, one leaning on a desk near the entrance to the hall while another sat by it. Their conversation was audible to the antifa inmates.

"Tell me about it," agreed the seated guard. "As my grandmother would have said, 'don't they have anything better to do with their lives?'"

"Exactly," said the leaning guard.

Saundra gripped two vertical bars and directed her unflinching stare upon the two policemen as she spoke. "You are complicit in state-sponsored terror. You are as guilty as the others in suppressing freedom. We will remember that."

"Oh, I'm *soo* scared," replied the guard, sarcastically. "Oh, please, have mercy on us for our many sins." He laughed. "What a joke."

"I mean, seriously," began the other guard, folding his arms as he still leaned on the desk. "What is it with these Gen Z people? There's no way we were that stupid when we were young. Of course, neither of us had to worry about that time of the month."

"Laugh all you like," she insisted. "But you cannot stop the resistance."

"Viva le France," said the sardonic one with a mocking salute, deliberately misstating the expression. He turned his attention back to his coworker. "I think they actually believe all that garbage."

"Well, if you want some more fun, go visit the Nazis on the southside holding cell."

"You know, that's an interesting idea," said the seated guard, feigning inspiration. "Maybe, between visits from the detectives, we take one of them," he said pointing at the cell full of antifa members, "and we dump them in with the Nazis. What do you think?"

"You know, that kind of sounds like fun," said the other guard, lacking any true plan to do so, but still going along as a way of messing with their jailed company. "And then we can all just leave the hall for about, say, ten minutes."

"Twenty."

"Even better!" said the leaning guard, who in his excitement rose to a fully standing posture. "We all take a break for twenty minutes and then come back."

"Oh, that would be hilarious. We'd have to bring a mop to remove all the blood."

"And seminal fluid," said the guard, crude humor generating outright laughter from himself and his coworker.

"Shut up, both of you!" declared Saundra.

"You know, I think we just got our first volunteer!" said the seated guard, still laughing.

"Definitely."

Saundra was about to shout back more valiant rhetoric, but then Rudd Yansk took her by the arm, drawing her attention away from the guffawing policemen. "Don't waste your time. You're just encouraging them."

"At least it's something to do. We've been here all day. I'm getting sick of this," Saundra complained, letting go of the bars and walking away.

"Look at it this way," assured Rudd. "I know it doesn't look that way, but we succeeded in our job. The workers got protection. Aside from a few locked in here with us, everyone else got away successfully. None of them got hurt or killed."

"There is that," she conceded.

Carla kept silent. She had talked with some of the others early on, but did not feel a need to continue conversation beyond the basic. She was a little amused by the whole situation. Of all the things she had done with her life, of all the lives terminated, facilities broken into, destruction wrought, her first arrest came because of a fist fight. Many of her peers may have seen this as the biggest struggle they had ever encountered; she ranked it much lower. Still, it was bearing on her in different ways when combined with the overall experience, the past few weeks to a month that had gone by since she began this cover.

"Let go of me, you Nazi pig!" shouted Jessie Phelier, attempting to wrestle her arms free from the dark blue uniformed policeman and the business casual detective bringing her back to the cell. "Let me go!"

The seated jailer arose from his seat, requiring no verbal cue for his mandated action. He had been doing it often since the work day began. Jessie decreased her resistance as the cell door opened and she was pushed into the small crowd. While the protestors were still wearing their hoodies, none of them concealed their faces. The shoestrings for their boots had been removed as they were processed, as were any belts. The two men who dragged Jessie back made a quick survey of who remained to be talked to. The detective, a white male in his late thirties with faded red hair, pointed at Carla.

"You're next," he stated, emotionless. Carla took a breath and offered no struggle as she walked between the two men, the jailer closing and locking the cell door as she went by.

"Don't tell them anything, Carla!" shouted Jessie. "Stay strong! Stay woke!"

As the guard returned to his seat, his buddy tapped him on the shoulder and then pointed at Jessie. "You know, maybe we should send her to the Nazi cell, instead." Both laughed at the idea as a troubled Jessie went to the bench to sit down.

Each man held an arm as they walked through the station, Carla seeing a collage of people differing in race, age, size, and side of the law. They went by cubicles where detectives followed up on leads, lawyers with clients were speaking with policemen, and suspects in other cases were led to different cells. Passing the crowds, the duo took Carla down a more solitary hallway. Their grip on her arms loosened as they took her obedience for granted. Their faith was well-founded, for Carla did not intend to attempt violent escape. The detective let go of her while the policeman kept control. He knocked on a windowless door to their right before opening the portal and bringing the supposed activist inside.

It was a small and simple room, containing a table with three chairs, none of which were occupied. The metal table held a few recorders, devices whose audio could be automatically transcribed by a computer program later on. To Carla's right were three people, dressed in button-up shirts, ties, and slacks. They each had badges on lanyards and guns in holsters. The leader of the group stood in the middle of the trio, fists leaning on the tabletop. He was about six feet tall, African-American, with short black hair and a thick mustache. He was also visibly seething.

Carla was directed to the lone chair on the side of the table opposite the three waiting authorities. The detective and the policeman remained standing behind her as she pulled back the chair and sat down, arms resting on the table. She was looking down at the gray surface, seeing from the corners of her eyes fingers pushing buttons on the recorders. The interrogation was beginning. She kept looking down at the table in silence. Then the chief slammed both fists onto the table, prompting her to look up at him.

"Now listen, you ungrateful little fanatic," he growled, his rage and frustration channeling through his words. "Now I've spent my whole Saturday having to listen to spoiled little brats like you call me a Nazi, a fascist, a tyrant, Hitler, Mussolini, Pinochet, and a bunch of other dictators, and I am absolutely tired of it. You do not understand just how *pissed off* I am right now. I am *this close* to taking you rotten children and throwing you into prison for the rest of your life!" Carla said nothing, remaining reserved. "So here's what's going to happen. You are going to start talking. And you *damn well* better say something different from the last bunch of putrid activists or I am going to throw absolutely every single *damn book* I can at you, and you'll never see the outside world again. DO YOU UNDERSTAND ME?" He did not wait for an answer, nor did she give one. "Now, with all of that out of the way, what do you have to say to me?"

Carla took a breath, decided it was the proper time, and in a monotone voice responded, "I am an undercover agent with the FBI, and I need to contact my superiors."

The man's expression instantly changed from rage to confusion. His gaping mouth and widened eyes bordered on the comical. The detective standing next to him leaned inwards and said, "Well, that *was* different."

* * *

She made her call, then she waited, in the interrogation room with the detectives, the officer who had escorted her, and the chief of the station. They were slightly rattled when the two federal government employees arrived. One was Caucasian and the other Latino, the latter having tan skin and well-combed black hair. He was shorter than his white peer and entered the room a little behind him. The local authorities all turned their attention from the suspected antifa radical to the newcomers. Carla stood up with a clear expression of relief, smiling at the duo as they entered the isolated chamber.

"Detective Michael Zambo, Federal Bureau of Investigation," the taller man stated, showing his badge to those gathered in the room. Alfredo Hernandez said nothing at the time. "And before anyone asks the question, yes, she works for me." He pointed at Carla as he spoke.

"I see," noted the chief in a much calmer tone.

"Gee whiz, Carla," stated an amused Hernandez. "I leave you alone for a few weeks and you get yourself into this mess."

"For what it's worth, Al, they attacked first," stressed Carla. "One of the Neo-Nazis threw a firecracker at us and it exploded. The blast threw everything into chaos and that was when the fighting began."

"Do you believe her?" the chief asked the duo.

"Agent Sharp has been a valuable asset in our undercover operation," noted Zambo. "I have no reason to believe she would lie."

"I am her immediate superior," chimed in Hernandez. "She is trustworthy and accurate. So I echo Detective Zambo's sentiment."

"Even if she were lying, I need her and the other antifa activists free as soon as possible. It is vital to our ongoing investigation."

"So you need them released, huh?" asked the chief.

"Yes, sir. For your troubles, the Bureau will compensate your department."

"Free federal funds, I can't argue with that," he commented. "What else do you need?"

"We would like some time alone with our agent. Some of the matters we need to discuss might be of a confidential nature."

"Understood," nodded the chief. "Let us know when you are done." The occasionally ill-tempered chief did not verbally apologize to Carla. Just before leaving the room, he turned to her, expressing remorse through a look and a nod, then left. The other local law enforcement personnel joined him outside the interrogation room, leaving only Carla, Zambo, and Hernandez. The three stood around the table.

"All right, now that we don't have an audience, what else can you tell me?"

"Tell you?"

"You have an update, right?" enquired Zambo, a raised eyebrow expressing elevated annoyance. "Some more information on this cell? What it plans to do?"

"No, not really."

"Not really?"

"I have already told you about Jessie, Saundra, and Rudd, have I not?"

"Yes. Your background information on Phelier, Jaspers, and Yansk has been very useful. Anything new on who Robespierre is?"

"Nope. Like I said before, he has a connection to the university. But again, he could be an alumnus, and giving these orders from halfway across the country."

"Or the world," added Hernandez. Zambo's withheld frustration increased.

"So, wait," began Zambo with a hand raised. "If you have nothing new, then why did you call us? Aside from wanting us to set you and the others free, of course?"

"That might have been sufficient," Hernandez said to Zambo. However, Carla was not going to allow that explanation to stand alone. She felt obligated.

"No, I did not just call you to get me sprung from jail," she said, taking a breath before continuing. "I want out." She paused, her dumbfounded audience waiting for more. Carla granted their tacit request. "I hate this. I hate being away from family for so long, being unable to call my husband, my grandfather. My friends. I ... I am struggling to keep it together. I am forming friendships with some of the antifa people. I feel like I am wrongly hurting them, because I know my friendship is based on a lie. And the idea that I am stuck doing this until I find something ... I can barely stand the thought. So I am asking, I am begging, I am *demanding* that you pull me out."

Zambo shook his head. He was skeptical of her distress. "Hold on, Agent Sharp. You just finished spending over a month undercover in Latin America."

"Exactly!" she struck back. "I just spent over a month overseas. And I thought I was going to have a few weeks at home with family. Furthermore, when I was abroad, I regularly talked with my giddo. There was no restriction."

"Listen, Sharp, I explained before—"

"I know, I know," Carla interrupted. "I understand why I cannot talk to them. But it is still the same end result. And I hate this end result. I want out."

"Carla," replied an increasingly desperate Zambo. "You have to keep at this. I just know there is something grander at work. Something far more sinister than shouting down some rightwing pundit, or playing fisticuffs with bigots. I need you to stay embedded with them. I just know you will find the proof I need to get the Bureau's notice. If you leave this, I lose my chance of stopping whatever they're planning."

"How long must I do this?" she demanded. "How long until you are convinced that there is nothing here but a bunch of small time activists?"

Zambo was about to respond, intending the growingly heated exchange, yet Hernandez cut him off. "One more week." Carla and Zambo turned to face their diminutive associate. Hernandez looked at Carla. "You stay undercover for another seven days and if you find no proof of a grand conspiracy, then Michael here will be the one who personally drives you to the airport." Hernandez turns to Zambo. "Right, Michael?"

Zambo grudgingly nodded.

"Carla?" asked Hernandez, focusing on the undercover agent. She was silent, discerning much with each inhale and exhale. She looked down at the table, speedily going through the positives and negatives of the offer. They were patient, trying to let her decide without any more pressure. She bent her right index finger and tapped the digit a few times on the tabletop.

"One more week," she said. "One more week and if I find nothing, no evidence of stolen explosives and guns, I get to go home?"

"Yes, one more week," said Hernandez, who smiled as he added, "and you will get home in time for Thanksgiving."

Carla paused. She thought a few seconds more. Then she slowly lifted her head to face the two federal government figures before her. "Okay. Okay, I can do one more week. Knowing that's it, that should get me through it."

"Excellent!" declared Hernandez with a big smile.

"Thank you, Carla," said a relieved Zambo. "For a moment, I thought I was going to have to pull rank or something."

"Pull rank on a wet boy?" she asked.

"She's got a point there," added Hernandez, playfully jabbing his friend with his elbow.

"Now then," concluded Zambo. "Let's get you and your friends out of jail."

* * *

Carla was starting to figure it out. She had suspicions going back to two hours previously, when Hernandez showed up on campus. He rolled down his car window, engine still running, and told her to get in. He offered no clear answers. Only talk about a "reunión importante" that they had to have eighty miles north of the university. She explained that doing so would cause her to miss an afternoon class; he responded with a gentle reminder about her not technically being a student.

The journey was at times beautiful. They took the route along the coast, with the Pacific Ocean in view from the heights. They stopped twice, once for a bathroom break for Carla and again for an early dinner. Other times, the journey was arduous. A rare thunderstorm touched down two-thirds of the way there. It was a relief for the drought-fearing locals, but a burden for Carla and Hernandez, slowing down the traffic. Carla clocked an extra thirty minutes tacked on to the nonspecific little adventure.

The sun was dipping low when they finally reached the city and one of its hotels. As they parked, she was all the more certain about the real purpose of the meeting. She had suspected it from the onset, an inevitable hopeful entertaining of a longshot idea. She kept ruling it out, not wanting to let herself down when it was revealed to be business. Hernandez rarely talked during this final part in the journey. This alone made Carla figure that he was trying to give her an unexpected surprise.

"Come on, Al, I think I know what this is really about," she said, smiling. The two were walking down an elegant hotel hallway on the third floor. The carpeting below them had ornate designs of gold, silver, purple, sapphire, and scarlet. The walls were painted white, with pillars carved into the woodwork. Colonial-style dentil molding lined the juncture of walls and ceiling. Each door was a pristinely polished wooden barrier with a five-inch tall golden number on the upper half.

"Do you?" asked a skeptical Hernandez.

"I am pretty sure I know who I am meeting here."

"I bet you do."

"You might as well tell me."

"And spoil the surprise?" joked Hernandez as the two stopped before an unopened door. While still smiling at Carla, he knocked on the door. "You want to take a last-minute guess?"

"No," said Carla. "But I will say that I appreciate it a lot."

"No problem," said Hernandez, taking a couple of steps back as the door opened to reveal Josiah Sharp. Her unspoken theory was revealed to be true. Husband and wife reunited, their happiness growing. Josiah moved across the threshold to embrace Carla, who in turn had moved toward the threshold to receive him. Their focus was interrupted only briefly by Hernandez. "I'll be downstairs enjoying a cancer-stick or two, if you need me. Just remember, though, that you need to be back later tonight."

"Of course," said Carla. "Thanks, Al." Hernandez simply smiled and waved before going back down the hallway.

"Did Alfredo really fly you out here just to make me feel better?" asked Carla as the two entered the hotel room, Josiah closing the door behind them.

"If only," replied Josiah as the two made their way to the king-sized bed at the center of the main room. "I'm in town for a governors' convention being held at the Jerry Brown Coliseum. Not to brag," he said, jokingly brushing invisible lint off of his shoulder, "but I am the keynote speaker."

"Really?" asked Carla in genuine amazement.

"Well, one of the keynote speakers. Specifically, for the first day."

"I see," nodded Carla. "Still impressive."

"I guess that happens when you are one of the youngest governor-elects in history. They want me to take the center stage."

"Do you have a speech ready?" she asked as the two sat down on the bed.

"Obviously," he said with a smile. "It's uploaded to the teleprompter and everything."

"I am happy for you," she said, looking down before continuing. "Isn't it a little early for the convention?"

"You remember my cousin Bobby and his family from the wedding?"

She nodded.

"They live out here. I thought I would pay them a visit before the convention starts."

"I see," she said, again looking down. "Like I said, I am happy for you. For everything. This, you winning the election. I was thrilled when I saw the news that you won."

"I missed you."

She smiled, looking down again. "Same here."

"I am not going to complain about your job tonight. Hernandez assured me that that was the last thing you needed."

"Good. After all, there is no point in complaining about something that cannot be changed."

"At least, not changed for the time being."

"Josiah," she said with some anger.

He backed off, physically and verbally. "Sorry, sorry. Bad habit." He drew close again, the two eventually holding each other. "So, what do you want to do?"

"Things I cannot do when I am undercover," she said. Josiah did not answer with words, but actions. The two grew ever closer, slowly kissing a few times before gently descending to the mattress. Carla's back was on the top cover while Josiah was above her. Moments of intimacy, genuine sentiments, flowed within her. For the first time in what seemed a great expanse of lost weeks, she fostered fully honest relations. Yet, even then, there was a sense of restriction, of limits. "I can only go so far tonight. I have to be back soon. I have to do more research, then talk to Zambo."

"I understand," said Josiah. He kissed her yet again. "We can save such a celebration for when you are finally done."

"Yeah," she smiled, moving her fingers along his cheeks. "Sounds good to me."

"So," said Josiah, as he remained over her in an intimate embrace. "What else do you want to do before you have to return?"

"Watch TV," she admitted. She smiled nervously as the banal request, then laughed in embarrassment. "I know that must sound really awful, but they never gave me one for my apartment. I think I have withdrawal symptoms."

"I get it, I get it," he said with some laughter of his own. "Then we can watch some TV. I'll get the remote and the guide." Josiah got up from the bed while she scooted back to where the pillows were. She finally took off her shoes to get more comfortable. Josiah soon joined her on the bed, sitting beside her, an arm over her shoulders as they cuddled before the high definition screen.

Their chatter became idle, minor, topically insignificant. Through the guide they got halfway into a cheesy action film. It was so over-the-top as to be unintentionally humorous. It all felt better. Carla was relaxed, amused, and at ease. For a time, she even let her consciousness abandon her obligations. The burden was temporarily lifted for the next three segments of the commercial-laden program. Then her phone buzzed. Taking a look at the small screen, she saw the text message from her superior. It hurt to know that duty was returning. So with a healed yet burdened heart, she said good-bye to her husband once again and returned to an apocryphal existence.

* * *

Jessie Phelier did not require an understudy. Despite the tumult of last Saturday, by Wednesday's full-dress rehearsal she was in professional form. Opening night, a Thursday evening in which many students lacking a Friday class attended, she remembered all her lines and all the proper stage cues. The same was said of the overall ensemble, many of whom saw theatre as their political expression. And so it was that *Julius Caesar* was performed for an intrigued audience.

Phelier's play company had put their own spin on the production. For time reasons, they chopped out several scenes and some of the windier monologues.

Due to numerical constraints, some minor characters were removed. The setting for their rendition was a high-end resort in Florida. Each of the major characters wore fashions reflecting the rich playboy class, with khaki shorts, collared shirts, fancy shades, and polo jackets abounding. Rome was a company rather than an empire, with Caesar an aggressive CEO about to be betrayed by the other members of the board of directors.

"Pardon, Caesar, Caesar, pardon," spoke Jessie as Cassius. They kept the original dialogue for the sake of art. "As low as to thy foot doth Cassius fall, to beg enfranchisement for Publius Caesar." Stage makeup outlined her eyes and lips; extra touches of blush and contour had been given to her cheeks. All makeup had been applied to prevent her face from looking featureless due to the flood lights hanging behind the audience, aimed directly at the actors.

"I could be well moved if I were as you," replied the actor portraying Caesar. He wore a bowtie and had a sweater with its arms loosely tied around his neck. "If I could pray to move, prayers would move me. But I am constant as the Northern Star."

Carla and Rudd Yansk were in the audience. He drove her to the performance, assuring her that this was simply a friendly get-together and not a date. Unless, of course, she wanted it to be a date. She accepted the ambivalent version of the gathering. They met a few others from the antifa chapter before the beginning of Act I. The space was not a formal one; specifically, it was a rented box theatre, lacking fixed chairs or workable curtains. The production had to set up the seats and some drapery before opening the doors. Fewer than a hundred showed up, but that was expected. With ticket prices and local businesses paying for ad space in the playbill, the production still turned a profit.

"Hence! Wilt thou lift up Olympus?" asked Caesar.

"We're nearing the fun part," whispered Rudd to Carla. She smiled and faintly nodded to confirm that she received the message.

A few lines later and the theatrical knives were drawn by the players. Each blade was raised high, then brought down upon Caesar. Each stab involved the supposed blade actually retracting into the handle when pushed against the victim. There was cheering in the audience as the tyrant was felled, a reflection of the cultural climate of the viewers. Carla and Rudd cheered with them as the wounded Caesar gave his final remarks, including the famous "Et Tu, Brute?" before finally falling downstage center. The actor rolled onto his side so he could breathe with impunity as the scene continued. It also prevented the audience from seeing him getting the fake blood ready for the other performers.

"Some to the common pulpits," declared Jessie in character, holding up her blade as she looked directly at the darkened audience. "And cry out: 'Liberty, freedom, enfranchisement!'" The crowd humored her, and chanted as directed, contributing their little bit to the performance like a sports crowd cheering on the home team.

"She's really good at this," whispered Carla to Rudd.

He nodded. "I know. She once told me that it's very easy for her to pretend to be someone else. That's why she's so good."

"Yeah."

Carla was enjoying herself at the play. She felt a sense of comfort comparable to that felt earlier in the week when she saw her husband. It was not an adulterous sentiment; her heart was not shifting away from Josiah and toward Rudd. Nevertheless, she felt a communal, fraternal affection. Once again, she was part of the tribe. They accepted her even without fully knowing where she came from. They were a ragtag collection of do-gooders seeking to rid the world of tyranny, like Brutus and Cassius as seen on the stage. They gathered around the fallen Caesar in their triumph.

"Stoop, Romans, stoop," commanded Brutus. "And let us bathe our hands in Caesar's blood. Up to the elbows and besmear our swords."

"Jessie told me this was going to be the gory part," Rudd quietly spoke to Carla, who nodded with a smile. Both kept their gaze upon the actors, doing as the Brutus character so ordered. By the time they knelt down, the actor playing the fallen Caesar had set forth a small dish with fake blood for the other three actors on stage to dip their hands and arms in. They simulated the motion of washing their hands, lathering themselves with the substance, its composition including corn syrup and red coloring.

Portraying Cassius, Jessie arose from the fallen Caesar. Both of her hands were drenched in the red liquid, as well as parts of her arms. She had them raised in a posture similar to surrendering with hands-up. Her eyes stared forward, their glance of menace looking not far from where Carla and Rudd were seated in the dark. Unflinching and unafraid, she gave a sinister smile and delivered her ominous lines. "How many ages hence shall this our lofty scene be acted over, in states unborn and accents yet unknown."

Then the comfort of community vanished. Carla again felt disconnected. She was reminded, through the lines of an Elizabethan era play, of what she was doing and what she was seeking to discover. In the darkness, she saw a whole host of young people who thought nothing of cheering the brutal murder of another due to political differences. Most of them cheered when learning that fellow human beings were sent to the hospital because of their protests. They celebrated anarchy, revolution, beheading the reactionaries, censoring the dissenters, and painfully moving society forward.

A performance, an act, and yet, Carla knew that Jessie had put herself into that statement, channeling her own drive for radicalism into the character of that ancient assassin. A fantasy openly entertained; theatre was the means for them to honor that which, in polite society, would garner repulsion. If ever called to account, they could always back away and simply state that it was only a play. It was only escapism. Nothing more. Carla knew better. She knew who these people were, and had a grim idea of what they would do to her if they ever found her out. And all the while, they would chant "Revolution," "Liberty," and "Equality."

And yet, as the play continued, the scenes changed, and the characters started getting killed off, one then another, she lacked anything concrete. As the play ended, she applauded like the others. The show had been entertaining overall. The interpretation was a strong one, even if jarring in that one moment. Carla kept up her façade, congratulating Jessie when they all hung out following the curtain call. There was still nothing actionable, no evidence that they were doing anything near to their aspirations. They were violent, they were active, and they were hostile. Yet unlike the revolutionary courts they dreamt of applying to their fascist enemies, they remained innocent until proven guilty.

* * *

Carla got home around 10:00 PM. She had caught up with Jessie after her second performance and they had dinner, along with a few mutual friends and acquaintances. Saundra was not among them. She had made herself scarce since Saturday, when they were all arrested. This was expected, as Saundra had specifically encouraged the various activists to lay low for a time. Earlier in the week, when Carla made a small grocery shopping trip, she had briefly encountered the activist leader. She spotted her dirty blonde dreadlocks across the produce aisle. They only had brief conversation. It seemed like Saundra was unusually reserved, though maybe that had to do with staying low.

Carla entered a dark apartment. She had gotten accustomed to going to her left and finding the light. Turning it on, she saw her lack of concern confirmed by the absence of vile creatures. She then went back to the open door and shut it, removing the light from the hallway. Taking her shoes off and laying them beside the entrance, she yawned as she walked across the living room to the attached kitchen. She opened the refrigerator door to look for juice or soda to drink that night.

There were not many items in the fridge. When living alone at an apartment, Carla normally kept a moderately-filled refrigerator. The operation complicated things. What's more, her cover as a college student led her to create a more believable atmosphere. Suspicion could fall on her if she had plenty of food in stock. One of the few things in there was a glass jar of tomato sauce. Elsewhere in her kitchen, she had virgin olive oil, salt, and some uncooked spaghetti. There was also some garlic bread stored in her small freezer. She planned to cook it all for her last evening.

She drank a few swigs from the soda before she went to her laptop, charging on the floor in the corner of the living room. Unplugging it, she took it to the couch, where she lifted the screen and turned on the device. She watched a few entertaining viral videos before she got a message from her Bureau superior. Carla had mixed emotions about answering the communication from Zambo. She was relieved that yet another day had gone by without incident, but she loathed having to bring him more bad news. She clicked on the icon. A new window appeared, showing Zambo from the shoulders up.

"Tell me you have something."

Carla paused, looking down before answering. "Sorry."

"Damn it," said Zambo to himself. He shook his head before responding. "You mean they haven't told you anything? Any new plots? *Anything?*"

"Well, there is some talk about us revisiting the dockyard. The workers there are going to stage another demonstration and they want us to serve as security."

"Nothing new about Robespierre? No clues about his identity?"

"None."

"Agent Sharp," began Zambo, who paused as he tried to collect his phrasing. "This is, um, a hard thing for me to ask. I have to ask, though. Please do not take offense. But I wonder. Are you trying hard enough to find more information?"

"I am trying," she assured him, suppressing her annoyance. "I have talked with many of them. Especially Jessie and Rudd. I keep asking what is next, what is coming. But all they tell me are possible protests, possible demonstrations. Nothing terrorist, or genocidal, or anything like that. Just the usual local activism."

"Have you been keeping track of social media? Maybe something has come up on the chat rooms or closed groups."

"I check and I double check," she said firmly. "Also, I have encouraged Jessie to tell me about anything coming up. Again, there is nothing happening that local law enforcement could not handle. I am sorry, but I cannot find anything."

Zambo appeared to mouth some profanity before he spoke again. "Well, all right. Keep looking tomorrow. Keep talking to people. Do everything you can to find something that links the stolen munitions, this Robespierre fellow, and any possible threats to national security. I just know there is something coming up."

"I will do what I can. Just like I have been doing."

"Thank you," said Zambo, sounding exhausted. "I will call you around eleven tomorrow night. If you find nothing, then I guess I have to drive to your place and get you home."

"Yes, that was our agreement."

"Okay," sighed Zambo. "Good night." He ended his call before she could reciprocate the valediction.

Despite drinking a caffeinated soda, Carla was tired by the arrival of the eleven o'clock hour. It had been a long day. Spending hours researching the antifa chapter she had infiltrated to find evidence of the conspiracy Zambo held in his mind, spending considerable time on campus to at least appear to study for classes, seeing members of the antifa chapter and socializing without giving away her real identity. All this bore heavily upon her energy supply. She made her preparations for bed quickly, brushing teeth, shutting down the laptop, turning off the lights, double-checking the lock, prayers, and then to sleep.

She saw Tiffany. Her friend from the Cicero Organization. The last time she saw her, she was murdered in front of her. Carla's mind showed the face, the opened eyes betraying a last moment shock. The bullet hole in her forehead, the blood flooding behind her head where the projectile had escaped. Her dead eyes looked. Then they became the eyes of Jessie. She was there. Bullet hole in her forehead, blood escaping. She was alive, or so acted that way. Disappointment, fear, sadness, and other cruel emotions displayed before.

Then to Tiffany. A moment smiling, another moment confused, and then again with the bullet to the brain. The gory scene switched back to Jessie. She was just standing there, frightened at the sight of Carla. Carla found herself holding a handgun toward her. The finger was pressing on the trigger. Carla was shaking her head, she was trying to stop it. She could not. Again the gun shots. No sound, no blast, but the holes emerged. Jessie was crying, crying for Carla to stop. Carla failed to. She kept firing. Again there was Tiffany. Again the staring corpse of her former friend. A noise. A screeching buzzing noise. Carla did not know what it was at first. It flooded her mind.

Then she realized it was the buzzer for her apartment, and fully regained consciousness. The buzzing continued for another second, then stopped. Carla looked up at the plain ceiling in the dark room. Then the buzzer sounded again. She was fully awake by then, and knew it not to be a mental fabrication. Carla threw aside her blankets and put her pants on. She unlocked her bedroom door and walked to the answering system attached to the wall in the living room. The buzzer sounded a third time for a few seconds before she reached the system panel and pushed a button so she could answer.

"Who is it?" asked Carla, letting go of the button so she could hear an answer.

"It's Jessie."

"Okay, I will buzz you in," said Carla, pushing another button that unlocked the front door. Carla was more confused than worried that Jessie was visiting her at such a late hour. She turned on a lamp so she could better navigate the living room. She yawned as she headed for the apartment door, knowing that Jessie would be there soon.

Just as she was nearing the door, she heard a few knocks. She looked through the peep hole to see that it was Jessie, who had rushed up the stairs. Carla unbolted the lock, turned the knob, and swung open the door. There was Jessie with a smile. She was in no way threatening, though because she was wearing boots and Carla was still barefoot, she appeared taller.

"Jessie, this is a surprise," said Carla. "Come on in."

"No, I didn't come here to hang out," she said with excitement. "Get ready, and let's go. We're heading out."

"Oh? Out where?"

"To see him. To see Robespierre," she said, and with glee added, "you finally get to meet Robespierre. So come on, hurry up, and get ready. He hates to wait."

IX

"Wake up," said Jessie Phelier. She was driving Carla to the abandoned church building, the same edifice where the antifa chapter held many of its meetings. "We're almost there."

"I wasn't asleep," insisted Carla. "Just resting my eyes." She had been leaning drowsily toward the passenger door as Jessie operated the vehicle. She grew more awake as they pulled up to the darkened structure, parking across the vacant street. Were it not for the street lights and some stars, the block would be a void.

Jessie put the automobile in park and turned off the engine, followed by the lights. The two got out of the vehicle and walked quietly toward the former church. The hour was late enough that the calendar date had changed. It was the final day that Carla was scheduled to be undercover—unless she could find a tangible lead. Jessie walked a step ahead of her, still exuding excitement.

"This is a big honor," Jessie explained. "Robespierre doesn't let just anyone meet him in person. He doesn't like to bring in anyone except those who are most committed to the movement. You should be proud."

"I will try to beam with pride," said Carla. Jessie smiled, amused by her friend's quip. The church door was unlocked. Jessie held it open for Carla, who thanked her as she walked into the former narthex. Having been there multiple times for antifa meetings, Carla began to curve toward the sanctuary.

"No, Carla, not there," clarified Jessie. Carla stopped and turned to face Jessie, who kept walking forward, toward the opposite end of the narthex. "Robespierre prefers to have the first encounter under the surface." Carla nodded and followed her friend to the other end of the space. Nearby was a wooden door that led to the cellar. Jessie took an old-fashioned key, about five inches long, from her hip pocket. She jostled the instrument into the elderly lock and with a jolt, opened the portal to the basement.

"That was loud."

"It is meant to be that way. Robespierre likes to know when people are coming."

"I see."

Jessie led the way down a flight of creaking wooden stairs. The course was poorly lit, but thankfully had two railings to give the traveler a safe descent. Soon Carla was on solid ground, a cold bare floor that flooded in heavy rainfall. Like the worship space above, the cellar had a vaulted ceiling and places for candles to be lit. No windows, though. At the very end of the cellar, there were several artificial lights placed on boxes. These lights colored the background for a few shadowy persons.

While looking around the space, Carla saw a curious if not alarming sight. Several crates were stacked upon one another. There were no markings on them, nothing to specify what they held—yet, to Carla, they seemed all too familiar. She remembered the weapons facilities that the Cicero Organization oversaw. While that part of their operation was outside of her former purview, she had still visited a few sites. A better examination would have been beneficial, but she did not want to appear to be staring.

They got closer to the lit side of the cellar, where there were four people present. First was a young man she knew only as Nick. He had a short beard and acne. They had socialized a few times, though they were barely acquaintances. Second was Rudd Yansk. He gave her a smile and a nod at her arrival. And then there was Saundra Jaspers. She gave Carla an acknowledgement, but more stoically so. Carla was a little surprised to see that she now had a shaved head, as though she had gone into basic training. At the end of the room, a few feet from the wall, was a man whose back was to the others. He was wearing casual clothing and slowly lifted his head as he heard the two new people come closer. At Jessie's silent command, she and Carla both stopped within a few yards of the man.

"Robespierre," began Jessie. "I brought Carla, just as you asked."

The man nodded and then slowly turned around. Carla saw that he was under forty but over thirty-five, fairly slim, with a youthful sparkle in his eyes. Far from having a monstrous appearance, he seemed approachable and fairly handsome. He was about six feet tall, though a little shorter than Rudd. He appeared fit and seemed familiar to Carla. She was not immediately certain of where she had seen him before. Her recent memory was still fathoming the mildly lit face before her. All the while, he got closer.

"A pleasure to finally meet you, Carla Wexler." He offered his hand. She shook it. "You are trying to figure out where you have seen me before, right?"

"Yes," she admitted.

"You are a student at Pacific Coast State University, are you not?"

"I am, yes."

"I am a professor there. A lofty, meaningless title, but one I bear." He got a few steps closer. "Soon, there will come a time when such titles are no more." He smiled. "I wanted to thank you for all your hard work. I have been told by those around us that you have excelled in fighting for the revolution."

"I try to do my best, Robespierre."

"And I very grateful," said the man with a lustful smile. He turned to the others. "Leave us. I would like to talk to Carla alone."

The three consented to leaving. "I'll wait upstairs for you so that I can drive you home," stated Jessie on her way out.

"Thank you," replied Carla, turning her back to the man so she could wave at her friend. When she faced the front once more, she noticed that Robespierre was a little closer.

"I need to examine you."

"Excuse me?"

"Nothing depraved, just a look over you. I want to know what I can find out about you that might explain how you became you."

"Um, okay," replied an uneasy Carla. He got closer while she remained still, almost at attention. He was drawing nigh, stopping when he was a few inches away. Carla tried to look forward, almost through him. She was not quite sure what was going to happen. She was not particularly frightened for her life. It appeared he was unarmed. What's more, she had taken down enemies larger and more muscular than the man before her. Gently, he took hold of her left hand. He raised up the arm with both hands, staring at her digits. He studied them in silence for a few moments.

"There is an imprint on the wedding ring finger."

"I was engaged."

"Was?"

"Yes."

"I see," observed Robespierre, speaking like a doctor analyzing a patient. "Rudd mentioned you having a sour relationship in your recent history." He let go of the hand, which Carla returned to her side. He looked deeper into her face. His proximity was past her preferred comfort zone. She resisted the urge to push him away, not sure of what might happen in response. Then he discovered something, something that led him to draw away a few inches. Instead, his fingers slowly ascended and then glided along the barely visible scar that went from her forehead down to the corner of her eye. "This is no wrinkle. This is a scar. It was deep when it was first struck."

"And that is why I left him," she stated, cold and implacable.

"Ah, I see," he replied. He frowned. "A horrible thing to do to a woman. A scoundrel would not appreciate such beauty. Such intense, carnal, beauty. So, so attractive." His fingers were gliding along her face. She was being caressed by the stranger. Each pet seemed like he felt more orgasmic. She could not take it. Forsaking any fear of backlash, as he was about to caress her a third time, she grabbed his wrist and stopped him, holding his hand away from her face, with obvious anger.

At first he was shocked by the sudden defense. Yet he offered no resistance to the rejection, but merely laughed. It was a happy laugh though, masking any sign of nervousness. The gripped hand waved a little, as to imply that he would halt his touching. Carla cautiously let go and was relieved to see him take a couple of steps back. He held his gripped wrist, not so much from pain but to get a feel for the moment of resistance from the otherwise obedient activist. He then took one step forward.

"Tell me, Carla," he asked. "Do you believe in God?"

"Yes."

"Religion is the opiate of the masses. God is dead. If there were no god, it would be necessary to invent him. Religion is an illusion without much of a future."

"Are you trying to convert me?"

"Hardly," he assured. "With all the respect in the world for my fellow revolutionaries, I believe there must be some divine being out there. Life is too intricate a joke to not have been crafted by a great comedian." He began to pace in front of Carla, who remained still. "I mention these various words of these various intellectuals to make a point. You see, Marx, Nietzsche, Voltaire, and Freud had the right idea when they uttered their little phrases. They knew that

139

an important abstract concept was untrue. However, they were a little off. They had the right critiques, but the wrong target."

"What is the correct target, then?"

"*Reason*," he said with guttural rage. "Reason. Reason is the enemy. Reason is the opiate of the people. Reason is something that if nonexistent, would be necessary to invent. Reason does not have much of a future, because with your help and my vision, reason will soon be dead." Carla was perplexed but interested in his words. "I know you probably thought that joining this movement meant destroying Nazis. It does, but I want more. We cannot simply treat symptoms when we can cure the disease."

"The disease is reason," Carla flatly stated.

"Yes, yes, you learn quickly," he nodded with excitement. "Reason is a disease. It is a tool of oppression. Weak elites use this idea to control the people, to manipulate and deceive the lower classes, to foster division and warfare, torment and conformity. Reason is what keeps all these oppressors and patriarchs in control of society. We cannot legislate them out of this, because the delusion of reason exceeds the power of the political. We will do something beyond the body politic. And it will happen soon."

"What will we do? What must I do?"

"I will answer all of your questions tomorrow evening," he assured her. "Only know that come Monday, reason will be doomed."

"Yes, Robespierre."

"You may go now. Go and sleep, with the joy of knowing that you will help usher in a new age of human history. You will help destroy the era of reason and bring forth the era of revolution!"

* * *

"I knew it, I knew it, I knew it, I knew it," rambled Detective Michael Zambo in exuberance. "I knew there was something going on and I was right!"

Zambo, Carla, and Alfredo Hernandez occupied a simple meeting room at the San Francisco field office of the Federal Bureau of Investigation. Hernandez had driven all the way down to Carla's apartment near the campus to pick her up. Carla and her superior from the Agency sat down at a well-polished table in plush office chairs watching their excited companion react to the news she had given him. Neither of the two seated figures quite knew how to grasp the sudden development.

140

"Now, before you get too overwhelmed with joy, good buddy," interjected Hernandez, prompting Zambo to stop his celebratory moving about and focus on his friend, "what Carla found was not definitive."

"True," he conceded, "but it was far more than nothing." He looked at her, an outstretched hand prompting her as he spoke. "Tell him, Carla; tell him again about the crates you found stocked in the basement."

"Well, as I said, they looked like the kind of packaging for weapons. I cannot say with absolute confidence that is what they were, but I can say they looked suspicious."

"You do not know for sure," pointed out Hernandez.

"I feared that if I looked at them too long, they would start to wonder why I was so interested in them."

"No markings?"

"None that I saw, but that does not mean they did not remove them somehow."

"Which is my point, Alfredo," Zambo explained, preventing Carla from answering further. "And the mysterious figure and his dooms-date intrigue me."

"It took me a little bit to figure out who it was, but after checking all the profiles on the university website, I could tell that Robespierre is Mack Channing, a professor."

"A mad professor, at that," declared Zambo, whose animated behavior was starting to remind Hernandez of himself. "And Monday is the day he strikes."

"But where?"

"I assume the governor's convention," explained Carla. "It begins on Monday, after all. And there are no other major events scheduled in the state on that day."

"So, unless they're going to attack Vegas, we should be keen on the convention," observed Zambo, finally beginning to contain his excitement. "Better yet, I can now bring something of substance to my superiors at Quantico, and they can give me more resources. Like keeping an eye on Channing. Where he goes, what he does. Also, I can have the tech team see what they can find out about his search engine history, possibly hack his emails ... You know monitor his cyber-life."

"All legal, of course," said Hernandez.

"More legal than the stuff you do for the Agency," quipped Zambo, getting a wry smile from his acquaintance.

"Do you still need me to be undercover?" asked Carla.

"I would very much prefer it," said Zambo, who turned his gaze to Alfredo as though looking for him to break a tie vote. "What do you think?"

"I defer to Carla," he said. Both men turned to face the undercover agent. She was still in the garb expected of her character, wearing black cargo pants and boots, with a gothic band T-shirt. Pondering, weighing options, she thought about it. Looking down at the table, she slowly nodded her head in the affirmative.

"Yes," she said, raising her face to behold Hernandez and Zambo. "Yes, I can do this for another few days. Besides, I am scheduled to meet Robespierre— that is to say, Channing—late this evening. He should give more information."

"Excellent!" said both men in unplanned unison.

"Then I should get you back to your place, tan pronto como posible."

"Yes," she agreed.

"Well, if there is nothing else you need to disclose, then I will get on the line to Quantico and let them know about this breakthrough," said Zambo. As he neared the door, he stopped and added, "Still very excited!" before leaving.

"Usually, I'm the enthusiastic one," observed Hernandez, Carla in agreement. "I'm not that annoying when I get excited, am I?"

"No, not at all."

"Oh, Carla, you are just trying to make me feel better."

"Maybe."

* * *

Jessie Phelier and Saundra Jaspers shared the longer couch in the living room of the apartment at the terraced building, while Rudd Yansk had the shorter couch to himself. This was typical. Each was buried in a laptop, occasionally shifting their seated positons so as to alleviate the stress of sitting down for so long while doing their online activism. A trio of keyboard warriors, their present efforts were geared toward research. Halfway across the country, a Neo-Nazi group had held a rally that included marching through a mostly Jewish neighborhood. Photos and videos of the daytime march were all over the internet.

"Have you gotten any hits?" Saundra asked Rudd, her eyes not leaving her screen.

"Nothing of value," answered Rudd. "Some folks are posting comments about how awful those people are, but no one seems to know who they are."

"Well, keep searching social media. Someone has to know those guys."

"Yes, Saundra."

"Jessie," said the de facto leader to her peer. The bespectacled Jessie looked up in curiosity. "It would help if you could get us more information on the people involved in the rally."

"You know I'm working on it, Saundra. They must have some smart tech people in their ranks, because the last few accounts I thought I could access were all encrypted. Like high quality encryption. An army of bots couldn't break those codes."

"Well, keep looking for a weak spot. They can't all be that careful."

"Yeah, I know."

For the next several minutes, there was a general quiet. Each activist was doing their part by posting photos to chat rooms and social media, asking people to identify the marchers. Video links and screen grabs alike were used for the effort. Searches were conducted about the event, with strenuous exploration for any proper names of those involved. They examined profiles when it looked possible that they had a lead. Eye strain ensued as they stared at the digital images, comparing marcher with suspect. None of them wanted to ruin the reputation of someone who just happened to look like a Neo-Nazi.

The leaders they knew; it was the foot soldiers they were trying to oust. Those figureheads at the helm of the small column were able to support themselves with their hate literature and nasty broadcasts. Their well-being would be unaffected by being outed. It was the others, those who worked for more enlightened bosses or did business with socially conscious enterprises, who were the best targets. Leaders were impotent if they had a following unwilling to participate over fear of exposure.

Jessie spoke up. "I think I have something." The other two looked away from their laptops, directing their attention to their ally. "Someone uploaded another video of the march. This time, it looks like it's a sympathizer." She continued to type away, trying to dig deeper as she engaged in conversation with the others.

"And what of this sympathizer?" Saundra asked.

"He might be connected to the group that did the march."

"Or he might just be another bigot."

"Yeah," admitted Jessie. "Checking his profile now." The person who had uploaded the video did not give his real name, but that did not matter. Through the power of her technological savvy, Jessie was able to locate an email address. From there, she got into his lightly defended account. She grinned as the information poured in. "Well, he's probably not in the group, but he definitely knows them."

"Really?" asked an impressed Saundra.

"He sent a fan letter to some of them, and they responded. Let me shoot you an email with the names he drops."

"Sounds good."

"Gals, someone on my end might recognize one of the Neo-Nazis," noted Rudd. "A person in the chat room said it might some guy they go to high school with. A real loner, introvert. You know the kind."

"Yeah, I do," acknowledged Saundra. "Keep looking into it. The sooner you all can give me stuff, the sooner I can tell thousands of others."

A minute later and Saundra had a new email from Jessie. Nearly all of the named people in the email correspondence had social media accounts. Fewer than ten minutes went by before they were able to confirm the identities of eight of the Neo-Nazis who had attended the march. All were male and none of them were older than thirty. Rudd's lead also turned out to be correct, adding a ninth confirmed identity. Rudd went a little further, noting that in the video that ninth person stayed close to another spiteful young man. Some quick social media searching and he had found a tenth confirmed identity.

"Good, good," said Saundra, concentrating on the tasks before her in multiple digital windows. "I'm posting the information to the message boards now. Jessie?"

"Yes?"

"Send me the info on the person who uploaded the video. The one who agrees with the Nazis. It doesn't seem right that he shouldn't be 'rewarded' for his associations."

"You got that right," said Jessie with a big smile. She sent Saundra the link to the uploader's profile, along with his email address. Over the next few days, the man who had unintentionally helped lead the antifa trio to expose the others would get hundreds of emails threatening the well-being of himself and his family.

On the social media platforms for the antifa chapter, within a few minutes, numerous fellow activists and allies were sharing their posts about the identified Neo-Nazis. Others took an offline approach, making scores of phone calls to the schools and employers of the angry young men whose images had been captured online and used against them. By the end of the month, half of them would either be fired or suspended by their employers; three were punished at school, with one of that number being expelled.

With others taking over their work, the three began to relax. Jessie removed her glasses and put them away, closing her laptop. Rudd gently placed his technological device on the floor, fingers pushing against his eyelids. Saundra got up to increase the blood-flow in her legs. She paced about behind the couch while Jessie conquered the freed-up space on the sofa.

"Another successful Saturday for justice," commented Rudd, getting tacit agreement from Jessie, but only cautious optimism from Saundra.

"I will share your sentiment when I get word that these bigots lose their jobs or their safety because of what they did. There must always be accountability for people acting like that in public."

"Amen, sister," replied Rudd.

"Here, here, as they used to say."

"Is that from one of your plays, Jessie?"

"Maybe," she responded. "You know, it's not like I keep every line I have ever memorized in my head. Eventually, I lose most of my lines and cues. That way, I can fill my head with more lines from different plays."

"I see."

"However, I guess it is always possible that I retain some of it subconsciously, you know, floating around my brain and all that."

"In other words, you don't know," flatly stated Rudd.

"Basically, yeah," she admitted.

Saundra's phone went off. It was a text message. She pulled the mobile device from her pants pocket, unlocked it, and checked the alert. She looked at Jessie. "Robespierre just texted me. He told me that you need to pick up Carla and drive her to the church at eleven PM. He'll be there waiting."

"Okay," obeyed Jessie. "Eleven o'clock. Got it." Jessie thought for a moment. "You know, I need to run some errands before tonight. Since we are at a stopping place, perhaps I should go ahead and get to it."

"Yeah, sure," nodded Saundra. "Take care, Jessie."

"Bye!" Rudd waved as Jessie left the apartment. The two remaining people waited a few moments before speaking. "Did you really have to shave your head for this?"

"I need to look different," responded Saundra, standing behind the longer couch with her arms folded. "Why haven't you done anything to change your appearance?"

"I'm pretty banal-looking as it is."

"Change something. Anything. I don't care."

"All right, all right," conceded Rudd, hands raised. "I will make sure something is changed by Monday. Scouts' honor."

"The Scouts are fascists."

"You know what I mean."

"Yes."

"Saundra," enquired Rudd. "Do we really need to keep Jessie out of the loop? She's been with us for a few years now."

"Yes," she stated firmly. "She's close to Carla. They are good friends now. And I do not believe either can keep a secret."

"All right."

"You know, while we are airing out our grievances," began Saundra, pacing behind the couch once more, "you didn't need to protest so much in front of Robespierre. I could tell he did not like it."

"Well, I didn't like what he wanted me to do."

"I get that you don't like this assignment. No one really likes it. But we all have to give up things to make this work. My hair, your convictions. Our safety. It means nothing compared to the chance to begin the next stage of history."

"I understand."

"And Carla will be part of it also, ushering in that new age. Even though we both know she will be just as hesitant, if not more so."

"Yes," said Rudd. "If not more so."

* * *

Carla and Jessie talked about their classes as the latter drove them up to the abandoned church building. Jessie was tasked with writing a term paper on anti-feminist tropes in entertainment. Given her theatrical background, she was planning to begin her essay quoting from the infamous monologue given near the close of *The Taming of the Shrew*, in which Katherine speaks of her husband as being her lord and master. Carla had to write an essay analyzing the radical politics of Guatemala, Cuba, Chile, or Nicaragua. She had final say over which tumultuous history she got to write about.

Unlike the first time Jessie came to her apartment to drive her to the former church, Carla was awake and ready to go. Jessie did not even have to go to Carla's door. A ringing from the system, a confirmation of who it was waiting outside, and Carla darted out the door, careful to lock it behind her. The car trip went without incident, with neither long red lights nor crowded traffic hindering their progress. The mood was easy, even though the meeting was of immense importance.

As Jessie slowed the vehicle to a stop, Carla noticed that there were two light-colored vans parked beside the church building. She did not recall seeing them previously when coming for antifa chapter meetings or the first encounter with Robespierre. They channeled suspicion for her, yet she had received no word from her fellow federal investigators over there being a need for action. Surely, they would have warned her if they had spotted something newly dangerous for her. Then again, maybe they did not consider the two vans a point of concern. For Carla, such a lack of worry seemed ridiculous.

"Here we are," said Jessie as the two unfastened their respective seatbelts and left the car. "Robespierre should be where he usually is."

"You got the key, I assume?"

"Of course."

"I guess if you did not have it, you could always hack the lock, right?"

"Yeah," laughed Jessie as the two walked toward the entrance. The two doors that led to the former narthex were unlocked. Carla and her friend walked from the end of that space to the next, Jessie lightly commending Carla for remembering not to enter the former sanctuary. She then took out the large key, unlocked the door, and opened it for Carla. "I'll be waiting up here like last night."

"Thanks," said Carla with an appreciative smile before descending the dark stairway into the basement. Down there, Carla's initial discomfort over the two vans grew when she noticed that none of the crates were there anymore. She fought the instinct to stare at the empty wing of the cellar, instead, focusing her attention to the shadow of a man waiting amid lit candles for her arrival. "I am here, Robespierre."

"Yes," he agreed, turning to face the newcomer. "You are alone, correct?"

"Well, Jessie is waiting upstairs."

"But she cannot hear us," explained the professor. "I know, because I tested out these things before making this my little clandestine meeting place. With the door shut, anyone upstairs might as well be deaf."

"Understood."

Robespierre slowly approached her with a smile. Mack Channing had a kind face full of charm. He wore blue jeans and an autumn jacket. His feet were covered with athletic socks and used sneakers. He halted within a few feet of Carla, the two standing directly opposite each other as though some invisible wall was erected between them. Carla assumed that his hesitation to move closer was over her previous hostility to his touching her face. His smile grew wider. He kept staring at her, as though studying her. She was beginning to feel uncomfortable and started to look away. Somehow, without engaging in physical contact, he seemed to be touching her in an undesired way.

"Do you feel uncomfortable?" he asked. "Go on, tell me honestly."

"Yes."

"You do not like it when I stare at you?"

"No, I do not."

"You do not like it when I touch you?"

"Right."

"Would you rather not be here?"

"Hard to say."

"What do you mean by that?"

"I do not feel comfortable right now, but I want to do something. Something to change the world. I want to start the revolution. And I want to know what you want me to do."

"Good, I like that," said Robespierre. "I like your willingness to get into an uncomfortable space in order to make the world better. If only more young people acted that way. Hell, if only more old people acted that way, too."

"Yes, Robespierre."

"You want to help me destroy the oppressive institution that is the myth of reason. Am I correct?"

"Yes, I do."

"Then you will help me do so on Monday."

"What will I do on Monday?"

"Before I tell you, Carla, I want you to know a key rule. What I tell you is between you and me only. No one in our little antifa operation knows what the other person is doing. Everyone just knows their part, like that old tale of the seven blind men who each feel a different part of the elephant."

"So which part of the elephant is mine?"

"I will let you know," Robespierre assured her, beginning to pace. "But first, I will tell you about the elephant. The elephant never forgets. The elephant will never forget what we do to it on Monday evening. That elephant will be the governor's convention. And the goal, the way in which we will destroy reason, will be the assassination of the very first speaker, on the very first day of the convention. I believe his name is Sharp. Yes, Josiah Sharp. A newly-elected governor and passionate young man. I almost respect him for his work among the poor, and for holding so many elitist pigs to account. Still, we must often sacrifice that which we love to the altar of change. And he shall be sacrificed."

"Do you want me to kill him?"

"Oh, no, no," Channing immediately replied, almost cutting off Carla's question. "I already have someone else for that assignment. Oh no, you will have an important part. Just not that."

"Then what?"

"Your part of the elephant will be monitoring," said the professor, taking a few steps closer to Carla. She thought about moving back, but decided to hold her ground. He took out an envelope from his jacket and handed it to her. "These are your credentials for the convention. Carla Wexler will be a volunteer who will help with convention security. In reality, you will be keeping track of other convention security personnel. If it sounds like they have found the person I assigned to kill Sharp, then you will alert that person."

"How will I do that if I do not know who they are?"

"In the envelope is a number to a burner phone. You will text message that number with any important updates. That is all you need to do. But even that little bit will make you a hero to the liberated masses."

"Yes, Robespierre."

"Now go, get ready for Monday. The time is coming for this age to end, and for a new stage of history to begin. Blood will soon flow and reason will soon perish."

X

"When I was growing up," Josiah Sharp explained to his wife, "I was raised with the idea that it was the husband who served as protector of the family." Carla al-Hassan Sharp smirked at the comment. "We keep messing that up, don't we?"

"Well, Josiah," replied Carla, "whenever you want to take a bullet for me, you are free to do so." He smiled at the comment, as did Alfredo Hernandez and Michael Zambo, standing in the same room and listening in amusement.

It was a break from the serious conversation taking place at that late hour. It was well after midnight, the sun several hours away from making an appearance. However, when Carla left the presence of Professor Mack Channing and was driven back to her apartment by Jessie Phelier, she had immediately contacted Zambo. From there, Hernandez was brought in and immediately suggested that Josiah be added to the meeting. They came together in a meeting room at the FBI headquarters. An aide provided coffee and donuts. Joining these items on the table were some napkins and paper cups.

"And he gave you a forged pass?"

"Yes," said Carla. She took the lanyard with ID badge affixed out of her pants pocket and put it on the table. Zambo, picked up the object and studied it, turning it over several times. He was impressed.

"They did a good job," observed Zambo. "Looks authentic." He handed it back to Carla. "They also did a good job hacking into the system. According to the tech guy here, 'Carla Wexler' is indeed on all digital copies of the convention personnel list."

"Later today, Jessie is going to lend me a set of 'good clothes' for my cover. We are about the same size, so it should be a fairly easy fit for me."

"So we know the target," began Hernandez, a faint smoke smell wafting from his clothes. "We know when they are going to attack ... During Sharp's speech, correct?"

"Correct," Carla affirmed.

"Location, person, time. Yet we still do not know who and how. Very annoying, if I say so myself."

"Robespierre would not tell you who?" asked Zambo.

"No. He said no one will know what other people are doing. Theoretically, whoever the assassin is will not know it is me serving as lookout."

"Interesting," commented Hernandez. "So there is no way anyone can rat anyone else out. You are all quite ignorant of the guilt of others."

"Yes."

"Well, Mr. Sharp," said Hernandez, turning to face the man seated to his left. "Once again, you can be the bait to catch a group of bad guys. What do you say?"

"Same answer as last time," stated the committed governor-elect. "I am not going to run from these things. If you need me in the crosshairs, then I will be there."

"Josiah, this is not like last time," Carla warned her husband, grabbing his hand. "We know even less about how these people are going to try and kill you. Hell, we do not even know who will kill you or how."

"Ignorance is bliss?"

"There has got to be a way to prevent this," insisted Carla, directing her attention to Zambo and Hernandez, standing opposite. "I told you about the two vans. They should be enough to bring down Robespierre before the convention begins."

"No, they weren't," said Zambo with a sigh. "While you and Hernandez were driving up here, I contacted state police and they tracked them down. They searched both vehicles and found nothing suspicious. No explosives, no guns, nothing."

"But the crates were not there this time. There was nothing there. I saw it. They could not have just made them vanish."

"Well, whatever they did with those crates, they didn't do it through those vans. Sorry."

"It will be all right, Carla," assured Josiah, this time being the one who grabbed her hand. "I trust you will stop whoever is coming after me."

"For what it's worth, Mrs. Sharp," Zambo explained, "Quantico has given this office the green light to field more agents on this case. Plenty of folks are working to find enough evidence to arrest Professor Channing, and if possible, those antifa activists you've been informing on."

"*Lying to*," she stated. "I have been lying to them. They offered me friendship and support in a cause, and I lied to them. Often."

"Look, Carla—"

"When you arrest them, I want them to get merciful treatment."

"Merciful treatment?" asked Zambo, critically. "These are domestic terrorists. They are planning to kill your husband!"

"Only one of them will try to do it. The others, people like Jessie and Rudd, they are basically good people. They just ended up with the wrong group and the wrong leader. I want you—, no, I *demand* that you take that into consideration."

"How about we talk about this more once this whole crazy episode is over, okay?" Hernandez interjected, stretching his upper body between Zambo and Carla with a nervous smile and two thumbs up. Carla backed off and so did his good friend Michael. "Excellent! Well then, everyone knows what they have to do. Tomorrow should be the most exciting Monday I've had in a very long time!"

"Yes, everyone needs to go home, get some rest, and be ready for tomorrow evening," noted Zambo. "Meeting dismissed." The other aides and agents exited the room, two of them getting some donuts and refills on coffee for the road. A few opted to remain at the office and begin their research for the case. One of them was kind enough to hold the door open for the first three out of the room. As soon as the door closed, another detective with a small paper bag containing two donuts and a small coffee cup in one hand grabbed the knob with his free hand. He held the door for another FBI employee.

"I better get you back to campus," said Hernandez. "You are fortunate. In my youth, I used to drive long hours into the evening. Saw my share of sunrises."

"And then he got a life," quipped Zambo, garnering amusement from both Carla and Alfredo. "What passes for one, anyway."

"Passes by yours quite often, actually," countered Hernandez, Zambo waving him off and directing his next words toward Carla.

"I appreciate all your work in this. We have gotten a lot of valuable information on antifa thanks to your efforts. And if we get some of these other figures arrested, I will be only too happy to cut them a deal in return for further details."

"I will be happy to tell them that, when the time comes."

"Anyway, like I said, sleep well tonight."

"According to my wristwatch, its already morning."

"I'll believe that when I see the sunrise," replied Zambo, gathering his things and exiting the room.

"I will leave you two alone," said Hernandez. "But do not take too long. The night is no longer young." They said their brief good-byes and he exited, leaving only man and wife inside the meeting room.

Carla's arms were folded. "How did I know you would say yes to being a target?"

"Because you know me very well."

"Yeah," she said looking down. He approached her. They were face to face, his hands rubbing her arms.

"It's almost over."

"It is almost over," she said.

"To clarify, I mean the assignment, not my life. I hope," he said with a smile. She remained reserved.

"You just have to joke about it. Why do you have to joke about it?"

"Because I know, by faith, that this will end well—no matter what happens. So, I am at peace with the whole idea, and you should be, too."

"The peace that transcends all understanding, right?"

"Right. I assume Orthodox believe in that, also."

"Well, in that case," concluded Carla, "maybe I will just let the assassin kill you."

Josiah paused, but then got the idea. "Now that's more like it." The two embraced.

"I better leave now. Hernandez will barge in to drag me away if I do not."

They embraced once more, longer this time. Both found it hard to let go. "Well, as the old hymn goes ..."

"God be with you till we meet again," Carla finished, Josiah nodding in agreement.

* * *

Rudd Yansk was praying in the sanctuary. The former worship space lacked the ornate décor that it once had in abundance when the parish was functioning. Statues had been removed, as had paintings of the saints. The altar was still there, yet stripped of all the trappings of high church elegance. Not even a crucifix remained. Some of the stained glass had been removed as well, taken by other congregations in need of new materials. Much of it still remained, though only a few simpler images of faith represented. Yansk had once joked to Carla that it looked very Protestant.

Still, he was there, treating the space as serving its intended purpose. Some of the barrier between the nave and the apse, with their cushioned kneelers, remained. Yansk had brought a rosary with him, and was nearing the end of a decade. His hair was bleached blond and his eyes were covered with bright blue contacts. Rather than his usual activist uniform of black clothing, he wore denim work clothes for a job he did not have. He felt some guilt over presenting himself in his fabricated manner. Yet his distraught feelings were centered more on what he was going to be a part of than what he looked like.

Saundra Jaspers walked into the sanctuary from the narthex through the propped opened doors, moving toward him up the middle aisle. She offered nothing sacred to the occasion, strolling down the stone walkway as though it were any other large meeting room. Saundra passed by the rows of pews, organized in two columns that had once looked identical; thanks to neglect, they varied in their warped imagery. Some had been removed, again taken to other churches in the diocese for their usage. Others were damaged, either by accident or vandalistic purpose. Yansk heard her coming, but kept saying his prayers.

"Are you almost done?" she asked impatiently. Rudd answered by staying in the kneeling position, eyes closed, hands clasped around the rosary. Saundra folded her arms and stood there for several awkward moments. Finally, he crossed himself in the Roman fashion and rose from the kneeler. He placed the rosary in his pocket.

"I am ready," he said. He walked down the center aisle, Saundra keeping pace. "Are the others ready, also?"

"That they are. They've been ready since last night when they moved two of the four vans several blocks away and let the cops trail the other two, thinking they had us. That is the brilliance of Robespierre."

"Yes, he knows his stuff," Rudd conceded. The two entered the narthex, then veered right to get to the cellar. Its door was wide open. "I am still a little hesitant about doing this."

"You got the easy part."

"That depends on what they do to me when I'm captured."

"You really should say 'if,'" advised Saundra as the two neared the door. "There's always a chance that you can do your job and escape."

"I lack your optimism."

Saundra and Rudd descended the noisy wooden stairs. Down in the cellar, about a dozen others awaited them. They all had hoods and bandanas, ranging in age from 19 to 33. Jessie was among them, giving the pair a contented smile when seeing them appear. Without orders, they halted their conversations and approached the stairway. Rudd stood at the foot of the stairs while Saundra remained a few steps from the cellar floor. Even then, she was slightly shorter than her counterpart. Mack Channing was not among them. He had a class that met at the same time as the meeting.

"All right then," began Saundra. "Everyone here knows what they must do today. We all know our part of the plan. Normally, when I address you and other likeminded activists, I lay out the rules of engagement. But you already know the rules. Robespierre or myself or Rudd here have told you what you must do. I have confidence that you will do it. And in doing it, you will usher in the next stage of human evolution, the next era of human flourishing, and end of the fascist plague once and forever.

"This is not like our other actions. There has never been a guarantee that you would walk away from what we are doing. They have no rules; they have no qualms about hurting or even killing us. But I will admit, this plan is different. The danger is much greater. The margin for error is far smaller. You all already accept the fact that this might be your last day among the living. You very well may die for your beliefs. I may die for my beliefs. But never forget, never ever forget, that in our sacrifice will come not just a setback for the Nazis and the tyrants, but the very end of their cause. Within twelve hours from now, we win. Not just for the time, not just for now. We win, period. We win."

Saundra was getting emotional. She fought back tears as she spoke those last words, softer than usual in the delivery. Rudd kept up a stoic front, hiding his misgivings within his conscience. Most nodded in response to Saundra's words; yet some were more overt in their pathos. However, Saundra was not going to end on the lighter note. "So are you ready to destroy the fascists!"

"Yes!"

"Are you ready to destroy patriarchy?"

"Yes!"

"Are you ready to destroy white supremacy?"

"Yes!"

"Then let's get to it!"

They cheered with her last comments. Everyone went to their own assignments passionately rushing up the cellar stairs. Jessie slipped ahead of the other listeners and joined her comrades Rudd and Saundra. Behind them were intermittent shouts of enthusiasm. They were all ready. They knew their objectives; they knew their parts of the mission. There was no practice run for any of it, per se, but each activist had their job well thought out. Nerves gave way to ecstasy as they got to the narthex and fanned out from there.

"Here's your badge," Jessie told Rudd, handing him another lanyard with forged identification. "Sorry it took me a little longer. Apparently, they put an extra watermark on the photo for approved operations crew."

"Thanks," said Rudd, taking the ID and dropping it around his neck. "The important point was that you got it to me before I had to go."

"Now if you will excuse me, I have to pick up Carla and drive her to the convention center," Jessie said, exchanging good-bye waves with Rudd and Saundra. Exiting the narthex, she went to the former church's parking lot to her compact car. Like most of the others, Rudd and Saundra walked a few more blocks to the two vans that the authorities did not know existed, let alone that they contained the stolen weaponry.

* * *

Named for a long-serving governor, the Jerry Brown Convention Center was built after the start of the twenty-first century. It fit the typical layout for a stadium, with an ovular form to its large main chamber, several open pathways for guests to come and go, a wide indoor area filled with assorted vendors offering overpriced food, and enough seats in the main room for 20,000 people. It was the site of many events of varied types, from sports to politics, to theatrical entertainment and graduations.

The grand structure was crowded on the first day of the governors' convention. In addition to the governors and governors-elect, there were aides and state employees, elected officials from California, campaign volunteers, friends of campaign volunteers, family, friends of family, local activists, and aspiring future elected officials. On the agenda were speeches, presentations, panel discussions—and that was just the main stage. Breakout sessions in other meeting rooms in the facility on a host of topics covered by individual presenters and panels, were also on the agenda.

Carla was making another round of the infinite hallway that surrounded the main gathering space. Many different kinds of people walked by or beside her. Some were moving fast, some slower. She saw ages ranging from small children on up to grandparents. There were even a few wheelchair-bound individuals riding by, their hands pushing the joysticks forward. Food places were open along the way, offering ice cream, hot dogs, pizza, chicken fried or grilled, sandwiches, funnel cakes, bottled waters, and other drinks. Carla seldom went to any sporting events, yet she felt that this environment strongly resembled such an occasion.

For the first time in weeks, Carla was in business-appropriate fashion. Jessie had loaned her a pantsuit with a white blouse and flats. Carla was surprised that Jessie had such clothing in her closet. The neckline and the waistline were both a little snug; however, the outfit worked overall. The lanyard with her volunteer badge hung around her neck while her pockets included a wallet in one and a phone in another. Occasionally she took out the device, and with the blessing of Zambo, sent text messages to the burner number, updating the unknown figure about any and all security developments.

There were few to report. As governors came and went, they had their own security detachments assigned. She sent a few messages about that, but then realized that this was redundant. At one point, she heard about a possible disturbance in one of the men's bathrooms on the main floor. She sent a text about that. When this turned to be nothing of lasting value, she sent another text following up. She never got any return messages, making her wonder if anyone was actually reading her texts.

"Agent Sharp," said a familiar voice from behind. Carla turned and saw Zambo standing with another man. Both were in ties and slacks, with lanyards identifying their professional status. The fellow next to Zambo was a little shorter than he, with a balding scalp and a gut created by beer drinking.

"Hello, Detective Zambo."

"Carla, this is Mr. Evans. He is chief of security here at the convention center."

"Evans," she said, offering her hand, which he shook.

"If you have any issues and I am not around, talk to him."

"Will do."

"Evans, this is my agent, Carla Sharp. She has been at the forefront of this investigation for some time. If she needs anything, you listen to her, okay?"

"Of course, Detective Zambo, anything."

"Good," nodded Zambo, who then looked at Carla. "Anything new?"

"Nothing. I send the messages and I get no response. I find nothing odd and I see no one around here whom I remember from the antifa chapter."

"Well, keep looking," advised Zambo. "Evans, your men have all the images of the antifa members, correct?"

"Just the ones who got mugshots."

"Well, that is basically all the ones we need to look out for."

"They will likely be in disguise," noted Carla. "I know Saundra shaved her head recently."

"Saundra?" asked a confused Evans.

"Jaspers," clarified Zambo, Evans' nodded his understanding. "Anyhow, I need to step away and give Quantico an update. I'll see you around."

"Take care."

"Bye," said Carla as Zambo left. "Anyway, I am going to keep walking around the outskirts and see if I find anything amiss."

"I'll do the same. In fact, why don't you go one way and I go the opposite? That way, we occasionally see each other and can provide fairly regular updates."

"Sounds simple enough. Sure."

"Happy hunting!" said Evans as he walked past Carla to do his patrol. As requested, Carla walked in the opposite direction.

More and more attendees were heading to the main gathering space. There were no individually assigned seats, though the governors and other important guests had their own reserved sections. Carla was getting fewer and fewer suspects for the crime. No one familiar had arrived. What is more, she wondered how they could get in without incident. After all, each center entrance had armed security with metal detectors. Unless they had a ceramic weapon, they were bound to be nabbed. And since Zambo had made no mention of such specialized tools of death being among the stolen supplies, Carla doubted that any of them had access to such a firearm. Still, she was cautious. She remembered to send another minor update to her unknown assassin accomplice.

"Buried in your phone, I see," said Josiah, pleasantly surprising Carla. She smiled as she sent off the message and looked up to see her husband, flanked by security, and with an unopened soda in each hand.

"It was business, I assure you."

"Of course."

"So what are you doing here?"

"I still have a few minutes before they need me backstage," explained Josiah. "A drink?"

"Yes, please," she responded. Josiah handed her the soda, the two opting to lean back on the painted brick wall behind them as they spoke and sipped.

"I take it you haven't caught the bad guy yet."

"I do not even know if it is a bad guy or a bad girl. You know it could be either."

"True," nodded Josiah. "I have had to deal with both."

Carla smiled. "A part of me wants to believe whoever it was might have gotten scared and decided to not show up."

"That's possible."

"It would explain why security has not reported anything suspicious, or stopped anyone with a metal detector. I want to believe that, but ..."

"Yes?"

"You know how it is, Josiah. We're never that fortunate."

"Probably not," he said, taking another swig. Then he smiled and lifted his can toward Carla. "How about a toast to never being that fortunate?"

"And to having humor under fire," she added, gently tapping his can with hers. A short while later, Josiah's phone sounded off. He took the device out of his pocket and checked the message. "What is it?"

"Time to go behind the scenes," he said. Josiah gave Carla a peck on the cheek. "Lord willing, I'll talk to you later."

"Lord willing," she agreed, taking a deep breath he and his security detail quickly walked away.

* * *

He got in without a problem. His uniform and badge passively proclaimed that he was a maintenance crew member. An unremarkable member of the operations department, the mostly working-class folks who put together and took apart stages, set up chairs, recorded with cameras, and moved around the lights. Security beheld his equipment, a variety of plastic and metal contained in a tool case, and allowed it in with little examination. They were unaware of the false bottom. He made it past the interior guards without incident. After all, they reasoned, he had already passed through the first layer of protection alarming no one.

From there he went upwards, joining other crewmen well above even the highest of the convention seats. The stage, with its banners and screens, seemed so small from his vantage point, the people moving around the floor and rows looked like figurines. They were far enough away to appear no grander than a few inches tall, yet not so far that a well-aimed shot could not effectively end a life. His view allowed him to see the legions of guests and honorees flowing into the space, like a bathtub filling with water.

Carefully he moved along the rafters, holding whatever railing was available with one hand while maintaining a determined grip on his case. There was little communication between him and the others up there. They talked more with each other, brushing him off as yet another person brought in to help with the convention. He had done his research. He knew they were going to leave soon. With them absent, he would finalize his preparations for the assignment he had grudgingly accepted.

"Still nothing new, huh?" asked Evans as he and Carla once again crossed paths. At this point, the circular hall had more security and ushers than it did guests. Carla shook her head. "Me, neither."

"We must be missing something."

"But what? I have a line on security, you and the FBI have been checking things, too. What are we missing?"

"You have been here since before the doors opened, right?"

"Yes," Evans replied. The two started to walk side by side down the hall.

"Did you check everyone who came in?"

"Security did. Yes."

"What about workers? You know, people who work at the convention center?"

"We checked them. We checked what people brought in. We checked everyone."

Carla looked inside the great meeting space. Things were quieting down. As it turned out, the color guard for the event was making its march down the central aisle at the floor space. Four Marines, two with rifles and two with flags, one American and the other that of the Corps. She could see them from the entrance. She took a few steps into the space and looked up. She then beckoned Evans to approach.

"What about that box up there?" she inquired with a whisper, pointing at the spotlight booth. The cubic quarters used for audio-visual elements perched high above opposite the main stage.

"Oh the booth? Yeah, we make sure that thing is always under strict guard."

"You sure?"

"Yup, ever since 1962."

"1962?"

"That was when *The Manchurian Candidate* came out. The original one, which was way better than the remake."

"Okay," noted Carla. "And what about the rafters?"

"Again, we check people out before they can go up there."

"Would there be a way to check and see if anyone is still up there? Or maybe went up there recently?"

"You think your man is up there?"

"It is still the best place for a sniper."

He saw the tiny soldiers presenting the colors, then heard the National Anthem performed by an operatic voice on the stage. Such patriotic showings did not move him to contemplation. Rather, he returned to work, opening the case and then the false bottom. He put the rifle pieces together, having practiced for hours in advance of the assignment. Every click made him closer to success. Finally, into the chamber went a lone bullet. He took a deep breath and waited for the opening speaker to begin. That was going to be hardest part for him: the wait, the dread, the angst.

"You checked out *everyone* who came up to the rafters, correct?" asked an increasingly impatient Carla. The Star-Spangled Banner was almost over and she knew her husband was going to speak soon.

"Yes ma'am. Everyone had the right ID and no one brought up any weapons," responded the middle-aged operations manager. He stood with his back to one of the entrances to the walkways above the audience. Beside Carla were Evans and Zambo, who had joined them a short while ago.

"Was there anyone who did not seem familiar?" Carla asked the operations manager, desperately looking for any clues.

"Actually, come to think of it, there was a fellow." He paused to think. "I mean, I don't really know everyone and I don't want someone to get into trouble who don't deserve it."

"We will figure that part out later. Just tell us about him," ordered Zambo.

"Okay then. He was, you know, a little tall. Bleached-blond hair. He had the right ID. I assumed he was with the convention crew."

"Bleached-blond hair?" asked Carla. "Like it was dyed?"

"Yeah, I guess."

Carla looked at Zambo, who nodded. He pulled out his smartphone and quickly brought up the images of booked antifa members for the operations manager to go through. A man was speaking inside the convention space. Carla knew it was not Josiah, but she could tell he was introducing him to the audience. The manager used his left index finger to swipe through the mugshots on the small screen. Then he stopped, looked closely and showed the image to the three others. "That's definitely him."

"We need to get up there. And now."

"Gotcha," said the manager, turning to unlock the door to the rafters.

"Do you have a spare gun, Zambo?" Carla asked the FBI detective, who nodded and knelt down to get a smaller caliber piece he kept under his pants leg, strapped near the ankle.

Loud applause masked any noise he made high above them. It was time. He avoided the spotlight booth, that cubic structure high above the seats that was eye level to him. Those manning the beams were unaware of him as he stood in the dark. He chose a walkway above the stage, hidden by all the lights being thrown at the speakers under him. With hesitation, he took hold of the rifle, breathing hard as he leaned over the top of the railing, right eye peering through the scope at the top of Josiah's head.

"Remind me, why are we starting on this side of the convention center?" asked Zambo, as he ascended the service staircase with Carla and Evans. She was at the front, the two men walking close behind. "Why are we starting on this side of the convention center?"

"From where we were, I did not see anyone on the walkways near the booth. And if the place is as well guarded as Evans says, then he would not be there."

"Which leaves the stage-side rafters," responded Zambo.

"Yeah."

They were a dozen steps away from the entrance to the rafters. She stopped briefly, the trio hastily preparing their attack in muted whispers. Nodding in agreement, Carla again took the lead, this time lightly stepping on each stair. Zambo and Evans did likewise, each person in the small group holding a handgun at the ready. He was waiting. He knew someone would come eventually. His aim was steady, his scoped rifle pointed down at the governor-elect. He even adjusted the scope, allowing for a magnified gaze. At that moment, he could almost make out the individual's facial expressions. It would have been a perfect shot.

"Stop! Drop the gun!" shouted Carla as the three charged through the unlocked door. "Drop it right now!"

By the second command, he removed one hand from the rifle. With the other hand, he lifted the gun upwards before taking a step back and gently placing the stolen weapon onto the grated surface of the walkway. From there he slowly returned to a standing posture, hands raised. His face was still looking away from the three newcomers, a full head of bleached hair their only view of his head. Yet she knew who it was; Evans had pointed him out. Seeing him from behind, she recognized the body type, confirming the identification.

"Turn around, slowly," ordered Zambo. The man obliged, gradually revealing himself to be Rudd Yansk.

"Carla," he muttered, almost unheard through the crowd noise as Josiah delivered yet another applause line without any violent interruptions.

* * *

Security took control of many of the smaller meeting rooms attached to the convention center. People walked through the curved hall without giving these quarters much thought. Some of them were used by employees, others for minor social functions like birthday parties or retirement celebrations. They were constructed of large painted bricks, with generic chairs and a long table in the center. Unlike the outer wall of the convention center with its large glass barriers, they lacked windows.

Carla, Josiah, Zambo, Evans, and Hernandez had gathered in one of these rooms, laughing and talking about the successful apprehension of Yansk. The mood was lighter, with the group sharing bottles of water and snacks set out for volunteers. True to her word, Carla returned the gun to Zambo, the minor weapon placed back in the holster around his ankle. There was much relief, even as Carla wondered about certain things. Her contemplations were still simmering as the banter continued.

"Well, to be honest, I was a lot more relieved after I got through the first couple paragraphs," explained Josiah as he took another drink of water. "I figured, if he hadn't shot me yet, he was never going to shoot me."

"Or he was waiting for you to die on stage," Hernandez quipped.

"Oh, come on, my CIA friend, did I really do that bad a job with my speech? The audience sure seemed to like it."

"Eh, it was passable," replied Hernandez. Josiah smiled and lifted his bottle as a salute to the faint praise. "You probably did better than I would have."

"You? But you have no fear of others."

"Maybe one on one, or in a small group. But thousands of folks, plus cameras? I don't know about that."

"Remember, Mr. Sharp," added Zambo, "there is a reason my friend here picked the most antisocial federal agency to work for. Isn't that right, Alfredo?"

"Sí, señor."

"Going back to the speech," said Josiah. "I knew I was going to give it my all, because I knew Carla was making sure I was safe." He followed up his comment by rubbing his hand up and down her back.

"What happens to Rudd?" asked Carla, more somber than the others. She was still looking down at the table, drawing invisible semi-circles with her finger.

"Well, for the time being, I plan to let him rot in jail," explained Zambo. "Let him simmer, and then go in and start the interrogation."

"Are you going to hurt him?"

"I might give him a verbal thrashing, maybe make sure others do the same through the night, you know to keep him uncomfortable. But we at the Bureau don't do waterboarding."

"Yes, Carla. Fortunately for Mr. Yansk, the Agency is not overseeing this one," said Hernandez, dryly.

"You will try and give him a deal, yes? After all, there are other antifa extremists out there. He will know things that I do not know."

"We will see what happens. No promises, but I will try," said Zambo. "And on that note, I should probably see to it sooner than later."

"Oh, oh, can I come along? Can I come along?" asked a theatrical Hernandez. Zambo laughed at his friend.

"Like I could ever stop you."

"Wonderful! This should be fun," said Hernandez with a smile. "Anyway, I am glad to see both of you are in good health. So I say, vaya con Dios y buenas noches."

"Adiós," stated Carla.

"Bye!" added Josiah, as the two federal agents left the room. "Have I ever told you how glad I am that Hernandez is on our side?"

"Yeah."

"Granted, I do not always like what he does or how he has such a grip on your life, but still. At least he is not actively trying to destroy us, am I right?"

"Yeah."

Josiah was getting concerned. His wife was surprisingly sedate for the occasion. She had not made eye contact for some time. He put his arm around her, but her stance remained unaltered. Lacking better insight into the strange behavior, he tried prompting her again with conversation. "You were amazing tonight. A part of me would have loved to have seen his face when you showed up."

"The look on his face ..."

"Pardon?"

"His expression, the look he gave me, what he said," Carla noted, finally looking up at Josiah. "He was not surprised to see me. There was no shock, no outrage. Just a slight affirmation of my presence. Nothing more."

"I see."

"Why was he not surprised to see me?" she asked, with some frustration in her voice. "It was like he knew it would be me."

"Did you tell him that you were there?"

"No. According to Robespierre, no one knew other people's parts in the assassination attempt. Rudd should not have expected me."

"Either way, I am glad you stopped him. And just in time, since you all told me he had the gun aimed at me and everything."

"He hates guns," she said softly.

"I am sorry?"

"He hates guns," she repeated with more energy. "He hates guns!"

"Rudd hates guns?"

"Awhile back, Rudd told me that he first got involved in political activism when he campaigned for increased gun regulation." Things were manifesting within Carla. "He is pro-life, all the way. He hates abortion, the death penalty, war, and he hates the idea of killing people. And he hates guns."

"Maybe he finally compromised his principles," countered Josiah. "Take it for what you will, but the French revolutionary Robespierre was originally opposed to the death penalty, only to compromise that principle later on."

"Not Rudd. He does not compromise. Ever."

"So what are you saying? You think he has a twin or something?"

Carla felt the impulse to act. "Josiah, do you still carry your revolver?"

"Yes?" he answered, perplexed.

"I need it," she declared.

"Okay," he said, lifting his jacket so he could get at the concealed holster. "What do you need my gun for?"

"I have to go back and find out what is really going on."

"What are you talking about?"

"There is something very wrong right now and I have to find out what it is," she said, rising to her feet while tucking the gun between her pants and her lower back. "If Zambo or Hernandez show up, tell them I went back to campus."

"Back to campus? You mean the attempt on my life was not the end of the mission?"

"Josiah," said Carla before she rushed out of the convention center, "if my intuition is correct, your life was never in danger."

XI

Carla al-Hassan Sharp borrowed a vehicle from convention security. It had an almost full gas tank, allowing her to return to the campus area with great speed. The late hour meant fewer cars on the road, also aiding in her effort to get back before something unforeseen came to pass. She thought of contacting Alfredo Hernandez or Michael Zambo about her worries, yet ultimately decided against it. This might all be unfounded. Perchance Josiah Sharp was the only target. Perchance the battle had been won and all that remained was to get Rudd Yansk to point out the other conspirators.

Yet as she neared her off-campus apartment the nagging questions continued. There were too many unresolved points for Carla to let things stand. The answers had to be at Pacific Coast State University. It was the epicenter for everything: Professor Mack Channing, the antifa chapter, her cover. Everything was demanding that she go back to the campus, go back to the starting point. Recognizing the value of the Wexler cover, she parked the sports car a couple of blocks away. Her character had claimed enmity against vehicles.

As she neared the front of her apartment complex, she saw it. Her passing glance at the neighboring campus was a brief, instinctual turn, prompted by nothing in particular. Yet with the look, Carla saw a triggering sight: a white van. It could have been owned by anyone and used for any purpose. Nothing obvious about it led her heart to increase its pace. Yet she just knew that this had to be evidence of their presence. The other two must have been decoys, planted to distract authorities.

Carla took a few steps forward, moving to the edge of the sidewalk. Would looking away cause it to disappear? Was she seeing things? No, it was real. It had to be real and it must have been there for nefarious purposes. No repair man, maintenance team, delivery boy or delivery girl, electrician, painter, plumber or any other member of the service economy was going to service a locale at such a late hour. Maybe for an emergency, some late-night crisis that required rectification, yet the ideas did not hold weight in Carla's mind. This was too coincidental to be dismissed.

Carla looked down at her clothing. The business attire and convention ID lanyard did not strike her as the proper outfit for an investigation. More than a fashion issue, she was feeling untrusting of the PCSU antifa, and preferred an outfit that was able to conceal her identity among peers. The hood and bandana combination was ideal. She entered the apartment complex and rushed up the stairs, nearly slamming her door into the wall when entering her apartment. An internal darkness lit only by outdoor lights, she changed into the coal-hued cargo pants, black hoodie, boots, and black-and-white bandana. She kept the revolver, tucked at the small of her back and covered by her sweatshirt.

She blended with the hour. Barely noticeable amid the darkness, she was revealed only when walking by a street light. Carla kept her right hand near the hidden pistol. She centered her attention on the white cargo van, the type of vehicle seen so often that people passed it on the roads with little attention. A basic automobile parked at the campus. As she neared it, a person dressed much like she was walked around the side. The person was obscured by the hood and the bandana, but their figure was highly visible behind the van. Neither person knew who the other was when they saw each other.

"Who are you?" the person asked Carla, distrust underlying their query.

"I'm here for the plan."

"No, you're not," he declared. "I know everyone who is supposed to be here. I don't know you, your voice."

"Listen, Robespierre told me to be here," she began, one hand outstretched to appeal to him. It was not working, he was reaching for his side. Carla soon realized he was going for a handgun.

She drew faster, not waiting to aim the revolver to before squeezing off a single loud shot. He was struck in the middle of the chest, his body flying into the van's frame then falling forward, expiring soon after. Only the obstruction of her oversized sweatshirt helped to muffle the blast, tearing a hole a couple of inches in diameter in the side of her hoodie. Carla looked around to see if anyone had been stirred by the noise. Amazingly, no lights came on, nor did any sirens begin to blare in the background. It was the city. There was much going around. Maybe a mix of the shirt fabric and the thick walls of the surrounding buildings had helped block the echoes from the ears of any concerned citizenry.

Carla rushed to the body to learn more. Removal of the hood and bandana revealed that it was Nick. She never knew him very well, and felt little emotion in ending his life. His weapon had been a 9mm handgun with a full clip of ammunition and a silencer affixed. Carla did not want to draw more attention. If there were other armed antifa extremists running around campus, Carla concluded that it would be best if the sleeping campus community was ignorant of such a danger and kept to their dorms. Carla stuffed the revolver into the pocket of her hoodie, opting to use the newly acquired weapon.

The van was unlocked. Carla opened the back doors to examine the interior. No one was inside. Rather, she found vindication. Several crates were stacked to the side. Carla climbed into the back of the van and approached the crates. She removed the top of one and then another, finding devices for explosives. Drawing upon her own background in planting bombs, she figured that these were the charges. Gently placing two of the crates down, she looked inside other boxes and found similar items. The explosive compounds must have been elsewhere.

She heard a jingle. The noise rang forth again. Carla heard it emanating from the back of the van, outside. She turned to the open doors, handgun pointed into the night. Another jingle. She figured out that it was coming from the same side as the body. She loosened up a bit as she started to think that the noise was coming from the body, rather than a new hostile. Nevertheless, she exited the van with caution. Getting out, she quickly swung to her right with the gun held with both hands. No one living was present. The jingle rang again. This time, Carla saw that it was Nick's phone, the screen brightening up with each received message, shining through his sweatpants.

Carla knelt beside the body, placing the gun on the pavement, and dug into his pocket to get the mobile device. Fortunately, there was no code required to use the phone. A swipe of her finger removed the stand-by mode. There was a text message thread displayed that included the young man she had killed. She was automatically guided to the most recent messages; which Nick was tagged in to get his attention. Carla read the succinct demands:

Where are u!??

Get to the park ASAP!

We need the charges.

Carla pressed the line at the bottom of the screen. From there, a small keyboard appeared on the screen, which she used to respond: *Sorry.* Message sent. *Got delayed.* Second message sent. *Be there soon.*

* * *

Carla was not well-acquainted with Sacramento Park. It was the location for the on-campus freshman dormitories, a collection of basic buildings that served as living quarters for the young pupils. The structures surrounded a grassy field used for outdoor reading and pickup soccer games, as well as community-building functions like concerts and ice cream socials. In the rare times that the white stuff fell in California, the Park was the best spot for a good large-scale snowball fight.

Yet Carla was knowledgeable enough about the campus to know what the antifa types were talking about when mentioning a "park." Things were starting to look more horrifying. At a normal walking pace, the distance from the east side of campus and the park took about five to eight minutes. Carla was going faster, fearful of what they were doing among the complexes full of sleeping teenagers. Occasionally the jingle chimed, signifying another text. She assured them that "Nick" was almost there. In the thread, she also saw a few people talking about a "Van 2" that was located near the park. That made four; two decoys and two genuine. Yet Carla still did not know how they knew to make decoys.

Finally, two of the freshman dormitories came into view. They had brick walls, rectangular windows, and metal doors painted blue. Each corner had a pair of lights mounted up high, and a security camera. Carla found it odd that a camera was also mounted not far from where she encountered and killed Nick, yet she had seen no campus police and heard no alarms. The university continued to sleep through it all. Carla soon saw two more dark figures in the eventide. They were situated at one of the corners of the freshman dorm to her right. One was kneeling, apparently fixing something on the wall. The other was leaning over, helping and making sure that they got whatever they were doing correct.

Silently moving closer, Carla saw that they were attaching a device to the side of the building. It had its share of wires and what looked to be sticks of dynamite. Exact details remained murky due to the evening hour. Regardless, she knew what the device was and its purpose. At this point, Carla did not know how to approach the duo. She could end them quickly, as they still did not know she was nigh. Or she could try and get closer, learn more, and possibly get their help. There had to be others around campus, doing the same explosive setup. They could point them out.

Yet before she could make a decision, all three of them had their phones go off. It was a text message telling them that someone had found Nick's body. The sound of the jingle from Carla's pocket warned them of her coming. Both turned to see her, both appeared to be ready for a fight, and both were taken out with head shots. Carla did it automatically, sending a bullet into each forehead, blood shooting out of the wounds to show the direction of the deadly payload. The two collapsed onto the paved walkway surrounding the building. Carla jogged over to them and confirmed their deaths. She also got a good look at the explosives attached to the building. After a brief study, she saw that they required more parts to be fatal; the very parts she had left behind at the first van.

More text messages were being sent. Carla put the phone on mute. Someone nearby had not done the same. She had to act. There was no way to be merciful; she could not guard prisoners and pursue any others alone. "God help me," she muttered under her breath before turning the corner, seeing two more hooded figures. She killed them both instantly with headshots as they tried and failed to attack her first. Carla rushed toward them, seeing that one was wearing a backpack. Carla turned him over and unzipped it, revealing more explosives. The other corpse had tape in one hand and a gun in the other.

Both hands gripping the gun, finger touching the trigger, Carla darted to the adjacent freshman dorm without incident. There she saw more explosives secured to the sides of the building, like a demolition job, ready to obliterate the structure. She also noticed something else: these destructive packages had timers. Carla did not notice one on the first attached device. Then again, she did not get a good enough look. Maybe, it had yet to be added by someone else. As the two bodies buzzed with text messages, Carla made sure that the attached explosive was not armed. To her relief, it was also lacking parts required for detonation. Crouched in the corner with a gun raised, she checked Nick's phone for more messages.

We need to get outta here.

Someone is bumping us off!

We got the charges. We will be at the park asap.

Somebody was coming. In fact, more than one was coming. Carla did not know who or how many, yet she had a good idea of where they were coming from. Putting the phone away she went along the side of the dorm, turning left at the corner. She stopped at the opposing corner, hidden by the darkness. Her view allowed her to see the grassy area, well-lit sidewalks, and the wide paved walkway she had used to get to that part of campus. While waiting, Carla saw that there were still no police around. Not even a patrol car. Across the park she saw a light come on in one of the windows of a dorm, but it was turned off soon after. She was amazed that the battle was still unknown.

Three hooded figures showed up, taking the walkway she had used minutes earlier before discovering the pair of antifa members attaching explosives to a building. They were racing to the park, each carrying a backpack, presumably filled with charges. Two of them had guns, while the third was carrying two additional packs. They veered off to the side, going to the very corner where Carla shot two of them dead. With a deep breath, Carla did an about face and jogged alongside the building before getting to the side where the newcomers were starting to do their terroristic work.

As she got closer, one of them spotted her. Carla opened fire, striking that person in the neck. A long spurt of blood shot outwards from where the bullet landed. Carla realized that she had no cover, spotting some bushes t her left. She rushed into them as a second person fired at her. The dark hues of her clothes aided in the camouflage, making the shots wildly miss her by a wide margin. By contrast, the shooter was clearly visible by the glow of the exterior building lights. The armed antifa member took a few steps out from the protection of the building corner. Carla fired a single shot into their right temple.

Seeing an opportunity, Carla ran back toward the corner, but soon came under fire from the third person. More shots, the noise deadened by a silencer, darted through the air. Bullets buried themselves in the ground under the bushes or punctured the paved walkway. Again, the shooter had poor aim and Carla reached cover unscathed. However, the figure kept firing, chipping off small bits of the dormitory's corner. Carla fired a few more shots before her weapon ran out of bullets. She tossed the gun behind her and yanked the revolver from her pocket, gripping it with her right hand. Her back was to the side of the building where she had been seeking cover from the gunfire. Her eyes and the revolver were aimed at the space in front of her, the attached explosive taped to the wall near her midsection.

Carla thought about doubling back, trying to take the unknown hostile party from behind. Yet before she turned, the building lights again helped her strategy. Carla saw a shadow rising. Then she heard the panting. The figure was getting closer, faster and faster. Carla held her ground, waiting for the person to clear the corner and be in range. Apparently, the mysterious assailant did not figure out that the enemy was waiting for them. Carla did not have to wait for more than a minute. Before the hooded figure could react to the surprisingly close enemy, Carla fired, sending a powerful shot into the head, tearing up hood and flesh alike.

Thrown by the blast, the unknown person was launched over the bodies of comrades, unceremoniously slamming into the paved walkway. The body landed on its side, a good deal of blood and brain matter oozing from the hood covering. All became still. Carla expected the campus police or even local authorities to show up. Someone had to have heard the commotion. Then again, the shot was virtually point blank; it was possible that the fabric once again muffled it just enough that the noise, while heard, may have been dismissed as another phenomenon, like a motorcycle or a firecracker.

Carla cautiously turned the corner, gun raised. She looked for movement at different angles, pointing the gun at each one. No one was there; only her and the dead. The first two people she killed by the explosive device. The unarmed one who had borne several packs of charges. The person who she shot in the neck who expired by the time she saw him again. And the two with guns that came trying to finish the job. She studied their bodies, confirming their expiration. Removing hoods, she recognized a couple of them as fellow radicals who had met in the former church and even shouted down that conservative speaker.

Then she came to the last body. There was little need to remove the bandana or the hood. She was smaller than the others and slim overall. Thanks to the building lights, Carla saw her fingerless gloves, each marked with a red anarchist symbol. It was clearly Saundra Jaspers. A mere formality, Carla pulled back the hood to verify what she already knew. Saundra's eyes remained open, the shot being that quick. A large bloody wound splattered crimson and light pinkish chunks over that side of her head, yet the identification was easy enough. She was remembering her recurring nightmare. She was becoming the nightmare. Carla suppressed the emotions, knowing she had to go to the second van. She needed answers, she needed to protect the campus.

* * *

Is anybody left?

There was no emotion to the text message, just the question. A short sentence. An enquiry to the silent thread. Yet Carla knew that behind the stoic letters, the simple query, the robotic popping up of the message, there was fear. Panic. Terror. And she was the author of all those emotions. Carla hastily searched the rest of Sacramento Park. To her relief, none of the explosives had been completed. Therefore, none of them were functional. An added relief came with the text messages of people leaving, interspersed with the blankness of others giving no response. She felt a sense of victory with each fretful comment.

Someone say something!

Much of it was coming from the same number. No one had their names listed. Yet numbers abounded. None of the others were sending new messages. Most of them were incapable of contributing to the thread after encountering Carla. She divided her time checking the messages and scanning the surrounding campus area. So quiet. She could not understand why not so much as a single student left their dorms to figure out what the commotion was outside. Surely, given the many young people who stay up all night, someone should have seen something and reported it to authorities. Yet Carla seemed to rule it all.

A new message came. Same number as the last two. *Door's open to van 2.* Then a follow-up statement. *Come quickly. I am alone.* Throughout the sentences no one seemed to grasp that their unknown menace had taken one of their phones and was reading their every message. Maybe it was because those who reported finding Nick's body did not mention details like his phone being taken. And since no one seemed to have names associated with numbers, no one would find it strange that "Nick" was still sending messages. Regardless, Carla had benefitted from their ignorance.

The second van strongly resembled the first one. The coloring varied a little, with some extra dents on the surface, and a different license plate. Otherwise, the vans shared a strong similarity. Carla noted that this van was parked on the exact opposite side of the campus; one was northwest, the other southeast. Carla approached the vehicle in caution, just in case there were more antifa members coming toward the vehicle. None were present. The text message told no lie, as one of the two backdoors was ajar.

Carla saw that there was no one in the front seats. Whoever was still there was in the windowless back. Only the somewhat open door gave evidence for another human presence. Was it a trap? How many were waiting? Carla was unsure. She thought about pushing against the door, closing it, and forcing the people inside to make a move instead. She considered firing rounds into the side, knowing that the shots could probably penetrate the frame and wound the hostiles. Yet she did not know if hostiles were even in there. She knew nothing about who was in there, either. Maybe it was just a lone, unarmed frightened teenager, desperate to get out of a mess beyond their comprehension. She chose mercy; she chose to swing the door open and point the revolver.

Jessie Phelier saw the masked hooded person appear with a gun pointed directly at her. She was in solitude in the back of the van, a laptop placed on a miniature table and glasses on her face. When the person appeared, she raised her hands in surrender, breathing with terror. Her lip quivered, her pores began to exude sweat. She was without hooded sweatshirt or bandana, instead wearing sneakers, a dark T-shirt, and dark pants. "Please ... Don't kill me ... I don't want to die ... I give up ... Whatever you want, just take it! *Please!*"

Carla was seeing her nightmare. The visions that plagued her many times in her sleep over the past month were manifesting before her. She had to suppress the heart-wrenching thoughts. She had control. She could be merciful. While still pointing the pistol at Jessie, Carla pulled back her hood and lowered her bandana. Jessie's facial expression went from fear to confusion. She attempted to form words, struggling to verbalize all that was afflicting her simultaneously.

"Carla," she finally stated. "What the hell are you doing?"

Carla remained silent. While not as obvious, she was also dealing with the challenge of explaining it all.

"Did you kill them?" Carla was about to offer an explanation, but Jessie angrily interrupted. "You killed them! Why the hell did you do that? What's wrong with you?"

"Jessie," she began. "I am an undercover agent with the government. I was assigned to infiltrate your antifa chapter. I was—"

"You're a fascist spy! You're one of *them*! You're Hitler!" While she kept her hands up, Jessie had lost all fear to anger. "I can't believe I thought you were my friend. You lying bitch!"

"Jessie, listen to me! Yes, I killed the antifa people on campus. But they tried to kill me first. I do not know why, but they saw me as an enemy—"

"As they should! I can't believe this. Nazi trash did this to me, to my friends! I will never forgive you for this. You're a murderer!"

"*I'm* a murderer?" Carla struck back. "After what you and your friends were about to do, you have the audacity to call *me* a murderer?"

"What are you talking about? We weren't going to kill anybody."

"Oh really?"

"Really! All we were going to do was blow up a couple of buildings. The library, the registrar's office, the economics department," she declared, almost shouting. "The reason why we came out so late was so that no one was around. That way, when the bombs went off, no one got hurt."

Carla was legitimately confused. She knew her former friend was wrong. She also knew her former friend was capable of forging documents and online information. Yet looking into her eyes, hearing the passion, she seemed sincere in her comments. Carla lowered the revolver as she responded. "You really believe that?"

"Yes! Robespierre himself told me that was what we were doing." Jessie was calming down. "I was assigned to hack the campus security system. Keep alarms from sounding, put the cameras on loop. Make sure the police had no reason to stop by. And then you showed up and *started killing people!*" She shouted the last few words, anger overtaking her once more.

"Jessie, Jessie, listen to me," said Carla, resting the hand holding the revolver on the carpeted floor of the van. "Your friends were not trying to blow up the library or the registrar's office. They were trying to blow up the dorms at Sacramento Park."

"You're a Gestapo liar. I don't believe you."

"Do you have access to the security cameras?"

"Of course I do."

"Then check the cameras for the freshman apartments. Check Sacramento Park. Zoom in on the corners of the buildings. Tell me what you see."

Jessie offered no verbal retort. With tacit permission, she returned to the laptop and began typing. Through the code and the cybernetic journey, she located the proper camera feeds. Carla saw her expression change from hostility to discomfort and perplexity. Her mouth gaped open and then closed several times. Then she was still, contemplative, trying to figure out the undeniable images before her. All that the newly hated person had said was true.

"I-I don't understand," she finally uttered. "Robespierre told me that we were going to destroy, we were going to destroy ... I don't understand. It doesn't make sense." She turned to Carla. "First I find out you've been lying to me, now I see Robespierre lied to me. What is going on? Who can I trust?"

"Take me to Robespierre and we will find out everything."

Jessie slowly removed her glasses. Her eye balls moved rapidly from side to side, as though she were reading an in-depth think piece. After a few moments, she put her glasses away, closed her laptop, and put it aside so that she could get up. Carla was relieved when the radical nodded in agreement.

* * *

"Carla?" Jessie started to ask her something while driving the van. Then she laughed in frustration. "Is that even your name?"

"Carla is, yes," she replied. "I am an agent with the CIA. However, for this operation, I was working for the FBI."

"A fascist group by any other name," said Jessie. She slowed the van as they got within sight of the former church. A gloomy amber hue was shining through the sanctuary's tall windows. "What will you do to me?"

"I promise I will put a good word in for you and for Rudd."

"Rudd is still alive?"

"Yes. When I caught up with him, he immediately surrendered."

"Of course, he would."

"I know you do not believe me, Jessie, but please consider this," began Carla as Jessie parked, "I hated doing this assignment, because I felt genuine friendship, especially with you and Rudd. In the spirit of that friendship, I am going to do everything I can to make sure the authorities go easy on you both."

"Thanks," replied a stoic Jessie. "He'll be in the sanctuary. He told me that."

"Judging by the lights, I would say he did not lie to you on that point."

"Yes. He didn't lie that time."

"Let's go in."

Jessie nodded. The two unfastened their seatbelts and got out of the van. Jessie went around the front of the van to walk beside Carla. The agent was still unsure as to what to expect in the former church. However, she did not want to convey hostility to Professor Mack Channing, so she tucked the pistol in the back of her pants. It was a warm evening; Carla was finally starting to feel hot with the hoodie on, so she took it off and left it in the van. Underneath she wore a plain white T-shirt with a high neck to help fulfill her preference for modesty.

"I will do the talking," said Carla as the two neared the entrance. "I do not want him to know that his plan just got foiled."

"He'll figure it out. He can tell whenever someone is holding something back."

"You are a professional actress," stated Carla. "I think you can trick him."

"I will try. Only because I want answers and I think your way might be better."

"Not bad for a fascist spy, right?"

Jessie gave her a quick smirk just before opening the door. Both women entered the narthex, which was lit only by the light from the many candles in the sanctuary. They turned right to enter the former worship space. At the front of the space, a few feet in front of the first pews, stood Channing. His attention was directed to the tall window of those lining that side of the sanctuary. Its stained glass had been replaced by regular glass, giving him a perfect image of the outside. He was also checking his phone, looking not for any new messages or calls, but rather the time.

"Robespierre, we have returned from our mission," said Carla. She and Jessie continued to walk toward Channing. "I thought you would like to know—"

"Stop there, now!" said Channing, who to the shock of both pulled out a Glock and pointed it at Carla. "Another step and I blast you away!" Carla and Jessie stopped, standing side by side. Neither knew quite what to say.

"Robespierre, what are you—"

"Shut up! Shut up!" he roared. "I don't know which part of the deep state alphabet soup you come from, Wexler, but I know you are a government agent trying to stop the march of history. So if you make another move, I will have the displeasure of killing you before you see the end of an era."

"What are you talking about?"

"Don't play ignorant. I have known for some time now that you are an undercover agent and nothing you say now will convince me otherwise."

"But Robespierre," interjected Jessie, bringing the other two to look at her. "I did the research on Carla and found nothing wrong."

"And that was your problem, Jessie. You were looking for something wrong, while I was looking for nothing."

"Nothing?"

"Nothing," he confirmed. "Nothing. Nothing at all, from before a few months ago. No local news articles, no social media posts. Oh sure, some of the stuff was made to appear older, but I knew better. I have my own sources in the revolution. I know people in the movement based in the Great Lakes region. None of them knew of a 'Carla Wexler.' Best yet, one of my female sources confirmed that at least one photo of you protesting was doctored." He smiled. "Your head was added to her body."

"And now it all makes sense," admitted Carla. Proud of himself, Channing nodded in approval at each point Carla made. "You knew that as soon as I got back to the FBI, they would monitor those vans. So you switched them out, knowing that we would follow them instead of the real ones. You told me that everyone was sworn to secrecy on their part of the plan so I would not ask anyone else their assignments, thinking they were all involved in the governor's convention. You picked that event because you knew I would believe that a political assassination was the true goal. And it was very far away from your real target. And I would have been tricked into thinking that by stopping Rudd I had foiled your plans, while being ignorant of your real objective."

"Yes, good Carla, beautiful and intelligent," he said.

"The only thing I do not understand is why no campus police were around to stop the planting of the bombs."

"The benefit of being a professor who has the ear of the university powers that be," explained Robespierre. "I made sure a campus lockdown drill was scheduled for tonight. Students stay in, and cops stay away." He grinned sadistically. "And now you know all things. Truly a pity that I will not let you see the sunrise. But I will let you see the birth of a new era. A new age devoid of the pestilence that is reason."

"How does blowing up a few thousand teenagers make the world a better place?"

"By ending reason," he responded without flinching. "Mankind is a savage species, meant for liberation from the chains of intellectuality. The best way to break those chains is to fuel the savage beast within. And that is what will happen in a matter of minutes. 1:47 AM Pacific Time, to be exact. A time that is meaningless at present, yet, soon and very soon will have a great deal of meaning for hundreds of millions of people. Best of all, we should be able to see the explosions from this window."

"But, Robespierre, why? Why do they have to die?" Jessie asked.

"With their deaths, comes the death of reason," he answered, his excitement growing at the aforementioned time grew closer. "Thousands of parents, politicians, pundits, activists, lobbyists, and bloggers will all demand blood. The blood of the liberals, the blood of the far left. Any effort to impede their bloodlust will be met with greater rage, greater and greater violent insurrection. All will fall apart into tribalism and genocide. Words will become impotent, voices of intellect will be the first gunned down. Suppression, street violence, massacres, revenge terrorism. A grand deluge of destruction.

"And I have your beloved revolutionary faction to thank for it all." Jessie winced at Channing's comment. "I briefly thought of luring a local Neo-Nazi chapter into doing my bidding instead, yet they lack the pull on a college campus. Antifa had the connections I needed, plus the perfect balance of civilization and savagery. You antifa folks are the only ones I know of who are principled enough to advance a cause beyond your own survival, yet animalistic enough to do horrible things in its name."

"Rudd disagreed with you," countered Carla. "And Jessie had to be lied to. Maybe they are not all as 'animalistic' as you claim."

"True," acknowledged Channing, becoming more excited when he looked down at his phone screen and saw the time; a couple of minutes remaining and counting. "Rudd had too much of the civilization and not enough savagery. However, I was able to convince him to do the part that required no bloodshed."

"He was never going to shoot," Carla realized. "He was going to *pretend* to, so that he could get arrested and occupy our time until it was too late."

"Correct."

"I do feel sorry for you," said Channing. "You eventually figured it out. Yet here you are, too far away to stop the madness." Carla remained silent, as did Jessie. They had pulled off a successful act. He looked at his phone, his eyes brightening all the more. "Yes, yes. It is almost here. We are almost there. The moment is coming. Another minute and nearly three thousand students will learn if there really is an afterlife."

Carla was getting ready to strike. Channing kept balancing his attention between the window, the women, and the time on his phone. His glances at the phone screen and the outdoors were consuming more of his focus. Carla needed just enough distraction, just enough drawing away from them to move. She knew when it would happen, when she would get a moment to rush the gun-toting professor. "It is coming ... Twenty seconds ... The era of reason is ending ... fifteen seconds ...” A wide smile growing ever larger across his face. Jessie was repulsed by the man before her. Carla was about to attack. “Five ... four ... THREE ... TWO ... ONE!” Only silence.

Channing seemed disoriented, rapidly looking at the window, then his phone. Carla ran for him just as he turned to face them. He panicked, firing his Glock wildly before being tackled by Carla. He barely stayed on his feet, leaning backwards into the railing. He fired two more shots, the gun aimed at the ceiling as Carla held his hand upwards. Dust and small pieces of wood trickled down to the stone floor. Finally, Carla buried a knee into his gut, making him lose the ability to resist along with his breath. Then she gave him a strong punch to his head, imprinting her knuckles into the side of his face. He went backwards over the rail onto the floor, the back of his head slamming into the stone with a bounce that knocked him out. Channing’s grip on the Glock went limp, allowing Carla to easily take it from his possession and aim it at the unconscious professor. She felt a surge of elation with the victory.

Then she heard the moans behind her. Carla turned to see Jessie sitting on the floor, leaning against the front pew on the left. One of the frenzied shots had struck her in the upper chest. Blood flowed down her body, forming a small pool on the stone floor. Carla was horrified. “Jessie!”

She ran to the profusely bleeding woman. Carla quickly knelt beside her wounded friend, putting the gun down so she could press hard with both hands on the wound. Moans became a scream of pain. Jessie’s eyes closed in a wrinkled tightness, tears escaping along the edges. The back of her head thumped the seat of the pew in her wrenching agony. Carla’s hands were not enough. Jessie slowly opened her eyes, looking up at the damaged ceiling. Carla tried to assure her it was going to be okay, trying to get Jessie’s eyes to focus on hers. However, Jessie was looking past her, and then she looked no more. Nightmare fulfilled.

Carla was wracked by deep personal pain. Tears flowed from her eyes as she looked at her hands, bright red with Jessie’s blood. She tried to clean them off, rubbing them on her shirt, and drenching the ivory cotton surface with the crimson flood. “I am so sorry. I am sorry. I am so, so sorry ...” Carla stopped trying to speak to the dead, instead wrapping her arms around the recently deceased. She buried her head into Jessie’s neck and hair, saying good-bye in mournful embrace, doubtful she would ever see her friend again.

His mind was cloudy, his vision cloudier. He was coming to with a strong soreness in the back of his head. A gnawing headache throbbed there, as though he were hung over. On the floor he shuffled, his vision improving. The dark ceiling and the glowing candles became visible. Soreness also afflicted his stomach and his arm. One had been struck by the enemy and the other was injured when he landed badly on the stone floor. Channing, Robespierre, the man behind the mayhem, slowly lifted his upper body. Not quite sitting, he strained to see what was ahead of him. From his vantage point, he saw the back of Carla and her slow release of the dead. He saw her cross herself in the Orthodox fashion and heard her utter a simple prayer.

"God, please forgive me for what I am about to do," she said, crossing herself again to conclude the supplication. She took hold of the Glock and rose to a standing position, her face still hidden from the laid-out professor. Then she gradually turned to face the altar. Channing was filled with great terror when he saw her. She had a blank stare, the blood of the murdered one drenching her once white shirt and smudged on her left cheek. She saw the altar, then she looked down at the man responsible for the death of Jessie. She took a step, then another, and then another, solemnly moving toward the guilty party.

"No," he said, shaking his head. "No, please." He shook his head more adamantly. "No, please don't, please don't ..." As he pleaded, she only got closer. She heard him, but she did not listen. His begging continued while he began to shove himself backwards, using his legs to push away in a futile effort at escape. She easily caught up and gave a firm stomp to his right ankle when it was a few inches above the floor, spraining it. He let out a loud scream and stopped moving. She raised the firearm to point the barrel at the professor, expression unchanged. He raised his left hand, pleading for mercy. "Please, don't do this. Please, don't. I'm begging you, don't. No, please don't kill me. Please don't kill me. Please don't kill—"

"Professor Channing!" shouted Carla, the vaulted sanctuary amplifying her declaration. He halted his pleas, looking up at her. "Are you trying to appeal to my reason?"

She offered no smile nor smirk, no laugh nor guffaw. Nevertheless, he found it hilarious. Channing, the Robespierre, was laughing. A little at first, but then more and more. The outbursts drew strength from his gut, his billowing laughter negating any escape attempts. Just as he was catching his breath, he laughed more. His face was getting pink, his eyes blinking constantly. The spasms made tears flow down his cheeks. Amidst this great letting out of it all, Carla aimed the Glock at his head and blew him away.

XII

It was a rough evening for Rudd Yansk. Once the authorities arrested him in the rafters, he was handcuffed and rushed through the convention center with few noticing his plight. Without consideration for his personal comfort, he was stuffed into a security van packed with armed personnel. Several minutes later the van, along with a compact carrying FBI Detective Michael Zambo and CIA Agent Alfredo Hernandez, left the governors' event and eventually ended up at a Bureau office up north.

Rudd was then forced to quickly walk from the van to the building, and once in the building to a windowless interrogation room. There they handcuffed him to a metal bar bolted in the middle of a heavy hardwood table, which was itself bolted to the floor. For hours, he was verbally questioned and harassed by multiple agents, Zambo and Hernandez among them. They took turns, each getting some rest before returning to the interrogation room and continuing their barrage of words. Eventually, all save Zambo retired for the evening.

Rudd received no such respite. He was kept seated in the metal chair, given only two bathroom breaks in which he was forced to go to the facilities with a pair of guards watching. Each time getting up hurt, his behind and legs were screaming at him to find a better position. His eyelids got pinker and his eye balls strained as the hours grew longer. He was spared any direct corporal torture, however, and had plenty of water to drink. Those mercies, combined with the restroom trips, were the only points of relief through the night.

Finally, the last of the government personnel left the room. Rudd was not told whether he was supposed to remain seated. He knew he was handcuffed to the table and thus had no choice. As minutes with by with him alone in the room, he leaned onto the flat surface of the tabletop, folded his arms, and rested his head. His was in a light sleep, as he believed that at any point, the oral abuse could return. For a brief while he was at peace, feeling better even with the awkward resting pose.

Less than an hour after he began his light slumber, he was jarred from it through the opening of the lone door to the room. He blinked his eyes a few times, rubbing one to clear his view of the person before him. It was a familiar face. She was in the clothing a radical ally would wear, yet he knew better. The late Robespierre had told him about her covert intentions when he gave him the assignment. As he rose to a straight posture in the uncomfortable chair, he expressed no surprise at her presence.

"I don't even know what to call you," he said, a yawn escaping under his breath.

"Carla al-Hassan Sharp," she said, walking to the chair placed on the opposite side of the table and taking a seat. She carried a clipboard, clamped down on a yellow notepad with a manila envelope behind it.

"Al-Hassan Sharp?"

"Al-Hassan is my maiden name and Sharp is my married name."

"No matter," he said, looking away. "I have nothing to say to you. You are a traitor and a fascist. You might as well be the devil himself."

"I am sorry I had to lie to you, I really am. For most of my assignment I was cut off from family and friends. For what it is worth, being in community with you and the others was one of the few things keeping me sane."

"Well, now you can go back to your community," sighed Rudd. "Meanwhile, I have nothing left, thanks to you."

"What did you think you were going to have if Robespierre succeeded?" she asked, critically. "You were still going to be arrested. And with your connection to the massive terrorist attack, you would have been sent to Gitmo for the rest of your life."

"If you want to bash it across my head that I am culpable in what could have been the worst attack on US soil since 9/11, don't bother. I got that stupid lecture over and over all night. People who belong to a government that has killed plenty of people." Rudd stared at Carla with a mixture of anger and disappointment. "You're part of the problem. The government has people like you kill people like me. You murder. You end life."

"You are right," conceded Carla. "I do not like my work. I have hated it ever since I was recruited. I constantly wrestle with how to morally justify what I am doing. There are nights when I am convinced that God will judge me wicked and damn me upon death. You almost have a right to judge me. Almost." Rudd paid more attention as Carla continued. "Rudd, I am not like the other agents. I know you. I know and respect your beliefs, and your moral code. And unlike them, I know that this whole plan of Robespierre's sickened you. You hated every bit of it. You struggled like I always struggle. You would have felt horrible even if it succeeded, even if everything he said would happen did happen."

"Yes," the radical agreed. "Yes, I hated it. But I felt it had to be done."

"Now, you are finally thinking like me," she said softly. The two sat in silence. He wanted to rebuff the claim, but he found little energy and little ground to do so. "Except I have never had to rationalize killing thousands of young people, many of whom share your views. I never had to justify such an atrocity to myself. And you should never have to. I know that you want to make things better. And I have a way to help you do so."

Rudd expressed interest in what Carla said. She took the envelope from behind the notepad and gently pushed it toward the prisoner. He studied it briefly before looking back at the agent. "What is this?"

"An agreement I had Detective Zambo draw up for you," she responded. "You will get a reduced sentence in return for helping the Bureau track down other violent antifa elements. I did not get everybody tonight. Some escaped. They and their connections will try to do horrible things. You know where to find these people; you know the connections."

"Why should I help a government dominated by white supremacists and rightwing zealots track down the only line of defense for marginalized peoples?"

"One, because you know damn well that not everyone in the government is a 'white supremacist' or a 'rightwing zealot.' Two, because you know that what Robespierre wanted to have happen would have made you no better, and possibly even worse, than any of those awful government elements you speak of. And three, because peaceful resistance always does a better job at changing things. You know point number three better than all the others, and I know you know it."

"Yes ... yes, I do," Rudd said weakly, nodding. "So what is the catch?"

"There will not be one," Carla assured him. "My husband is a lawyer, and he personally reviewed the document for your benefit. Help the Bureau arrest violent extremists, and in return you not only get a reduced sentence, but peace of mind."

"I will think about it," Rudd said, holding the contract.

"Good," she said, rising from her seat. "Anyway, if you have any problems, you can contact me."

"I won't," he stated, then weakly smiled. "It would be too tempting." She smiled back. Carla nodded her good-bye, and he waved while looking down at the paperwork. Carla walked away from the radical, taking one more look as she opened the door. He was not looking at her, but rather scanning the text of the agreement instead.

* * *

Professor Holton Fillerhouse was in an unpleasant mood. The haggard, middle-aged man slouched as he sat in the waiting room. His hair, a majority gray, seemed to have grayed even more since the start of the semester. His face was scrunched into a burdened scowl. A heavy frame was covered by proper attire. That day, he wore a button-up collared shirt with tie, a dinner jacket, slacks, and black dress shoes. He ignored the various academic publications and college-centered magazines available for reading. Also taken for granted were the awards hung on the walls. A student receptionist paid attention to her computer screen, mixing the monitoring of a business email and social media exchanges.

Provost Juana Marciela opened her office door and quickly looked around before she found Fillerhouse. "Hey, have you been waiting long?"

He shook his head side to side.

"Come on in," she waved, an extra two inches to her diminutive height due to her heels. Fillerhouse slowly raised his large body and lumbered into the office after his superior. As he entered, he noted that she had already returned to her desk and sat down. He was not looking forward to the meeting. Both were aware of the subject matter, which was the petition that Mack Channing had promoted while alive. Fillerhouse had only heard rumors about its popularity. "Have any plans for Thanksgiving?"

"Seeing family in Kansas. I do that every year," he responded.

"I see. Driving or flying?"

"Driving, just like every year."

"Oh, okay," nodded Marciela. "All my family is in California, so I am staying pretty local." He nodded back. She took a breath and continued. "Of course, I did not bring you here to talk about holiday plans. I brought you here to talk about the petition."

"The petition," he stated without pathos.

"I hate to tell you this, but it has a lot of support."

"I shouldn't even be surprised."

"A lot of decent people signed on to it. Not just much of the faculty and the staff, but thousands of students launched their own online equivalent. I bet at least a quarter of the student body is on board by now. And the number is rising."

Fillerhouse shifted in his seat. "And so, no more conservatives because a vocal minority of the students and some hypocrite professors say so?"

"It is more than just them," noted Marciela. "Some alumni have caught wind of the petition and have voiced their support. No one has said overtly that they will pull their donations if we do not pass it—"

"Oh come on," declared an annoyed Fillerhouse.

"But they implied it when they contacted me," she finished.

"This is ridiculous."

"They have many sincere concerns over what is happening. They do not like seeing the upheaval caused every time a right of center speaker comes to campus."

"Then they should blame the fanatics who keep disrupting campus life!"

Marciela raised her hand to quiet the curmudgeonly academic. "I understand where you are coming from. And I want you to hear me out before you leave in anger."

"All right," said the professor to the provost.

"This is me speaking for myself. This is me telling you how I feel about it all and what I plan to do about this petition. Can you be patient and bear with me as I tell you about my background, and what I feel about this as a result?"

"Okay, okay," he grumped, trying not to roll his eyes. Fillerhouse expected another lecture about historically oppressed minorities and genders. Something about privilege and the inability to understand where someone who was neither white nor male was coming from. He had weathered such talking points for years, often tearing them apart in his lecture hall and in the occasional on-campus debate.

"It seems like a lifetime ago and then some, but there was a time when I was a student," explained Marciela. "At the time, the Israeli-Palestinian Conflict was a big source of on-campus debate. I had many Jewish friends growing up, so naturally I sided with Israel. Problem is, the campus had a large Muslim population, and many of them were Arab, so plenty of people supported Palestine.

"I was very active in the cause. I attended events with speakers, wrote the occasional opinion column, asked critical questions during any Q&A that the Pro-Palestinian student group sponsored, things of that nature. In short, we knew each other." She laughed briefly. "In fact, I remember when we would see each other walking across campus, we usually gave each other 'the look.' That was when we had nothing nice to say, but we knew each other. Nothing overtly hostile, just 'the look.'"

"The look," chimed in Fillerhouse in a relatable tone.

"Anyway, one semester they were holding a big cultural dinner and entertainment event. I had made a couple of friends among the Pro-Palestinian group and so I was invited. However, come the night of the event, they did not have enough people to help serve the food. I thought, 'why not?' and I helped out. I even got to serve a meal to the group's president, who in return made sure to set aside a meal for me. An added bonus was that none of my other friends who went there considered it political."

Fillerhouse smiled at the last sentence.

"I was just thinking about that night last week, when I first learned about this petition," explained Marciela. "I kept thinking to myself, 'what were we doing right?' I mean, back then, we were all in our late teens and early twenties. We were 'immature,' 'ignorant,' not the wise, intelligent, mature adults. And yet back then, we acted so much better than all of these educated elders. And these elders, as well as the current culture, are teaching the students to act like the so-called mature adults and not us so-called ignorant teens from years ago. I, for one, do not like this new direction. I want my student years to come back."

Fillerhouse smiled again. Never had Marciela seen her peer grin so much in so little time.

"I do not know if I can defeat this. I do not know if I can convince the faculty senate and the board of visitors to reject it, but I will try." She stood up and offered her hand.

Fillerhouse nodded in contentment, rose, and shook it. "And I swear to be by your side the whole way."

* * *

Where are you now?

Josiah Sharp had sent another text message to Carla al-Hassan Sharp. She knew the context of the query. She was in the passenger-side front seat of a compact car being driven by Alfredo Hernandez, her suitcase in the back seat. It had been nearly thirty minutes since his last update request. His anxiety had some justification, as her flight had experienced an unexpected delay. Despite knowledge of the intended meaning, Carla's mind wandered into other significances that could be attached to the question. He deserved an answer quickly though, so she tapped on the small screen and typed up one, pushing a button that sent it within a second of it being written.

Almost there. Turning off the highway.

Carla had enjoyed the rare treat of sleeping on the flight back. Hernandez was with her and had agreed to keep watch during their time in the clouds. She lost consciousness about fifteen minutes after takeoff, and only regained it as they neared the airport. The grogginess was gone by the time they were allowed to leave the confined vessel. She stayed awake for the car trip, speaking little as Hernandez picked the music. Carla kept looking outside, leaning her head against the window as the world blurred by.

OK! See you soon!

He was quick to respond. Josiah had also been quick to get back home. His convention involvement had only lasted two days. Meanwhile, Carla had to stay an extra two days to finalize her reports and handle some other operations minutiae. Zambo was still in California, putting the final details on the successful case. He gave overtures of gratitude over and over again to the undercover agent, even offering to buy her dinner at the best restaurant in the state. She kindly declined the honor and requested to go home.

"I am impressed with you," Hernandez spoke up after several minutes of quiet. Carla straightened up in her seat and faced her superior. "How did you do it?"

"Do what?"

"Convince Mr. Yansk to rat out some of his radical buddies," replied Hernandez. "I usually get my way with helpless interrogation subjects. I have scared plenty of guilty folks into cooperation. Pero, he did not budge for me. Hora después hora, I tried, only to have him refuse to cede any proverbial ground. One talk with you, though, and he was signing a plea bargain, pointing folks out. Amazing, simply amazing."

"Gracias, mi amigo."

"So, *how* did you do it?" asked Hernandez with greater emphasis. "Do not deprive me of such wonderful knowledge."

"Well, Al," she began as the car turned into her neighborhood. "My husband would call it 'moral suasion.'"

"Moral suasion?"

"Yes."

"Okay," nodded the driver as they got onto the correct street. "I can see that."

She got another text message, prompting her to cease her conversation with Hernandez and focus on Josiah's latest comment.

Is that your lights I see?

She smiled and responded immediately. *Yes.*

He texted a thumbs up emoji in response. Carla closed the text message app, believing that it was no longer necessary. Even in the darkness of night, she saw him standing outside of their home. The world stopped smearing together and the surrounding backdrops all became still. The houses were calm in the evening, their lights offering enclaves of vision for all passersby. Some of the brighter stars above were visible, though the street lamps made for some competition. There he was, waiting for her on the front lawn. Hernandez put the car in park and unlocked the doors.

"This time, you will get at least six weeks off," promised Hernandez. "I will make sure of it, if I have to kill all the bad guys myself."

"Thank you," she said with a tired smile. Getting out and opening the back door to get at her luggage, she said, "That means I can celebrate Thanksgiving and Christmas."

"Yes, it does," agreed Hernandez. "Vaya con Dios, mi amiga hermosa."

"Adiós, señor," she responded before slamming the door shut. She walked in front of the car, and waved good-bye after reaching the grass. Hernandez waved back and drove off, back to the airport. He still had another flight before he could be home.

Carla saw her husband. He was thrilled to see her and he approached her with a wide smile. Carla was still pondering. The sudden stop in motion, no longer fighting, no longer in the air, no longer in the automobile, made her thoughts flow within her. Josiah noticed her somber mood and cautiously embraced Carla. She seemed a little better, though still in her sense of troubled contemplation.

"What happened?" he asked. "Did things go wrong?"

"Of course they did not," she said, trying to convince herself while talking to Josiah. "The bad guys are all dead or on the run, thousands of good citizens were saved, a villain will terrorize people no longer, and we both made it out alive and at home. So, I guess it ended well ... And yet, I cannot feel well." She was starting to crumble, so Josiah moved in closer and gave her a stronger embrace, which she reciprocated.

"Things are better," he assured her. "You made them better."

"Thank you, Josiah," she said. "That helps." She was about to go for her suitcase, but Josiah took it with his left hand while putting his other arm around her shoulders.

"Come now," he said, his next words bringing her open amusement and growing comfort. "I believe I owe you another sleepless night."

Author's Note

Research for the portrayal of the Antifa chapter would not have been as complete were it not for two major sources: a Vice News video report titled "The Black Bloc: Inside America's Hard Left" uploaded to YouTube in November 2017, and the personal experiences of the author in high school and college associating with those along the spectrum of the American political left.

About the Author

Michael Gryboski was born and raised in the Washington, DC metropolitan area. He graduated from George Mason University with a Bachelor of Arts and then a Master's, both in history. He previously had seven novels released by the small California-based publisher, Inknbeans Press. In addition to writing fiction, Michael also writes news articles for an online publication based in DC, as well as other works including church hymns and the occasional opinion piece. Michael would rather be correct than widely accepted.

Feel free to follow Michael on social media at the following accounts:
www.facebook.com/MichaelCGryboski
www.twitter.com/MichaelGryboski
www.instagram.com/michaelgryboski

Coming Soon

Carla will return next year in
Carla: The Cherub of Death